Shadow Coast

Shadow Coast

Philip Haldeman

Hippocampus Press

New York

Except for certain details, the setting of *Shadow Coast* is genuine; however, the characters and events, past or present, are entirely fictional. Although some liberties have been taken with Native American mythology, the author has attempted to retain the basic elements of this fascinating region and its history.

The author wishes to thank S. T. Joshi for his exceptional generosity and assistance; Sarah Troiano for her valiant efforts in the Flatiron Building; Bill Nye for his early encouragement and technical advice; and Charles Beauclerk for attempting a London bridge.

Published by Hippocampus Press
P.O. Box 641, New York, NY 10156.
http://www.hippocampuspress.com
All rights reserved.
No part of this work may be reproduced in any form or by any means
without the written permission of the publisher.
Cover art and design by Cassie Barden. Photography by David Haldeman.
Hippocampus Press logo designed by Anastasia Damianakos.
First Edition
1 3 5 7 9 8 6 4 2

ISBN13 978-0-9771734-7-1
ISBN 0-9771734-7-X

For Ann

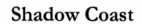

Shadow Coast

Chapter One

Waves rolled out of the darkness like black liquid mountains, the wind strained the rigging, and the deck shuddered with the yacht's tilting, headlong motion. As Mark Sayres steadied himself against the cabin bulkhead, he gazed toward the limit of the sloop's running lights and felt the discomforting sensation of being hurled through an endless, freezing tunnel. Before emerging topside, he had struggled for twenty frustrating minutes with the chart, re-checking his calculations, unable to find out what had gone wrong. He'd wanted only to be a passenger, but had hitched a ride with an owner who loved tradition. Old-fashioned navigating without GPS was a bit challenging, and he'd volunteered to be responsible. But now, according to the intractable geometries of the chart, he knew they shouldn't have passed within ten miles of the James Island Light.

Leaning harder against the bulkhead, he examined the compass. Still nothing wrong. He glanced over his shoulder at the owner and skipper, John Horn, who was in the cockpit working the tiller. The wood, chrome, cloth, and brass that made up the forty-six-foot sloop were slick with salt spray, and against the backdrop of night, Horn's middle-aged face was a plump white oval underneath a wet blue rain hood. Was it a hostile face? Maybe, or maybe not, thought Mark, but it demanded authority and was looking increasingly sullen after an unknown quantity of hip-flask whiskey. Being off course was bad enough, but the *Lenore* had just three on board. If her skipper got stubbornly drunk, that could be another problem. The northern part of the Pacific Northwest coast was a geologic fortress of high cliffs, massive boulders, sub-surface reefs, and towering off-shore sentinels of rock called sea stacks—no place to be within ten miles of shore after nightfall. Only when they sailed around Cape Flattery and turned east would they be safe.

Horn *must* have been steering off course, Mark thought. Their initial landfall, Neah Bay, was tucked in around the corner of Cape Flattery, and since Mark had no intention of drowning before getting there, diplomacy be damned. As the boat pitched, he stepped awkwardly into the cockpit toward Horn and raised his voice over the wind: "We're still too close to shore! Why not point her out to sea and let her self-steer? The wind-vane can handle her for a while, and that will correct the error."

Horn squinted into the heavy spray. "I'm selling this boat," he said, "and I'm sure as hell going to enjoy her for a few more hours!"

"We're too close to shore," Mark repeated.

Horn studied him in the manner of an unsatisfied chairman of the board. "Well, whose fault is it? What have you been doing down there?"

Mark stared back defensively. "The course I gave you was accurate. I've gone over it again and again. Have you kept her on course?"

Horn wiped the salt spray from his face. "I'm steering the course. What the hell kind of sailor do you think I am?"

Mark squelched a surge of irritation. "I don't know."

Horn's face turned red in the glow of the running lights, his voice an abrasion of contempt. "Go forward and help Craig with the heads'l. I'm sure you'll get along with him just fine. We've reefed the main. I'm replacing the genny with the storm jib out of the goodness of my bleeding heart, and I'm going to temporarily alter the course out to sea by thirty degrees. *That* ought to satisfy you. I'll tell you when I've resumed course. I'm not going to let you ruin my last few hours with this boat!"

Mark noted the time. It didn't matter who was right or wrong. A temporary change of thirty degrees would easily take care of the error, and after rounding Cape Flattery he would disembark at Neah Bay and leave these two jokers to continue on to Victoria themselves.

He held onto the port stanchions one at a time to keep his balance, made his way forward to the main hatch, and sat down hard against the ventilator. The wind howled and the deck shook like a giant pinball machine. He pulled his watch cap further down over his ears and took a second to fasten his safety line. Near him on the foredeck, Craig Ol-son, a shaggy-haired Norwegian with some limited crewing experience, was a shiny wet figure in yellow rain gear awkwardly preparing to haul in the genoa. Olson was Horn's twenty-six-year-old nephew, and Mark hoped the younger man could take the initiative away from his irascible uncle. Regardless of this, Mark intended to keep a closer watch on the compass.

Finding his footing amid the wind and spray, he began helping with the sail. "My D.R. was accurate. Your uncle's had too much to drink."

"He gets this way."

"Great. Can you at least try to get him off the tiller? We can switch to the vane, or one of us can take the helm."

"Fat chance." Breathing hard, Olson began hauling in the genoa.

"What kind of a man won't spend a little money on a hand-held GPS—not to mention personal safety lights?"

"The kind of traditional man who still plays tennis with a wooden racket—like my uncle. Look, don't worry, he'll probably get sick in an-other few minutes and I'll take over. We'll sail around Cape Flattery fine, drop you off as planned, and then my uncle and I'll anchor for the night."

Mark smiled sarcastically. "It seems your uncle isn't used to sailing at night. If we tried just a bit more, we could all get drowned first."

Olson returned the smile, sat down, and began tying the sail to the railing, working with both hands, bracing himself with his rubber boots to keep from sliding on the tilting deck. "We can always pray."

Mark looked at him. "Yeah, but the dead sailors prayed just as hard as the survivors."

In a minute, Olson half-heartedly tossed Mark a full sailbag.

After putting up the storm jib, the two made their way down the rolling deck to the cockpit.

Fighting off a touch of queasiness, Mark felt as if he were clinging to a raft. Before going below, he glanced at the compass again. The boat was keeping the modified course. Olson went to the tiller to offer Horn the services of a substitute helmsman, or barring that, to tell him they were going below to dry off. Mark, in his experience, had never seen such a bullheaded skipper. After departing Astoria just after dawn, he had begun to regret volunteering to navigate, and he was not beyond pulling Horn bodily from the helm if he discovered the boat drifting off the temporary heading.

Mark followed Craig Olson down into the damp, relatively warm cabin and closed the hatch. They removed their life jackets—which had safety harnesses—then their foul-weather gear, and tried to warm up by the kerosene heater. An overhead lamp illuminated the mahogany cabin, and a bottle of Red Hook rolled aimlessly across the floor. Given the angle of heel and the downwind teeter-totter ride, it wasn't especially comfortable, but it was better than huddling out on deck. In any case, Olson went forward to his bunk for some rest.

Mark sat down as best he could at the chart table, trying to think of anything but his stomach and a verging seasickness. He adjusted the tacks holding the chart, drew in the new course and looked to see if the *Lenore* might have any other problems. He couldn't see any. The coastline wouldn't present any difficulties until it curved back out to form Cape Flattery, the farthest northwest corner of the contiguous United States. The small town of Neah Bay on the Makah Indian Reservation was the only populated place within miles of the Cape. It lay on the north side, shielded from the harsher ocean environment, and would be a good place for Horn and Olson to start the last leg of their trip to Victoria, B.C., where they would deliver the yacht to its new owner.

Mark was on his way to see his wife, Maggie, who, because of her archaeological training, was ensconced somewhere along the rugged coastline well south of the Cape. As a summer volunteer, she had spent six weeks helping to dig up Native American artifacts. Mark had agreed to take care of their six-year-old daughter until the middle of September. He'd converted a spare bedroom into an architect's office, and although he had a year-long contract with the San Diego School District for some remodeling projects, finances were tight. He tremendously enjoyed his daughter, but found himself doing more parenting than he had time for. He hadn't wanted Maggie to go, but it seemed as if she needed an escape, and the coast peoples had been a special interest of hers in college.

Then he'd received a letter that annoyed him. It was in the wooden drawer near the yacht's chart table, where he kept a few personal things, and he hadn't known what to make of it:

Dear Mark,

Just a short note. They've discovered something up here. I'm learning a great deal, but I'll have to tell you later. I know it's been hard on you to take care of Erica by yourself, but I want to ask if it would it be all right if I stay here into the fall to help catalog and preserve some artifacts we've uncovered. When I go into Neah Bay, I'll call you.

Love, Maggie.

Had it ended there, he might have forgotten about it, even though Maggie didn't usually change her mind or go back on her word. He *was* getting tired of being a single parent; he also knew that the archaeological excavation was a rare opportunity for Maggie.

But after her phone call, everything changed. She was apparently in one of her dark moods—minor despondencies that had begun a few years ago. He initially thought they might have something to do with his staying in a high-unemployment profession. But she insisted their spotty financial situation was not the cause, and maybe because archaeology might have been even less dependable than architecture, she never complained. Yet things had gotten a little tough, and Mark couldn't entirely separate Maggie's transitory depressions from family economics. He'd accepted one job after another, with gaps between, and Maggie reluctantly went to work for a bank. They had become silent about the goals and dreams they'd once sought.

When she finally called from Neah Bay, she sounded not only depressed but frightened. Why? Nothing she said accounted for it. She didn't want to go back on her word to come home—that was all. She just felt a compelling urge to stay and learn more about the new artifacts.

He might have accepted that, but then an odd anxiety entered her voice, and she followed it with a puzzling remark: "Erica will be in school now and she needs you. I need to be *here*." After saying she loved him, she paused as if struggling with some inner emotion. Her voice was shaky and she seemed near tears. Then, after a minute, she hung up before even asking to speak to her daughter. Which was the last straw.

During the next two days, he went through all the paranoiac possibilities. Was she being mistreated? Had she met someone else up there? Did she want a new life? A divorce? Was she ill? It was crazy, but *some-*

thing was wrong, and his concern mixed with a growing resentment of her need to be away.

Finally, after much anxiety, he decided to leave Erica with his in-laws and travel to the site. A friend in Portland mentioned the yacht delivery and said they could use an extra crew member. Everything fit into place, and sailing up the coast would conveniently get him there two days after the student volunteers left at the end of the season. If something personal was at stake between him and Maggie, the fewer people at the dig, the more privacy. He flew from San Diego to Portland, then started to sail with Horn and Olson northward from Astoria.

The yacht was jolted harshly as it slammed through a wave, forcing his thoughts back to the present. He reached for the *Coast Pilot* and found a marked page. It said: "Between Cape Alava and Cape Flattery, the coast curves slightly in a series of bights, but continues as rugged as before. Numerous rocks and ledges are off shore as far as about a mile." He scanned further down the page. "The Devil's Pillar, 0.2 miles S of the W point of Cape Flattery, is a rocky column 157 feet high and 60 feet in diameter, leaning slightly NW, 150 yards off the face of the cliff. Cape Flattery, a bold, rocky head with cliffs 120 feet high, rises to nearly 1,500 feet about 2 miles back from the beach. Tide rips are particularly heavy off Cape Flattery." On another page, the descriptions were like something out of Homer, including a strange offshore formation called the Giant's Graveyard, made of dozens of pillars of rock spaced apart in the sea like colossal tombstones. The entire section was filled with descriptions of unusual formations. ". . . Some rock towers are as high as 100 to 195 feet, and many more are awash or covered by a fathom or less. The foul area continues past James Island . . ."

Foul area.

He put the book back on its safety shelf and reached for his gray rag-wool sweater. Shoving other thoughts aside, he wondered if Horn would pass out at the tiller.

"I'm going topside to check on the compass," he said.

Craig Olson was still in his bunk up forward. Mark perversely hoped the cocky Norwegian was feeling a little seasick himself.

"I think he'll be all right," said Olson. "He doesn't usually make mistakes."

"Neither do I," said Mark. He put on his jacket, tightened the laces high on his waterproof boots, stepped up the ladder and opened the hatch into the windy companionway. Without looking at Horn directly, he leaned up and looked at the compass. Almost exactly thirty degrees west of course. Soon they could resume their proper heading. He ducked back down into the cabin and closed the hatch. He looked through the brass-ringed porthole at Horn, who was mumbling to himself or to the sea. Mark could live with him for now. The man might be crazy, but it didn't matter. Only, he thought, I might have flown to Seattle and taken a float plane to Neah Bay.

The *Lenore* plunged and Mark was knocked off balance against the galley countertop.

"There was a good one!" said Olson, coming from the forward cabin to stand in the doorway. Smiling, he pushed back a huge clump of damp, sun-bleached hair. He reached up into a small compartment, brought out a blue baseball cap that said "Rutledge Technologies" across the front, and put it on. Then he took a cup down from the cupboard and poured himself some coffee, trying hard not to spill it. "Are you wondering why we're so anxious to be out here in this muck?"

"Well, I can see John Horn doesn't want to give up his boat."

"He had a lot of debts. He sold his Portland publishing business to a conglomerate." Olson leaned against the countertop and sipped his coffee, which kept slopping onto his hand. "Throw me a towel, will you? I got the damn thing too full. . . . Anyway, he was forced to sell his business. His contract said he could still stay on and manage reprints. There was nothing he liked more than reprinting old books. Can I get you some coffee?"

"No thanks. I'm getting queasy."

"When I was small, he gave me a book on Civil War memorabilia. I still collect old tintypes, you know. Anyway, the reprint part of the company didn't turn enough profit and my uncle was now controlling the unprofitable part. What happened was they fired him. The contract didn't say anything about indefinite employment. Personally, I think his lawyer should have been shot. Uncle John made all the reprint decisions he wanted until they fired him."

"What about the money he got for the company?"

"Well like I said, he was heavily in debt. Aside from a mortgaged house, this boat was all he had left."

Olson drank down the coffee, rinsed the cup, and returned it to its hook in the cupboard. "Sure I can't pour you a cup?"

"No, thanks."

"You know, he loved this boat and he wanted it to be like one he'd owned before. The first one, the *Eldorado*, had a tiller, so he had to have a tiller on the *Lenore*. As near as two weeks ago he didn't know he would have to give her up. He must have spent his last dime on that tiller."

"What do you mean?"

"She had a wheel, and he replaced it—the wheel, binnacle and all. I guess he just grew to like the feel of a tiller."

They felt the impact of another large wave, and Mark braced himself by putting his hands up against the ceiling.

"My uncle might be hard to get along with," Olson continued, "but he's been on a downhill slide. He has his reasons for being angry."

"People can act foolishly with or without reasons," said Mark, bracing himself as the yacht shook.

Olson considered this and then spoke earnestly. "We're going to be all right, regardless of my uncle. I'm a high-tech kind of guy, but I put faith in the Lord."

"Good," said Mark flatly.

Olson shook the blond hair away from his blue eyes. "Can I ask you a personal question?"

"Sure."

"Where did you learn to be so skeptical?"

Mark was amused, but wasn't sure how to answer. He always thought of his father when the subject of religion came up.

"When I was a boy," he said, "my father took me out on Mission Bay and taught me how to sail. On Sundays he'd wait for my mother and me to come home from church. Sometimes, I'd sit and talk with him. My mother was religious, but my father had an attitude. He told me: 'Believe in God, son, but question every word of the Bible.' This led to a lot of thinking in a ten-year-old."

"And a little insecurity, I can see."

Mark smiled. "More like self-reliance."

"Self-reliance is what my uncle is about," said Olson, and began putting his foul-weather gear back on. "I'll go topside. You get some rest. You were up early this morning plotting the course."

"I don't think . . ."

"Take it easy, man. The old man's been steering wrong, that's all. I'll check the heading again. Go and rest for a while. We'll be around the Cape in a couple of hours, and there's a little cafe at Neah Bay where we can have a good breakfast in the morning."

Mark watched Olson go through the hatch topside, then went forward to his berth. Maybe, he thought, he'd been a little outspoken with Olson, whom he had no reason to mistrust.

He lay in his berth for a long time, too tired even to take his boots off, drifting in and out of sleep. It wasn't easy, being knocked around the way they were. But the severity of the ocean distracted his thoughts away from Maggie for the time being, and after so many hours at sea, he was desperate to go ashore.

When he awoke, it still felt like riding a roller coaster, so he got up, came into the galley and looked at the clock—a nice Chelsea with a black enamel frame. It was late. He saw his watch cap on the floor and reached to pick it up while trying to keep his balance. As he reached down, his stomach churned, and he felt nausea lurch into his throat. Oh no, he thought, not this again. He refused to vomit. He hadn't eaten much, thank God. Fighting it off on deck might work. It might keep it from getting really bad. He tossed the cap on a bench, and by the time he put his jacket on, he heard a noise on deck—Olson's voice. Then Horn's, yelling.

Olson burst through the hatch. "Sayres, you'd better get up here."

"It better not be too tough. I'm getting sick."

"We changed the course back, and I know the time, but I think I heard breakers."

"What?!"

"Breakers. I'm not sure. Uncle won't listen to a word. I heard them, and then I didn't hear them in the darkness—to port. You really can't see a damn thing up here."

"Port? What the hell are you talking about?"

Mark quickly put on his life jacket and rushed up the companion-

way. The wind struck violently at his face. The sea was foaming in
white caps, and the yacht slid through them, plowing up and down like
a gray whale.

"Craig, I don't think you could have heard breakers, but you better
get out on the bow." Mark went to the port side, which was riding far
out of the water. He huddled down and listened to the sea and to the
boat rising and falling through the waves. Remaining there for many
minutes, he strained to hear something distant, but couldn't. Breakers
might have been associated with a sea stack, but after the course cor-
rection the boat must be far out to sea by now. Olson had let his
imagination get away with him. Still, the depth sounder could be
checked. He looked at Horn. Horn looked sarcastically back.

"What shall we do with the drunk-en say-lor?" sang Horn. He tried
to stand up, swaying, but fell back down, holding onto the tiller's gym-
bal extender. His life jacket was on and his safety line secure. "I am
very sick!" he shouted. "I'm going below. That's just the way it is. And
I don't want any complaints! Come and get this crap off of me." He
pulled at his safety line angrily. "Get it off of me."

Mark struggled across the sloping cockpit to where Horn sat. The
skipper stood up again, impressively able to keep his balance. "Put him
in the brig until he's so-ber!"

With his cold hands, Mark locked the tiller in place but decided
against leaving it unattended. The sea was too heavy and they were going too fast. One big wave and she might broach. And getting Horn below was now a two-man operation.

Horn raised his voice loudly to the wind. "During the whole of a
dull, dark, and soundless day in the autumn of the year," he quoted
with amazing lucidity, "when the clouds hung oppressively low in the
heavens, I had been passing alone, by horseback, through a singularly
dreary tract of country." Mark eased the tiller a bit to starboard and felt
the ship respond. He brought her slightly up into the wind. Horn sat
down, watched for a moment, then leaned forward and put his lined,
reddish face close to Mark's. He smiled bitterly. His voice was low and
full of sarcasm. "You've gone and put us off course," he said. "If you
were the best navigator there was, you'd still be wrong."

The stern lifted under them, the yacht started to heel over, then nosed in, catching an overtaken swell. Mark gripped the tiller and held her steady. But the water broke over the side near the bow, sweeping Olson off his feet. Mark saw him fall down and then crawl cautiously back toward them across a deck littered with lines, winches, blocks, and other obstacles.

"You'd better get below," Mark said, helping Horn unfasten his safety line.

Horn blinked at him. "You've spoiled everything," he slurred. "And you're insolent. I don't even know you. Don't order me around. You're a re'l son-of-a-bitch, y' know that?"

Mark reached out and held Horn gently but firmly by a chunk of his rain jacket. "We've all got problems," he said, "but I have somewhere important to get to, and I don't want you falling overboard. I can't hold onto both you and the tiller at the same time, so get below!"

While Mark strained to keep a hand on the tiller, Horn pulled free, hung onto the rail, and indecorously vomited over the side. Grabbing hold of Horn's jacket, Mark pulled him, drooling and spitting, back toward him.

"Go below! You've had it!"

Horn kneeled on all fours and crawled forward. When he got to the companionway, he folded his arms pitifully and leaned up against the hatch, moaning in unison with the wind. In a few minutes, Olson crept around the tilting cabin and came back to where Mark was manning the helm. They stood together looking toward the bow and into the blackness beyond. The deck seemed as long and narrow as an airport runway at night, lit in a ghostly white glow. All around, the sea rose and foamed.

"We'll double-reef the main," said Mark. "I'm going below to check the depth sounder. You stay with the tiller until I come back, then we'll take care of the sail. Let's come up into the wind a little more."

"There," said Olson.

"What is it?"

"I hear it again."

They stood still, staring as far ahead as they could while the yacht sped into the downwind darkness and the waves rushed past the hull. Though Mark was cold, he felt suddenly colder, for he believed he heard a low, distant sound, like faint crashing thunder.

"Craig, get below and start the engine."

Olson stepped quickly to the companionway leading down into the cabin, and over John Horn, who, still moaning, was trying to sit up.

Mark left the tiller and went over to the compass, which floated like a big eye in its calm liquid. He stared down at this glass-enclosed, floating black orb while Olson tried to start the engine.

At that instant, and for the first time in Mark's sailing experience, terror overcame the pangs of seasickness. It was as if he'd been struck in the face, or as if some nightmare had been resolved only to reveal another more horrifying nightmare beyond. As the engine tried to come alive deep down, the boat's running lights dimmed—and Mark saw the eye of the compass, drifting in its subtle liquid suspension, fluctuate almost ten degrees counterclockwise.

He stepped over Horn, shoved open the cabin door and went below to get a flashlight. "Olson! I'm leaving the hatch open so you can hear me! When I tell you, shut off the running lights for three seconds."

Coming back to the compass, he pointed the flashlight at the black dial, then leaned around the bulkhead and yelled down into the cabin. "Shut them off!" The lights went out, and under the beam of the flashlight the compass drifted a full twenty degrees counterclockwise.

He bent down to Horn. "*How* was this compass adjusted after it was moved? Who adjusted it?"

Horn looked up, pale and bloodless. "It was done just after I changed to the tiller," he said in an angry half-whisper, "when I had the compass mounted to the bulkhead." Olson came up out of the cabin: "What the hell is going on out here? I played with the lights. Now what?"

"The running lights dimmed when you tried to start the engine." Mark smashed his fist angrily into the cabin bulkhead next to the compass. "And the wiring for the running lights goes right through here."

Olson stared blankly at him. Mark looked down again at Horn. "The compass had been adjusted while the lights were off. I'll bet you haven't sailed at night since then. I'll bet no one even thought about the wiring's magnetic field inside this bulkhead. We've been steering off course since sunset."

"It isn't possible," yelled Horn angrily. "The wiring can't make that much of a difference—hardly any difference at all."

"It can," said Mark.

Olson became greatly irritated. "You sure?"

"Damn right. I saw it. We're miles off course, and this is why."

Olson stepped quickly back to the helm and unlocked the tiller.

Mark put his foot onto the combing, grabbed a handhold, stepped up onto the top of the cabin, but couldn't see very far into the darkness. If the sound had been constant, they'd have probably run aground by now. But Olson had been uncertain of the direction. The only explanation Mark could think of was that they'd passed some offshore rocks.

"We've got to start the engine," he shouted, "lower the main, and steer hard to port."

"Listen over there," yelled Olson, now pointing dead ahead.

Mark listened, and heard what he feared—the crashing sound of waves breaking against rocks.

He started to climb down off the cabin, then stopped. Straight ahead, at the very fringes of the running lights, about a hundred yards away and accompanied by a distant crescendo of breakers, something tall, black, and immense loomed up in the darkness. Like a guardian at the gates of hell, a huge sea stack, a towering wall of jagged vertical rock, appeared out of the night. White patches of water frothed and smashed against its base. They would collide with it in a matter of seconds.

"Bring her up!" he yelled. "Now! Now!"

Olson seemed confused or unable to see what was happening, but he yanked the tiller in panic, bringing her hard to port. The yacht heeled over, straining her rigging. Mark fell down to avoid the boom, his hip smashing onto the top of the cabin. He grabbed out for anything he could hold onto, and the *Lenore* broached wildly. He felt the force of the ocean roll under and try to tip the boat over. The whole starboard side came awash with a tremendous roar. Mark held on while the violent motion tried to throw him overboard. He saw the mast spreader just about touch down into the sea. The starboard stanchions dipped under water, and when he thought the whole boat would capsize, she miraculously righted herself, and the sea flowed off of her. He turned over on his side and shouted to Olson, "Leave the helm! Get that engine started!" He felt the sea pushing the boat closer to the rock tower, which was now directly to starboard. Horn had fallen into the cockpit, and as if drowned, lay face down in a pool of dark water. Olson tried to set him up against the combing. "I'll take care of him," yelled Mark. "Start the engine!"

Olson headed for the companionway, letting Horn fall into the water again. Mark's arm felt sprained, and he lowered himself painfully down from the top of the cabin. He knelt down, pulled Horn's face out of the water, and leaned him up against the combing. Horn choked something barely audible: "God, what's happened? Something is wrong. I am not myself."

"Get below!"

Mark hung onto the tiller. The wind moved against the sail again, and he tried to steer straight into it, and into the waves. She came around, luffed, and Mark looked back over the stern at the gigantic rock, but could only focus on the lethal white breakers. The engine roared to life, but at the same time there was another sound, and he felt the keel bump hard into something. Shit, he thought, there were smaller outcroppings of rock all around just below the surface. Goddamn it, move! move! A wave lifted the deck under his feet, and as the engine slipped into gear the yacht pitched sideways, putting the stern right up onto whatever they'd hit. Mark clenched his teeth and felt the blood leave his face. He heard and felt a crunching, tearing sound directly underneath him. Olson came up from the cabin. "Sayres, we're . . ."

"Get out a distress message."

Olson disappeared into the cabin. The wind tore across the deck, the boat seemed to break free, but then rolled back onto the hidden underwater edges, shuddering and breaking underneath. Mark guessed that if the boat sank, they would die in the freezing water or be smashed against the rocks like rag dolls. He felt Horn's hand grab onto his pant leg, and he reached down to help him. The older man stood up, holding onto the rail for support.

Olson yelled out, "She's taking on water fast."

"There's an electric pump," muttered Horn. He stumbled toward the cabin door.

"She's filling up!" yelled Olson.

Mark decided to let out the main sheet and let the sail flap in the wind, hoping the waves would roll her off the underwater rock. Then he heard the engine sputter and die.

"Olson!" But he knew the engine wouldn't start in a flooded compartment. In a second, the boat seemed to come free, but spun around, and he knew the only chance now was to sail toward the sea stack, get up speed downwind, then point her hard to starboard and try to steer around the stack on the inland side. She was already being shoved by the wind and waves. Mark took a deep breath.

He steered the *Lenore* toward the massive rock wall. He glanced down to the sheeting track below the rail. The waves could break over the side any time. She was listing heavily, and might sink quickly. He concentrated on her speed. He waited as long as he could, then brought the tiller firmly toward his hip. The boat began to respond, but not fast enough. The rock, as big and dark as an unlit office building, came up quickly, and he could just see around it into the blackness.

A wave came over the side, smashing him against the combing with an enormous slap. He managed to keep his right hand tight on the tiller, and stood up again. The boat slowed to a standstill, tossing in the waves, then began to move again. Horn and Olson stumbled out of the cabin, checking each other's life jackets. "We're gone!" yelled Olson.

"Where for Christssake is the life raft?"

"It's in the sail bins forward," Olson said. "But the cabin is flooded."

"We're still moving," growled Horn. "When we hit the rock we'll get swept around the other side."

Mark watched to port as the rocks got closer, now only about fifty feet away. In the dim reach of the running lights, he could see the wash of barnacles and seaweed which clung to the lower portions of rock. Water flooded over the side into the cockpit, swirling around them, sloshing into the companionway. A wave hit them hard abaft. The boat heeled, then came back upright, tilting erratically. The three men hung onto anything they could in the freezing wind and water.

"We'll get smashed to bits," said Olson. "We're moving with the waves, but if we get trapped alongside the rock, the waves will pound the shit out of us."

"The watertight compartment will keep her afloat," said Horn.

"Better get out on the foredeck," said Mark. "She's shifted back, going down by the stern."

"Swim down inside and get the life raft!" yelled Horn angrily. "If we can stay with her for only ten minutes we can get that sucker pumped up."

"Too dangerous," Mark snapped back. "She's flooded. I sure as hell don't want to get trapped down there if she decides to sink."

Mark lifted himself out of the water up onto the tottering cabin, then helped the other two up and out near the mast, where they re-attached their safety lines and decided to inflate their life jackets. The wind still held some command over the flapping sails, but in a few seconds they would unavoidably hit the base of the sea stack to port. Mark, now wet and cold, could only stare at the towering rock and at the waves which smashed against it. He saw the waves hit the base of the rock at an angle, and hoped that indeed, the boat would eventually be swept around the right side into what he assumed was open water. If the boat stayed afloat, they'd ride her toward the beach and swim ashore—if the shore was nearby, if the tide was going in the right direction, and if they didn't freeze to death.

"Here it comes!" yelled Horn. "Hang on!"

The dark waves rolled in and pushed the boat up against a jagged rock wall. The hull crunched like a piece of snapped Styrofoam, slid off, then hit again.

"We can fend her off with the spinnaker pole!" shouted Horn, trying to keep his balance.

"No! This isn't a rowboat!" yelled Mark. "The waves will push her around the corner."

Nevertheless, Horn and Olson detached their safety lines so they could quickly get the spinnaker pole and take it to the port side. From the foredeck, they awkwardly poked the pole out toward the rock as another wave hit, but it sprung jarringly back toward them, crashing on the deck. Horn dangerously grabbed for it, but missed, and it slid under the rail into the sea. Horn put his hand on the unsteady rail of strung cable, leaned out, made another grab for it, but failed.

"Let it go!" Mark yelled.

Another incoming wave hit hard, and the yacht rolled violently. In that moment of turbulence, Horn was caught off balance, leaning over the rail, and then he suddenly toppled over into the sea.

When the boat rolled up again like a heavy log, primed for the next big wave, Horn was floating by his life jacket in the swirling water, without a safety line, trapped between the hull and the wall of rock.

Mark realized with horror what was about to take place. He desperately looked around for a line to throw overboard. Olson was clinging for life to the ventilator funnel. The deck pitched harshly with the next wave, knocking Mark down. The water crashed over him, nearly sweeping him off the deck. He held tight to the hatch cover and balanced on hands and knees, gagging up salt water, clearing his nose, shaking his head. He got to his feet, swaying, weakly reached out for the port rail, and with a violent feeling in his stomach, looked for Horn again. He hadn't felt the boat collide with the rock that time.

Miraculously, Horn was hanging at arm's length onto the gunwale amidships, unable to raise himself up. His pleas for help were barely audible. Mark started toward him once more, but the boat was relentlessly shoved onto the rock again.

Horn was looking straight up, his mouth open in fear. He was trapped. He screamed in pain as his legs, like two sticks, were hopelessly crushed between the hull and the rock. From Horn's contorted face came a deep, hoarse wail. He hung in agony onto the hull as long as he could, then slid down into the water, again kept afloat by his life jacket. Mark had been washed down between the side of the cabin and the stanchions. All he could do was watch—and hang on for his own life.

In another second, Horn was caught against the rock again. Then, for a terrifying moment, as the boat rolled, he was out of sight. Nothing could be seen but the moving black water. Then he reappeared. His head was a smashed and bleeding travesty, blood flowing from his crushed jaw, mouth and nose. The life jacket, which had been torn against the rock, held him afloat for a few more seconds before he disappeared into the swirling liquid darkness.

Mark stared in horror, his breathing altered and unsteady. It was a swift, terrifying death—no appeal, no mercy. Gasping, he crawled back toward Olson, squeezed his eyes closed, trying to force what he'd seen into the back of his mind. He heard the hull shift and scrape and the wind blow irregularly in the sail. The boat was still drifting even as she scraped, even as the rock tore at her.

"Where is he?" yelled Olson.

"Dead."

Olson struggled to get up, but slipped back down into the water that flowed over the deck.

Mark grabbed onto the ventilator funnel and took Olson tightly by the arm. "He's gone."

Olson said nothing, but his expression hardened into a stare.

"Listen to me. We've got to get to the top of the cabin and ride it out as best we can. She's still being pulled."

Again, the boat was smashed into the rocks and dragged along. They hung onto the mast and listened to the crunching fiberglass of the hull. The running lights blinked and dimmed.

"We can't stay here until she breaks up," said Olson. "We can't do that."

"You can't swim against those waves. You'll end up getting washed right back against the rocks."

"Just what are we supposed to do?"

"Hold on and stay out of this cold water as long as possible."

Another wave hit the cabin, surging over them like a dark living thing, and Mark was washed down again between the cabin and the portside rail. In a moment of panic, he reached up, choking water, grabbed for anything his hands could find, and got hold of the cable.

Dropping by the stern, the whole yacht settled low in the water. Every second or third wave washed over the deck. It was impossible to stand.

They held onto the mast as the wind and waves worked to shove the hull around the sea stack. For a moment, the boat hung up on a jutting of rock, and just when Mark thought they'd break up, she swung partially around and broke free. Sinking, she was now swept around the rocks into the open water.

Mark now released his safety line, and he and Olson crawled out onto the bow as the yacht slipped under. In seconds, they found themselves in the freezing ocean, clinging to the chrome rail around the pulpit, the only part of the *Lenore* left above the surface. The water was so cold Mark wondered if they could stand it for more than a few minutes. John Horn's death assailed him. The ocean would now proceed to commit two more gruesome murders. Shivering uncontrollably, he could barely think. Around them was a void of chilling, universal blackness, and the mammoth waves, unseen, heaved up and down like melted ice.

Soon there was the sound of distant surf, and Mark desperately tried to recall whether or not the tide was going in the right direction. Slowly, he began to believe they would at least wash up on shore, dead or alive. Thoughts of his wife and daughter came to him. Would the future stop now? He imagined Maggie on a dark beach miles away, unaware of his death, and pondered the cruel irony of how her secretiveness had led to this. He tried to sustain himself with movements of his arms and legs.

Looking into the dark, he tried to talk to Olson: "Stay with me. Listen for the breakers."

No one answered.

He moved hand over frozen hand slowly around the pulpit rail, but there was no sign of Olson. Where *was* he? He yelled, but there was no reply. In an icy panic, he blindly reached out while still keeping hold of the rail.

"Olson!"

He yelled again and again into the rising and falling blackness—which returned no sign of life. The sound of the breakers, or what Mark thought were breakers, mixed with the blowing wind and spray. All around, the invisible ocean moved like the pounding of a monstrous cold heart. Then, in the midst of this wall of sound, he thought he heard Olson's voice at the faintest point of audibility, opposite the sound of the breakers. Oh, God, he thought. Was it real? Surrounded by noise, you'll sometimes hear a voice that isn't really there. Don't risk your life, goddamn it, until you *know*.

He stayed there in frozen agony, hanging onto the pulpit rail, staring into the blackness—and in a moment, the distant voice was gone. There was nothing he could do. Blood pounded in his head, and he forced himself to listen to what he hoped were breakers on a not-too-distant shore. After several more minutes, he couldn't wait. Taking the only chance for survival he had, he pushed away from the yacht's protruding bow and began to swim slowly and painfully toward the sound of crashing surf.

Chapter Two

Mark slowly curled his fingers in the sand. The sand was recognizable by resistance, not by touch, because his hands were numb. Every part of him was numb, perhaps every inner organ. Maybe, he thought, his blood was frozen or barely flowing. Disoriented, breathing heavily, he was in a damp, perilously cold night, but somehow had fought his way through the surf, had missed being smashed on the rocks, and crawled painfully up the beach after the waves had violently washed him ashore.

Now there was the sound of a barking dog.

Shivering uncontrollably, he opened his eyes and tried to force an upward gaze. The beach was dark but for a partial moon in a gap between the clouds, and there were cliffs lined with evergreen trees on a huge promontory above him. Was he dreaming or dead? He couldn't move and struggled to maintain a clear thought. The dog barked again, and its sharp sound mingled with the heavy roar of breakers.

Voices—and in a moment, a kind of shuffling sound--were very near. Someone was talking. Someone asked who he was. He couldn't respond or raise himself up. If they moved him, he thought, he would crack in two like a block of ice. He was overcome with fear. If they pulled on his arm, it would break off.

"Hang in there, pal." He heard this, but it wasn't in response to his fear. They didn't understand his condition. Someone was shining a flashlight on him.

"Let's get him up the stairs."

"It's a long way. He's shaking like hell."

"We've got to get him warmed up. You'd better go and get a heavy blanket. Michael, you go back up to the house with Sandra."

"Better call the Coast Guard station. There may be others."

Mark felt himself being lifted by the ankles and under the arms. Two men struggled awkwardly with him across the sand and then the rocks into the shadow of the promontory. In a few minutes, they began to ascend a set of wooden stairs, half carrying him while he tried to walk. The stairs had small landings where they rested.

"Try to stay awake," one of them said.

"Good, now, let's keep going," said the other. "Just take it easy, man. Don't say anything if you don't feel like it."

Mark did not feel like it.

Somewhere before the top, he passed out.

*   *   *

After an eternity of darkness, he awoke on a sofa, and across the room from him was a stone fireplace containing a crackling fire. The room was larger than average, and the ceiling was bordered with heavy crown molding. The windows were shaded closed. Lace curtains hung from a brass bar over the upper window frames, and the walls were covered in muted wallpaper with light-brown spaces between floral designs. A dining-room archway was cased in dark wooden molding. The room contained some late Victorian furniture and an antique clock on the mantelpiece. Mark could hear a ticking pendulum over the crackling of the fire. The contrast of surroundings and the lapse of time between the immense ocean and this domestic warmth was as profound a transition as he'd ever experienced.

Someone was speaking in a low voice. Mark closed his eyes. Whoever was in the room apparently hadn't noticed he was awake. He thought of the accident: the sinking of the sloop and the death of John Horn. The odd stairs ascending the cliff must have led to a small town on the Olympic Peninsula. The map, however, hadn't shown anything between La Push to the south and Neah Bay to the north. What time was it? The antique clock said 12:10. Was it A.M. or P.M.? As the person speaking rambled on, Mark felt secure under the warm blankets. He vaguely remembered being taken out of his wet clothes, toweled off, and put into a bathrobe and blankets. The numbness was gone, the shaking had abated into occasional spasms. His head began to clear to another stage of wakefulness, and he rolled stiffly over on his left side to feel his bruised knee under the covers. His fingers moved individually, and he forced himself to stretch his muscles before absurdly thinking: You'll be sore in the morning. He was already sore, and he would sure as hell be worse in the morning, if it wasn't morning already.

"I think he's awake."

Someone walked across the room.

"I should be going. Shall I take him with me?"

"No. It's all right." This was a woman's voice.

"Are you sure?"

"Of course. Lucky enough you were nearby."

"Well, looks like you guys saved him a helicopter trip to Port Angeles. The authorities want to talk to him, but I guess I'd rather he wasn't dragged out in the cold again, anyway."

"Can you tell us what to do after the warm tea?"

"Feed him when he's hungry. Give me a call at the Ozette ranger station if there's any problem. I'll be hanging around there tomorrow, then home to Port Angeles. And after you give him some tea, call the Coast Guard again. They'd probably like to know who the hell this guy is, where he came from, and if he was alone."

Mark's stomach felt squeezed and knotted. The sound of a door closing coincided with the clicking of a latch. He became aware that the feeling in his stomach wasn't pain, but emptiness. The feeling grew. He rolled on his back again.

"You still awake?" someone asked.

He looked up toward the ceiling. Sounding to himself as one does after awakening from anesthesia, he whispered, "Slightly." He reached around and felt his sore neck. The man standing over him was about fifty, tall and thin, with a gray-streaked beard.

"The doctor just left. He says you'll be fine." The man paused. "I'm Garman Hanley."

"Mark Sayres."

"I'm the minister of the First Missionary Church. I'm a visitor. You're in Sandra Torrel's house. She's fixing tea. Her husband is temporarily away. What happened to you? You were on the beach."

Mark detected annoyance in this man's voice and managed what he thought was a discernible smile.

"I must be keeping you all up."

Hanley looked at him blankly. "We're not accustomed to pulling people up from the beach in the middle of the night."

It was night, thought Mark, or early A.M., since no light shown behind the shades. "Night," said Mark aloud, and felt a kind of drunken assertiveness flow through him. Maybe mild hypothermia was causing him a little trouble, afflicting him with false emotion.

"Don't talk. It's all right," said Hanley.

Another man came over to the sofa. He was perhaps thirty-five, dark-complexioned, with straight black hair and heavy shoulders. He wore blue jeans, a red-plaid shirt and a dark brown, unbuttoned leather vest. The man stared down. He looked like a Native American. He grinned with a set of slightly uneven teeth, and his expression looked as if some small joke had been played on him inadvertently. "You got a little bit cold out there, man. Hell of a night for a swim."

"This is Jim Kallabush," said Hanley. "We carried you up from the beach less than two hours ago. When Sandra's dog didn't come back, I sent my son Michael to look for him. It was Michael and the dog who found you. You are lucky to be alive. A little one way or the other along the shore and you'd have been cut to pieces scraping the rocks."

Mark understood, and felt as though his stomach had become animated, contracting in hunger or pain, he couldn't tell which. Talking was almost too much for him. He closed his eyes for a moment.

"The Coast Guard spotted some wreckage that drifted into the rocks. Was that your boat?"

"I'm sorry, what . . . ?"

"I asked if the wreckage on the rocks was yours."

"It must be. It must be the sloop I was on. We were sailing up the coast."

"How many on board?"

"Just Horn and Olson . . ." A cold memory went through him. Something inside him collapsed. Horn was dead—but Olson had disappeared in the darkness. It didn't make sense. Wasn't Olson the strongest?

"Have they found Craig Olson?" he asked.

Hanley walked away, and a minute later Mark heard him talking on the telephone. When he returned, he looked even more concerned than previously. "You're the only one they've found."

"The boat went down. Olson was near me in the water. But something happened to him. I don't know what happened. He must have let go of the railing. Then he was gone."

"I'll tell them." Hanley went to the phone again.

". . . Tell them there were three of us. John Horn was lost overboard. Horn is dead. But Olson was alive."

Mark felt an intolerable pang of agony. He might have figured out the problem with the compass. He'd taken the navigator job. Now two men's lives were lost.

"I've told them," said Hanley when he returned. "They've got a Coast Guard helicopter doing a search. There isn't much more we can do. This is a remote area."

A quiet, blond-haired boy came over to the sofa. He looked about eight years old and wore a T-shirt imprinted with a faded green stegosaurus. Though he hadn't said anything so far, he now had a curious smile and looked as if he was delighted at Mark's survival.

"I found you," he said. "I'm glad you aren't dead."

Mark smiled weakly back. "I'm glad I'm not dead either. Thanks."

The boy continued to gaze at him as if impressed by his own handiwork. His smile broadened. Then Reverend Hanley came over to him and put a gentle hand on his shoulder.

"Michael did just the right thing," Hanley said, gazing at the boy, then addressed the two others in the room. "We can stay longer if you like."

"No, really. You'd better get Michael home to bed." This was apparently Sandra Torrel speaking. "I'm glad you came to visit tonight, but Jim here can hang around for a few more minutes. And it's late." Her tone was cool.

Hanley put on his coat, then buttoned Michael's coat. Sandra saw them to the door, and they were gone.

While a further layer of Mark's exhaustion peeled away, Jim and Sandra could be heard taking dishes into the kitchen. The drenching cold fingers of the ocean continued to loosen their grip. The warm room eased Mark's thoughts, and he adjusted the wool blankets. He felt like an intruder, though he began to resign himself to being a shipwreck victim. He still felt groggy, if not a little hallucinatory. The people and their voices seemed dreamlike and compressed in time. He concentrated on them as he would on people in a strange country. And he supposed he was in a strange country.

Jim Kallabush brought him a cup of spice tea. He managed to sip it, trying to keep his mind working. His host, Sandra Torrel, sat in a wingback chair to the left of the fire, her gaze often fixed on some unknown point in the dining room. A woman with black hair, slim and nicely proportioned, she might have been in her late twenties, Mark thought, but the firelight brought out the features of a slightly more mature face, like one of those pale yet attractive English beauties one sees in Shakespearean dramas. He searched for a sign of Native American because of her shiny black hair, but saw and heard only west coast Anglo-Saxon. Although her tone was accommodating, she seemed preoccupied. It was as if she'd waited until he had awakened, heard him say something resembling human speech, then casually decided to let him stay put and rest, all of which took kindness and hospitality. She might have let the doctor take him.

He painfully stretched to set the teacup on the coffee table next to the sofa, then lay back down and was thankful his mind was clear enough, or curious enough, to engage in this amateur analysis. He wondered how far Maggie was from here. His thoughts returned to her, the letter, and her strange phone call. The horrible incident at sea was put aside, temporarily suppressed. In a few minutes, drowsiness mixed with the warmth inside him and the lovely image of his accidental host in the wingback chair. He allowed himself to drift back into a sound sleep. He did not awaken until the morning light shown behind the lace curtains and the firewood had long since cooled to a black crumble of ash.

Chapter Three

The treacherous sea remained behind his eyes and in his stomach. The queasy motion of the yacht had not entirely subsided, even after a night's sleep, and he guessed that the details of the wreck would never leave at all.

He waited, then allowed himself to look at the ceiling. After a minute, he removed his blankets and slowly sat up. He was wearing a man's green terry-cloth bathrobe and a pair of thick wool socks they'd wrestled him into last night. He rubbed his bruised knee, then his neck. His muscles felt like knotted ropes. Along with everything, he was hungry and aching.

"You're moving around."

He turned toward the voice. Sandra Torrel leaned against the dining room archway. She was of medium height, with a smooth, pale complexion, that black, wavy, shoulder-length hair, and what looked from this distance to be light-gray eyes. She wore a dark-blue turtleneck and jeans. She was as beautiful as before, and it made him feel a little uncomfortable under the circumstances.

"You can use the shower. Go there to the entry hall and then up the stairs." She paused self-consciously. "Would you like sausage and eggs for breakfast?"

"Please don't go to the trouble."

"No, it's all right. I volunteered to let you stay here. It's quite far into town and you weren't in any shape to travel. How do you like your eggs?"

He could barely manage a smile. "Well then, like I feel. Scrambled."

"OK," she said, and walked into the kitchen.

He slowly stood up and found the staircase in the entry hall near one of those Victorian hall trees with an umbrella stand and an oval mirror. The house had history about the furnishings. He stiffly ascended the stairs to a second-story bathroom where he was able to shower, wash the sand and salt out of his hair, and take a more accurate stock of his cuts and bruises. In the shower, he had to shake off the horrible images of John Horn going down in the water, then Olson's voice in the darkness. Taking deep breaths, he tried to occupy himself in the moment, but aside from another flash of memory concerning Maggie's phone call, his thoughts didn't lead far from the sea, the wreck, and the dead and missing.

While drying himself, he noticed a man's razor lying on the porcelain sink, apparently Sandra's husband's, then noted that a bathroom will always make a person feel like a trespasser.

As the steam cleared from the mirror, he saw that his face was clean and ruddy from the hot shower. Maggie thought his eyes were subtle and expressive, "if you look closely," and he sometimes found that people considered him deep in thought even when he was focused on something trivial. Entering middle age meant little to him. There was almost no gray in the brown hair, but a slightly receding hairline that he hoped would cease its recession. He rinsed off a black comb he found on the sink, ran it through his hair, rinsed it off again. After the night's trauma, he felt he could face *whatever* problem Maggie was having. As his face got cooler, he marveled at the fact of his survival, thought of his daughter and hoped she was getting along with his in-laws.

After drying off and putting the bathrobe and the wool socks back on, he went downstairs into the kitchen, which smelled intensely of frying breakfast.

"Hello," he said. "I feel awkward."

Sandra managed a smile. "No need. It was a bad night. If the tide hadn't been coming in, or the beach wasn't sandy below us this year . . . well, you're lucky, that's all I can say. Did I mention we'd sent Reverend Hanley's son, Michael, out to look for my dog, and that's why we found you?"

"Yes. Where is he—I mean the dog."

"Barney's outside, but if I bring him in he'll put his muddy paws all over you and beg at the table."

She turned to the counter next to the stove. "The county sheriff called early this morning. He's coming to talk to you. And the Coast Guard helicopter was searching again this morning." She cracked four eggs into an earthenware bowl, added milk, and began to whip the eggs. "They may think you're a drug smuggler."

"What?"

She shrugged her shoulders innocently. "There've been a few incidents farther south. Someone shows up in a private boat along the shore at night and the authorities are going to be suspicious."

"How do you know I'm *not* a drug smuggler?"

"Well, you don't seem like one."

"How many smugglers do you know?"

Sandra smiled and poured the eggs into the frying pan.

Mark looked out the window toward the dense forest behind the house. The air was thick with a heavy drifting mist.

"Please sit down," she said. "Where are you from?"

"Thanks. San Diego. And I hate to be ignorant, but I don't know exactly where I am."

She put two slices of bread in the toaster. "Were you lost?"

"Yes, we were lost—well, in a manner of speaking. We were vaguely heading in the right direction."

"Well, you're on the Olympic Peninsula coast."

Mark nodded politely. "That part was right, anyway." Mrs. Torrel hadn't meant to insult him, but her information might have better applied to a shipwreck victim in the seventeenth century.

Sandra glanced at him suspiciously, then added, "You're a bit south of Point of the Arches. The Makah Indian Reservation is up north. This is an isolated area. There are no other houses around here, though we do have phone and electricity. This house was built a long time ago at the end of a private road in the 1920s by a wealthy lumberman."

"I see."

After she set his plate down on the table, she began cleaning around the stove and sink, eating her breakfast from a plate on the countertop. Was she afraid of him? he wondered. Possibly. But she was suddenly lost in thought, oblivious to him. He ate quickly, downing the scrambled eggs, four pieces of toast, bacon, some hash browns, and a large glass of orange juice between sips of coffee. Though he was sore and relatively immobile, he was beginning to feel mentally normal.

While cleaning up the dishes, she asked him about the sailing accident and his destination.

"I came up here to see my wife. She's a volunteer at an archaeology site."

Then he related the story of what happened on the yacht, and about the misadjusted compass. Sandra Torrel listened carefully but was oddly quiet.

After finishing with the dishes, she showed him how to use an old Kenmore dryer out in a small, enclosed back porch. His clothes had already been washed. She seemed less confident about what to do with him now. Perhaps they had been tiptoeing around some awkward points of etiquette, but he didn't know what those might be. He loaded his wet clothes into the dryer and returned to the living room to rest.

When he returned to the back porch, he dressed by taking his clothes directly from the dryer, stiffly moving his arms into his shirt, painfully bending his sore legs into his blue Levi's. His boots, which were mostly rubber, had been drying out near a heating vent in the dining room. Although they were still a bit damp inside, he put them on and returned to the back porch. Then he went into the yard where he briskly petted Barney, a brown and white sheltie. The barren yard was surrounded by huge evergreen trees, and the heavy mist continued to roll through the forest.

He played with the dog, then walked down along the north side of the house past the dining-room bay window and out to the front. A tire-rutted road came out of the woods from the northeast, smoothed out and curved around just in front of the house. He crossed this dirt road and headed toward the edge of the cliff. The wind was chilly. A picket fence had been strung along the cliff's edge but had partially fallen away. Three old, twisted spruce trees grew between the house and the cliff. The beginning of the wooden stairs to the beach lay at the north side of a shallow promontory beyond another wind-blown spruce. He was thankful the stairs had been maintained. He guessed it was forty or fifty feet down.

He stepped near the broken fence to get a better view. To the north, cliffs were curtained in mist and topped with densities of dark green trees. Rocks rose from the sea in colossal crags and fissures. It was a scene of dampness and diffuse gray light, of heavy ocean rumblings and shapeless clouds that blocked the sun. He shivered again at the sight of the ocean. The sea was a vast, rolling plain. Rock formations huddled in fog, while landward to the south, tree-lined bluffs vanished into the distance. The mist, sky, and ocean enveloped everything in an unearthly gray shroud.

Looking offshore about a half-mile, he saw the sea stack he assumed they'd encountered during the night—a big, tall, slate-colored rock formation that was actually a twin, one large and one smaller megalith violently pounded by distant waves. Far to the south was another formation, perhaps the cause of Olson's hearing breakers to port. Whatever the appearance of this mythic seacoast, it was strange and illuminating to see the puzzle of last night laid out in bare geologic elements.

He put his cold hands in his jeans pockets and looked back at the house. Considering the potential of the ocean view, the location of the house was somewhat unusual. A two-story, turn-of-the-century style, it stood far back in a large clearing, as if the builder had been overly concerned about getting too close to the cliff. The traditional bays, dormers, and thickly milled window frames gave it an imprint of ego and authority beyond its actual dimensions, though a decorative oval window in the second floor and a long front porch redeemed its general oppression. It was in the shingle style, thought Mark, and appeared of high quality. The shake roof looked almost new, and so did the muted earth-tone paint. The interior had been restored, he guessed, and it must have cost a lot of money considering the remote location.

As the chill was about to send him back, he heard a car engine. A dark green police S.U.V. came from the road out of the woods and parked in front of the house. It had a gold county sheriff's emblem on the side. A large, uniformed man got out, walked onto the porch and knocked on the door. Sandra let him in.

Returning by the back way, Mark stepped cautiously inside the closed porch. Whatever the reason for the sheriff's visit, he hoped there wouldn't be any legal trouble. Horn was dead and if Olson was still missing, there would be difficult questions to answer. They had been unaccountably close to shore in the middle of the night. If the sheriff did suspect drug smuggling, what would happen? Furthermore, Mark was the navigator. If he was suspected of negligence, he might have to call an attorney. These were self-centered thoughts, but uncontrollable. He also worried that being chilly might cause him to appear nervous or guilty, so he stayed in the kitchen for a minute to get warm. His gray sweater was still drying.

Voices came from the living room, and after he felt comfortable, Mark walked in and introduced himself. The officer was a tall, heavily built man, about fifty, with a large, rather severe face. He wore a light brown shirt with epaulets on the shoulders, a thick-textured leather belt, and a holstered gun.

"Deputy Sheriff Rick Hermann," he said, introducing himself.

Sandra excused herself, crossed toward the entry hall, and politely went upstairs.

"I have something to tell you, Mr. Sayres. I wonder if we could sit down and talk."

They sat in the two wingback chairs on either side of the darkened fireplace.

"First," said Hermann, "there's been no sign of your friend Olson, or of your skipper's body . . . who you indicated fell overboard at the rock. The Coast Guard called in a second helicopter from Port Angeles and searched the beach again early this morning. Your boat has broken up on the rocks. The Coast Guard's job ends with search and rescue, and they've done all they can. You may have been about a quarter-mile off shore. Can you tell me what you were doing a quarter-mile off shore?"

Mark guessed that the man would consider him a liar or a fool, whatever he said, so he took a deep breath and told him everything.

"The boat was sinking and then Olson and I were in the water. Then Olson was gone. I couldn't see him. He had let go of the bow railing for some reason. I yelled for him, but I didn't know what direction he'd gone; then I began to swim as best I could toward shore. I barely made it alive. That's it."

"We got the skipper's name from Reverend Hanley last night. You said the other man's name was Craig Olson."

"Yes. Horn had sold the boat and was delivering it to Victoria, B.C., from Astoria. I came up from San Diego to see my wife."

"You sailed here directly from Astoria, then? You haven't been up here before this—say in the last several days?"

"No. A friend in Portland who works for *The Oregonian* told me that Horn could use an extra hand to sail up the coast. I decided to sail. This was the first time I'd met Horn or his nephew."

The deputy sheriff stopped and looked at Mark as if trying to make up his mind about something.

Mark interrupted Hermann's rumination. "Sheriff, I'm not a criminal, and I didn't murder anyone, though in a way I might as well have. What can I tell you? I'm a stupid guy who couldn't figure out a problem with a compass until it was too late, and I'll foolishly blame myself for the rest of my life." So much for calling an attorney, he thought. With nothing more to say, he gazed toward the front window.

"Take it easy, Mr. Sayres. I didn't read you your rights yet. It's a pretty rugged coastline around here, and lots of chances for trouble. Also, lots of notches or caves for a drowned body or two to hide."

"I realize that."

Hermann leaned forward in the chair, forearms resting on his knees. A somber expression crossed his face. He looked down at the carpet, then at Mark.

"Without evidence to the contrary, and previous to an investigation, I am going to tentatively accept what you've told me—that you had nothing to do in a criminal sense with anyone's death." There was another awkward silence. "Actually, I came all the way out here because of your wife."

Mark was caught off guard. He looked at the sheriff in surprise.

"I knew your wife was staying at the archaeological diggings a little way south of here. We've been trying to get hold of you since Tuesday afternoon."

"What are you talking about?"

"I'm sorry to have to get to this in such a roundabout way, but I had to question you about your whereabouts. . . ." He sat up straighter and rested his elbows on the cushioned arms of the chair. "I'm sorry to tell you that your wife is missing."

Mark was stunned.

"I have a man coming here to meet . . ." the sheriff began.

"You mean you . . . know my wife? You know who I am?"

"Yes."

"I don't understand. Did Maggie leave the dig? What?"

"We don't know. Her things are still in one of the shacks. I'm sorry. Maybe I should have come out here last night, but considering what you've been through, it's probably good you got some rest after your accident."

Mark slowly shook his head in a gesture of incomprehension. He searched his shocked mind for a shred of explanation. For God's sake, Maggie. . . .

"She left without her backpack or her other clothes. The people at the dig spent a lot of time looking for her until they called us—and we organized a search."

The sheriff looked at him intently. "Oddly, someone said they saw your wife walking in the woods the day after she was missed. It was probably a mistaken identification, because she didn't return to the dig that night either, but the whole area was searched again."

Hermann shifted in his chair. "There's not much more to say except that we unsuccessfully tried to reach you. We eventually contacted your mother-in-law, who said you were on your way up here from Astoria. We searched for your wife for three days with about a hundred people. The helicopter flew over the beach a dozen times for several miles in each direction." The deputy's voice had risen in volume to a coarse resonance.

"I'd like to ask if you can tell us anything that would help explain her disappearance."

Mark could barely speak. "Nothing specific. I can't believe it. I was just coming to see her."

Hermann took a deep breath. "Was she depressed or upset?"

Mark felt his mind go numb. He recalled Maggie's phone conversation, painfully certain that something was wrong. "Yes. I don't know."

"Yes, you don't know?"

"No, I . . . She *was* depressed when she called me, but I don't know why. There wasn't anything specific." He felt inappropriately defensive.

"Don't get upset, Mr. Sayres. I'm sure you'll want to stay around for a few days, and of course we might need you."

"How do I get to the archaeology site?"

"There's a fellow coming here to take you. He's been helping down at the dig. His name is Jim Kallabush. I believe you met him last night."

"Yes."

"He's going to drive you. It's not far south of here." Hermann got up from the chair, but Mark was dizzy and couldn't get up. He couldn't pretend to be well. Why had Maggie left the dig without warning—without her things?

"Concerning the boat accident, there is still a problem here without either of the two bodies of the people you say had gone into the water. I emphatically want you to stay in the area for a few days."

Mark agreed numbly and thought of his daughter again. A gulf of emotion was opening up—then a spontaneous, clear, and bittersweet memory of when he'd first met Maggie on a summer evening. A young woman then, a stranger, had just finished listening to a chamber music concert in Balboa Park. He recalled the loneliness that had driven him to approach her. Her young face, blond hair, and summer dress seemed to invite him into a shadow, where he spoke to her about the music. During their conversation, he mentioned his interest in architecture, and she asked him if he'd ever had a desire to wander around the old houses, cathedrals, and historic places of Europe. They talked a lot—and laughed, and made a date to see each other again. The next week they went hiking, slept in the foothills of Mt. Palomar under the night sky, and fell in love. Their togetherness grew into marriage. They had a daughter, Erica.

Hermann stood up. "I'll be going now. Things have been kind of busy around here." He went into the entry hall and yelled upstairs. "Hello? You up there? I'm about done if I can use your phone."

Mark got up from the chair and stood awkwardly on the oriental carpet.

Sandra came downstairs while Hermann used the phone. She gave Mark an odd glance.

Hermann talked for a minute, then hung up. "Kallabush should be here any minute to pick you up. He's driving from his place near Sooes Beach. He's got a borrowed key for the logging gate at the south end of the reservation." Hermann attempted a shy smile, bringing out the wrinkles in his weathered face. There was an awkward silence. "Well, I'll be going now."

As Sandra showed him out, she stood on the porch for a while with the door ajar, speaking to him in half-whispers, the effect of which made Mark strangely uncomfortable.

Sandra came in, closed the door, and thrust her hands into the back pockets of her jeans.

"What did he tell you?" she asked.

Mark told her the story. She sat on an arm of the sofa, her face like a beautiful white sculpture.

"I'd heard that a woman was missing from the dig," she said when he was finished, "but I didn't know who, and when you told me about your wife . . . well, if I'd been smart, I might have connected it."

"There was no way you could have known." He was stumbling in a dense fog, saved from the sea only to be plunged into a worse nightmare. Heat seemed to rise into his head, and he broke into a mild sweat. He wanted to grab onto his life before it fell away.

"Look, if there's anything I can do. . . . Did Hermann say anything more?" she asked.

"No, not really."

With a pained expression on her face, Sandra started to say something else, but stopped. He was sure something was on her mind, but all she said was, "Jim will be here pretty soon."

*　　*　　*

After being sure he was calm, Mark removed a damp long-distance calling card from his wallet. He dialed Maggie's parents in San Diego.

After one ring, Maggie's mother, Dorothy, answered. Her voice filtered through the line. ". . . No, Erica can't hear me. I haven't told her anything. We can't tell her until we know what's happened. . . . We didn't know where you were. We couldn't get hold of you on your cell phone after that sheriff called us."

"I stupidly put the cell phone in my bag before I left for Astoria," said Mark. "I didn't check my messages that night and couldn't get them when we were out at sea. A lot has happened. I'll have to explain later." He paused and reflected that he hadn't said anything about the reasons for his trip in the first place. "And I may not be able to reach you for the next couple of days. I'll be down on a remote beach south of here, but I'll let you know anything as soon as possible. And tell Sam not to worry too much. Maggie probably just left without telling anyone."

"Why would Maggie do that? Something must have happened to her, but they're not reporting it here as a criminal investigation."

Mark felt a huge weight crushing him. "I don't know."

"Mark, what can we do?"

"I don't know. I'll do the best I can. Try to be patient."

He said goodbye and quickly got together what was left of his things, including the damp sweater, but not his life jacket, which he left for Sandra to dispose of. Sandra walked aimlessly around the living room, then went upstairs, found an unopened toothbrush package and a small travel kit, which she gave to him.

"It's funny," she said. "This is all I can do. I can't help you."

"You've been very gracious."

"Don't be too hard on yourself." Her eyes were a curiously imponderable watercolor.

A car horn sounded outdoors. Mark put on his jacket, put the token gifts in his pocket, took his sweater, and went outside.

Jim Kallabush nodded to him behind the window of an old, powder-blue Plymouth Valiant that flaunted a nasty dent over the front wheel-well. Mark got into the car and closed the door. Sandra Torrel stood on the front porch.

The car window was coated with dust and mist. Through the glass, Sandra's figure seemed indistinct, faded, lonely. A shroud of ocean fog passed like a moving curtain between the car and the house. She remained on the porch in the cold, watching as the car circled in front of the house and carried him into the forest.

Chapter Four

Kallabush flicked the wheel left and right as if he were playing a video game. The route he followed away from the Torrel house through the murky woods could barely be called a road; it was more a phenomenon of earth and gravel appearing around disintegrating logs, giant sword ferns, and swampy pools of skunk cabbage. The beam of the car's headlights through the mist produced the eerie effect of descending into a prehistoric bog. "Sandy's got a Land Rover in the garage. Around here, four-wheel drive is best on the old logging roads. They try to keep the roads maintained, but it can be a losing battle."

The car hit a pothole and Mark grabbed for the edge of the dashboard. "This is an old logging road?" he asked quietly.

"No, this is a private road first run through when Joseph Torrel built the house out here in 1922. He owned the lumber company 'til the late 1920s. I hear he was kind of a tyrant who didn't care much for Indians. Anyway, there's still logging going on around here, and it's the abandoned logging roads that let people get down near the archaeology site."

In another minute they came to an open gate. Kallabush stopped the car just beyond it, jumped out, and swung the gate closed behind them. He wrapped some chain around a post to keep it in place, wiped his hands on his jeans, and got back into the car. The private road joined a wider dirt and gravel road. After a turn or two in a generally eastward direction, Kallabush headed south. "These are true logging roads," he said. "Full of potholes as usual."

They were quiet for a while, perhaps self-consciously aware of the subject they'd failed to broach. Finally Kallabush said: "We all looked real hard for your wife. I didn't know who you were. I mean, I didn't recognize the name Sayres or I would have said something last night— well, maybe it was better for you to rest. I haven't been around the dig that much lately. I didn't know your wife well."

"Did they look everywhere possible?" A dumb question, but all he could think of.

"Yes. I think she'd have to have gone a long way off for us to have missed her, or a long way into the forest, far enough so that many more days of searching would prove nothing."

"How many people are at the dig?"

"Couple of days ago there were maybe six or eight. Now just Ken and me. Paul Radwick, the man who started the dig, he's coming back soon. I think he's at the University of Washington now. Dr. Radwick, he's kind of hoping we may have found another place like Ozette. We've found some things, but nothing real old like at Ozette. I mean nothing more than about a hundred years old."

"Maggie did graduate work at the U.W. in archaeology. She knew about Ozette."

"It's the major archaeological site farther south. It was a real discovery. They found the remains of a smokehouse that had been buried in a mudslide about five hundred years ago. The clay made it so the house was well preserved. Not just the house, but a lot of stuff inside— even baskets and cedar boxes—all sealed up in the mud and clay. It took a lot of trouble and a lot of people to excavate that site."

"Maggie told me about it a long time ago."

"It was a big deal, in the news and all that. We're talking about the oldest North American culture. Fifteen hundred years of it."

The mist was abating somewhat. Using the washer, Kallabush gave the windshield a swipe with the wiper blades. A second sweep cleared the water away. The narrowing road was wet, too, and they couldn't go any faster, steering around clusters of potholes, but at least the road was hard-packed earth and gravel.

"They find your friend yet, the one who disappeared in the water?"

"No."

Kallabush frowned. "Man, I've lived all my life near the sea, and sometimes it's like that. Sometimes a person is there, and then they are not there. Could be they did something stupid. Maybe not. It's all the same. Makahs were great whale and seal hunters, so we've had food when inland Indians were starving. But man, you better believe the ocean can take life away as well as give life. White men here, they know this too. Sometimes all you got is hope."

The car slowed down. "It's a little rough now. I really shouldn't take the car on this turnoff, but if I don't, it'll add about a mile to our hike."

"How long is the hike?"

"Not bad. A little over a mile, but we've got to get down a steep trail to the beach, which is a bit rough. Your boots looked waterproof."

"I bought them for both hiking and sailing."

Kallabush smiled. "OK. After we leave the trailhead, you can sail through the mud."

*   *   *

At the trailhead, Kallabush parked his car near a metallic-blue Nissan Pathfinder and an old red Honda Accord. The Honda was parked where the gravel left off and the black mud of the forest floor began. On the rear was a faded bumper sticker that announced, "You are on NATIVE AMERICAN LAND."

"Looks like we got company today," said Kallabush, staring at the partly rusted Accord. "Looks like Richard Walker drove all the way around."

"You mean from Neah Bay?"

"Yeah, but he must have taken the paved road east along the straits and then come all the way around through Ozette. You can't drive straight south from Neah Bay because there's a big metal gate at the southern boundary of the reservation."

"A gate?"

"Yeah, the land south is owned by a logging company. But it's the only road south, so the archaeologists got a couple of gate keys and loaned me one because I'm the off-season caretaker. Privileged guy, I am." He shut off the engine and opened his door, which groaned. Mark reached into the back seat for his sweater, then stepped out of the car and walked over to Kallabush who was busy inspecting the old Honda.

"Yeah, he sure keeps this old car running."

Mark nodded. But a scene of Maggie packing her suitcase while Erica constantly ran in and out of the bedroom came to his mind, and he felt another tightening of his stomach. He knew that when he got to the dig, he had to ask some questions and hang onto whatever hope he could. Deciding to tie his damp sweater around his waist, he zipped up his jacket and found himself looking down at the bumper sticker.

"Guy can't get off the warpath," said Kallabush, smiling. "Well, we'd better get hiking down to the beach."

Mark nodded. The fog had subsided, but it was the beginning of a chilly autumn on the outskirts of the Olympic rain forest. They hiked at a steady pace through a delicate grove of young alder, then into the darker forest. The narrow trail led into an enormous cavern of spruce, cedar, and hemlock, where only a few rays of light filtered through the canopy. The smell of the earth was damp and intense, but refreshing. Orange, brown, and white fungi grew in the hollows of stumps, and moss-covered logs rested like prehistoric wrecks on the forest floor. After a half-hour of hiking along the narrow trail, Mark was breathing more heavily. He repeated inwardly that Maggie could still be alive. He had to believe that.

"How much farther?"

"Not too far. We'll rest before we climb down to the beach."

The climb down was more awkward than difficult. They skirted along a rocky stream, waded through a thick growth of salal and salmonberry that had apparently grown back since the archaeology team had cleared it, and maneuvered around some boulders near the level of the beach. When they emerged into the open they were well above the winter high-tide line.

A monochromatic grayness enveloped the shore, the sea, and the distant breakers. Color seemed drained from the trees that grew atop the bluffs to the north and south. A cold wind blew inland. The scene was gloomy, and the thought that Maggie wanted to stay here longer was depressing. Mark forced himself to concentrate on what lay before him. Whatever had upset Maggie, he would have to depend on whoever was here to help.

Four small shacks were huddled in a cluster south of where the trail emerged from the woods, and closer to the beach. Kallabush led the

way toward these little structures that had apparently been built by the
scientific team out of boards and shingles.

A deep channel in the ground on the way to the shacks, about five
feet wide and maybe forty feet long, had been cut from a wide shelf of
land somewhat elevated from the beach. The channel had vertical sides
and stretched from near the first twisted spruce trees at the edge of the
forest to a shallow drop-off to the beach. The path stayed landward of
the channel, and Mark could see pin markers with eyelets sticking into
the dirt walls of the excavation. Had this been where Maggie was working? White string marked off squares along the walls of the trench, and a
variety of rocks and shells could be seen in the cross-section of earth.

A second channel, also perpendicular to the beach, had been dug,
and this broadened considerably at the landward end, forming a large
circular pit shallower than the channel itself. It looked as though the pit
had been abandoned. A cord had been strung around it about two feet
high, but no white string marked the sides. The pit was about three feet
deep compared to the connecting trench's four.

"You can see there's been a lot of digging," Kallabush remarked.

The tide was low, the beach was mildly sloped, and the breakers were
a fair distance away. As they made their way, the trail turned toward the
shacks and the beach. When they approached the first shack, a face appeared in a small window that had been crudely fitted into the flat siding
next to the door. The door, which faced south, opened, and out stepped
a man about thirty years old, Asian, with a wide, amused expression.

"Well, Kallabush, I thought I heard some voices out here."

"Just us," said Kallabush.

Inside the shack, Sayres and Kallabush removed their muddy boots
and set them beside the door. Mark scrutinized the room. Two other
people, a man and a woman, sat on a simple bench against one wall.
The interior was cramped, uninsulated, and about the size of an ordinary bedroom. A Coleman stove lay in one corner, a kerosene heater in
the middle of the room, and a card table stacked with books, papers,
and a hurricane lamp. Light came through the glass window by the
door, through an opposite window of stretched, clear plastic, and
through a small window looking toward the sea. Some crude shelves
had been made with rocks and boards.

The woman on the bench, a dark complexioned, plump, but not unattractive person wearing fine wooden beads around her neck, smiled. The man did not. He did not look especially Native American in facial structure or complexion, and he wore a black hat with a flat brim tilted jauntily. His brown wrinkled-leather coat was of the "flight jacket" variety, zipped up almost to the neck. He rested his black boots on the wooden floor near a sleeping bag that lay unrolled on a piece of egg-carton foam.

"This is Mark Sayres, Maggie Sayres's husband," said Kallabush.

"Oh?" said the Asian. "I . . . I'm very sorry you had to be here under these circumstances. I'm Ken Matsamura. This is Richard Walker and Judy Roundtree."

"Mark was in a boating accident last night," noted Kallabush.

"Really? We don't get much news out here. What happened?"

"The yacht I was on went down a little way north," said Mark. "One of us was lost overboard and another is missing."

Matsamura seemed a bit overwhelmed. "I can't believe it. Are they still searching for them?"

"I think so. I don't know about one of them. His name was Olson. The other, Horn, is dead."

"Coast Guard was out last night and this morning," said Kallabush.

"I'll be damned."

No one quite knew what to say next.

"Look, can I get you something to eat or drink?" asked Matsamura. Mark declined politely.

"Good choice," said the man on the bench. "This ain't no Ramada Inn for sure."

"True," said Matsamura to Sayres, "but you can stay as long as you want. This whole thing about your wife has got us all depressed. We thought she might have gone into Neah Bay with a couple of the women students, but when they came back in the morning, they said they hadn't seen her. The next day, after we knew she was missing, someone said they'd seen her in the forest. But she didn't come back that night either, so we guessed the person had been mistaken. All Maggie's belongings were still in the shack, so we had to assume something had happened. We carried out a huge search. I suppose you know

about it. There isn't much to add. The student volunteers left a couple
of days ago." Matsamura's expression was one of discomfort.

"Did she say anything about being upset?"

"Not that we know of."

"Where are Maggie's things?" asked Mark.

"Oh . . . yes, they're right over here." He lifted a canvas suitcase
from a dark corner.

As Mark took it out of Matsamura's hand, he remembered how
Maggie had looked when she said goodbye at the airport, and an over-
whelming sense of loss enveloped him. His eyes momentarily lost focus
as he put the terribly familiar old suitcase on the floor and opened the
lid. Quietly going through it, he found many recognizable items including the letters he had sent. In one corner of the suitcase was a pair of
leather workman's gloves he'd given her for the trip. They'd joked
about her becoming a ditch-digger. He fought back his emotion.

". . . I can't sleep," she had said. He remembered her head on the pillow, her profile dimly captured by the reflected light from a street lamp
under the window shade. "What's wrong?" he asked. Her eyes shim-
mered with moisture in the semi-darkness. She was silent, then shifted
under the covers. "I don't know." She turned away from him in the
night, toward the window, eventually falling asleep, disturbed by something inexpressible. It was a scene that repeated itself at different times.
Was Maggie depressed by something in their marriage, or by the world
outside? Maybe she had experienced a similar emotion here and had gone
for a walk in a state of depression. Or had she been victimized?

He carefully closed the suitcase.

"You can stay as long as you like," offered Matsamura again, "or at
least until we fold up shop for the winter. That's about two weeks
away. You can stay in 'Harpo,'" he said. "There's a couple of clean
sleeping bags in there. We have four shacks: Groucho, Chico, Harpo,
and Zeppo. We left out the other one. I can't remember him."

"Archaeologists know nothing about trivia," said Judy Roundtree.

"They don't know everything," said Richard Walker.

Matsamura shook his head. "You guys came down here to give me
a pain in the ass all right."

"That's for sure," agreed Kallabush. "I'm going to get a couple of folding chairs from next door." He went out.

"These here," said Matsamura, "are a couple of the local 'natives' from around here."

"Oh man," said Judy.

"This is the third time they've come to visit, and they're still giving us trouble."

Kallabush shoved his way through the door carrying some folding chairs. He gave one chair to Mark, unfolded his, and sat down.

"Gummo," he recalled. "The fifth brother."

Mark sat down in the chair and they were soon having soup and coffee heated on the small propane stove ventilated to the outside. They talked of the weather. The conversation avoided Maggie, but it was a natural avoidance, thought Mark. What could these people do that they hadn't done already? Everything seemed normal. He dug his wristwatch out of his pocket, but still couldn't get it to run. As the wind beat against the plastic window, he put the broken watch back, folded his arms over his chest, and closed his eyes. Maggie was logical, efficient, and reasonable. If she'd left the dig without telling anyone and meant not to return, why didn't she take her suitcase? Where was she? Desolation overcame him, and he tried to think. But after five minutes he found himself covering the same old territory he'd covered at home—ending with her nervous voice on the telephone. Finally he dozed off, and by the time he stopped ruminating and drifting in and out of wakefulness, the group's conversation had moved on.

". . . to understand the past," Kallabush was saying.

"Disturbing the land of our forefathers," said Richard Walker solemnly. "No more and no less than grave robbers."

"How can we learn about our ancestors unless we find out how they lived?" said Kallabush. "That is the important thing—to preserve our traditions, to discover what is lost."

Matsamura sat next to the card table, an unlit pipe hanging from his mouth.

Walker looked intently at Kallabush. "Preserving our traditions does not mean digging up the whole coast. You are a Native American. We have learned from the Ozette dig. There is no need to steal more so-called artifacts from our dead ancestors. These people who lived here were recent, is that right?"

"We have found things dating from different times," interrupted Matsamura. "We're taking a risk here, more so than at Ozette where they had more evidence about the nature of the place. They knew they were dealing with centuries of residency at that location. Here, we haven't found the quantity of items we'd hoped for."

"Jim, would your grandmother have wanted the whole coast dug up?" said Walker, becoming annoyed.

"We are not digging up the whole coast, and my grandmother is dead," said Kallabush. "Many Indian ways of thinking are dead."

"But we have caught whales again."

"Listen, Richard, I want to learn what the past has to offer—not bow down on the ground to it. I respect the land around here as much as you, and I want our sons and daughters to know how our ancestors lived and see the tools they took with them to hunt for whales, and know the old ways and know they are descended from a courageous and inventive people. What I don't want or need is to hang onto superstition."

"We're not talking about superstition. We've got to get back to the idea that the land is sacred. That is a way of living, not a superstition, and it works because it teaches us we are not separate from our surroundings."

"OK. We learn from the land. Now we should learn from our ancestors who lived and died on the land so that they won't stay silent forever."

"They are not silent," said Walker. "Go into the forest, onto the rocks near the sea, and hear them speak."

"They will not speak to those who know nothing of them," said Kallabush.

Walker shook his head, leaned back against the wall, and raised his coffee cup in a mock salute. Then he stretched his legs and rested his boots on their heels. "What will you do when you find the bones of the dead?" he continued. "Archaeologists think they can dig up dead Indians wherever they find them. What would happen if we went around digging up white graves?"

"The law has changed since the incidents you speak of, and you know that."

"Look what happened at Ozette."

"Those remains were preserved in a five-hundred-year-old mudslide."

"The mudslide was their resting place. They should not have been disturbed."

"The tribe was supportive of the Ozette dig, and they are supportive of us here."

"Not all."

"Of course, not all."

"It's never easy," Matsamura interjected, "to get everyone in agreement. The way things are going, this camp will be closed permanently. And take it from me, the money will run out before we can dig up the whole coastline. Besides, we're not technically on the reservation this far south."

"That means nothing," said Richard.

"We have to go, Richard," said Judy, sounding worried. "Won't be long before dark."

Walker set his cup down on the floor. "Can't argue with that."

"Why don't you stick around and use an extra shack?" said Matsamura. "There aren't any people except us now."

"Yeah," said Kallabush. "Guard your ancestors for the night. If we find any bones, you'll be the first to know."

Walker glanced at Judy. "You want to stay with these weirdoes, honey?"

Judy smiled. "I've got Dorothy Swenson taking care of the kids."

"She'll put them to bed, won't she," said Walker, "if we don't come back by nine or so?"

"If we don't come back she'll be worried."

"You mean because of the talk?"

Judy glanced at Mark, then back at Richard. "Doesn't matter. If we don't come back before nighttime she'll be worried."

"OK."

Walker nodded to everyone. "Thanks for the invitation anyway."

"Sure," said Matsamura.

The plastic window made a whipping noise and was moving in and out quite regularly now with the increasing gusts. Jim Kallabush opened the door for Richard and Judy.

"Plenty of light left for the hike back," he said, eyeing the sky. Then he looked at Mark. "How about if I set you up in 'Harpo' now? Better start up that kerosene heater. You don't know how cold it can get around here at night."

"I know something about it," said Mark.

"I guess you do," said Kallabush with a faint smile.

Mark and Jim followed Richard and Judy outside. The sky was darkening. It was starting to drizzle.

As Mark followed Kallabush along the little rut toward the end shack, he looked over his shoulder at the departing couple who made their way along the path toward the trail entrance. Judy seemed worried, and he mentally saw them through the woods, placing them comfortably in the Honda with the bumper sticker.

"Here's your shack," said Kallabush. "Sleeping bags inside. Pick either one. There are rolls of foam too. Oh hell, I guess I'd better come in and light that sucker up. You ever use a kerosene heater?"

"Yeah, but maybe you'd better do this one. I'd hate to burn the place down."

They went inside. While the wind and rain gusted against the thin cedar walls, Kallabush lit the heater. He did the same with a hurricane lamp on a small table against the wall. He familiarized Mark with the food supply and instructed him on outdoor toilet procedures. "Like Richard says, it's not the Ramada Inn."

"It's what I'm used to," said Mark.

Kallabush chuckled. "Yeah, right."

"One thing, though."

Kallabush held the door latch.

"What did Richard mean about the 'talk' at Neah Bay? Judy seemed worried."

"Oh, that," said Kallabush. "Nothing." A strange expression crossed his face. "Just some old Indian shit. Don't give it a thought." He opened the door to go out. "Get some sleep. You're starting to look like hell again."

Chapter Five

In the morning, they prepared breakfast in the main cabin. The idea of continuing to search for Maggie in the woods where others had searched made no sense. The big search had already taken place. Waiting for news was all that remained.

Matsamura kept Mark occupied by teaching him how to clean a few unearthed artifacts. To that end, Mark dutifully took a couple of green plastic buckets down to the beach to fill with sea water. Kallabush and Matsamura worked at the junction of the excavation where the deeper channel met the circular pit. This was in the wide, well-protected area above the winter high-tide line. Most of the digging was in earth, not sand. The driftwood thrown up along most of the beach was lower relative to the forest at this point. The deep shelf of land characterized by earth and underbrush, protected by bluffs covered in vegetation, was a good place for a small village.

The temptation for Mark to glance over his shoulder toward the trail entrance was strong. The deputy sheriff might wander in with news. There was no electricity, and the camp's emergency cell phone, which used a satellite service, needed recharging.

As Mark put the buckets down by his feet, he looked southward along the beach—a scene of stark, unspoiled beauty.

He saw something that distracted him. Down the beach under the cloudy sky, an isolated figure in a yellow rain jacket walked south along the margin of the cresting tide.

While the cold salt spray swept off the breakers and gradually drifted in, Mark found himself watching the figure in the distance. The man appeared to have shaggy blond hair. He was walking slowly but purposefully through the shoreline mist. Mark let a few seconds lapse, and as the waves rolled in, he allowed credence to an unlikely thought. He forced himself to wonder if, somehow, that man could be Craig Olson. From the back it looked like him. Might he have survived and by some remarkable circumstance was wandering around down here? It was hard to shake the absurd idea.

Leaving the buckets, he walked in the man's direction. It's ridiculous, he thought—crazy. But Olson had on yellow foul-weather gear, this guy's got on something that looks the same, and he has the same muscular build and blond hair.

The man was more than a city block down the hazy beach, and kept walking without turning around.

The rubber soles of Mark's boots were good for traversing beach terrain; they fit him well, and the sand just below the high tide line was firm enough that he could keep up a good, steady pace.

The farther he walked, the more wildly convinced he was that this really could *be* Olson—who might be walking around in some sort of daze. Mark quickened his pace, hands in pockets to keep warm, breathing steadily, trying to get within hailing distance. What difference would it make if he was mistaken? A little embarrassment, the consequences of desperate optimism.

Far down the beach was a rocky bluff jutting into the sea, waves heaving into it, cascading off. The man maintained his distance, a yellow blot of color on the landscape. Though it seemed useless to shout over the sound of the breakers, Mark cupped his hands to his mouth. "Olson!" he yelled. But he hadn't gained on the long-haired man at all, who must also be keeping a strong pace and who did not vary his path. Mark began to jog, leaning forward, looking up every few seconds to check his progress. What *explanation* could there be for Olson ending up so far south of where the boat went down, and how could the Coast Guard have missed him the night before? It was insane, but stranger things have happened, he told himself.

Though he sped up, he wasn't gaining on the man. Any moment now, this guy might turn and walk toward the forest; not that it would be hard to follow him, but for peace of mind Mark didn't want to risk it. He imagined having to call the Coast Guard or the police to report seeing Olson. They'd have to come out here. He didn't want that, and didn't know if he'd have the nerve to make such an improbable report.

Breathing hard, he slowed to a walk again. The guy was as far away as before. Had he been running? Mark completely stopped for a moment to catch his breath, a bit angry at himself—and also at the person in the distance, who he now suspected was intentionally trying to stay ahead. Had the man seen him?

Let's get this over with, thought Mark.

He hit a stretch of firm, wet sand and began to run fast and steadily, looking down, then ahead, occasionally tripping in the waves sluicing up the beach. He knew he couldn't keep this fast pace for more than a few minutes. He wasn't a good runner, though he felt in better shape since last night. The man did not run. The man continued walking as before.

Heart pounding, near exhaustion, Mark blinked ahead through the dampness of the ocean mist.

The truth invaded his mind in a hot wave of incomprehension. The man was *walking* and staying ahead of him. Mark had been running hard for over a minute. The man never ran. He walked—and like a mirage of water on a scorching summer highway, stayed ahead at whatever speed Mark chose to take.

Mark stood on the beach, perplexed, lungs burning.

The figure, a person in a yellow foul-weather jacket surrounded by heavy ocean mist, gray rocks and sand, was almost at the bouldered outcropping. He walked farther, but did not reach the outcropping. Neither did he turn.

Mark felt a chill crawl up his neck—not of fear, but of a deep confusion, the meaning of which was rooted in whatever conception of reality he ordinarily relied upon. The experience was so disorienting that he lost concentration and tried unsuccessfully to fend off dizziness. Something strange was happening now. The sound of the waves breaking on shore was amplified, unreal, and nearly unbearable. The color yellow, the swipe of meaning in the distance, became the forced, compelling center of attention. Mark saw nothing else, blocked everything else out, grew light-headed, faint, then nauseous. He kneeled on the beach and felt the dampness of the sand come through the knees of his pants. He bent his head down to keep from vomiting and tried to regain composure. He felt the warm blood flow back into his head almost immediately as he bent over, took a deep breath, and looked up again.

The man standing in the yellow foul-weather jacket turned and stared back from near the outcropping. His face was pale white, the blood gone from it, gazing soberly. *It was Olson.*

Mark shut his eyes, then put both palms flat down on the wet sand and tried to fight off the swirling nausea. After another second, he shuddered, then looked again.

The figure was gone.

The landscape was empty of visible life and drained of all movement but the mist and sea. Mark stood up and stared toward the sand and pebbles that marked the high tide line, at the field of cobble-like rocks that extended to the winter driftwood, then at the barrier of far trees. The sound of the breakers was tolerable again.

He brushed his hands off and took another deep breath. He felt the cold breeze, thinking he must be ill, must be affected by some weird post-hypothermia. The tide was peaking and in a moment washed over his boots. It was also erasing whatever imprints might have remained on the sand, yet Mark knew there would be no footprints except his own. The man could not have physically gone anywhere. God in heaven, he thought, it was a hallucination. He tried to reconcile himself to this disconcerting event as he turned back in the direction of the shacks.

Another thought seized him. He remembered that they told him Maggie had been *seen* the day after she disappeared. This coincidence materialized like the sighting of a distant, dangerous animal. It hung in morbid suspension, an impossible enigma, until it lapsed into the prosaic realm of suggestibility.

Brushing the sand off his pants, making sure he was no longer light-headed, he walked back. You're not over the trauma of the yachting accident, he told himself.

In a few minutes, he retrieved the plastic buckets, walked past the cross-sections of earth where Kallabush and Matsamura were hunched down with their hand tools, and went to his cabin. Inside, he sat down on a wooden bench, leaned up against the wall, and tried to get hold of himself. He pressed his temples with his fingers. He hadn't seen Craig Olson. He repeated this in his mind. There was no physical explanation. If another man in a yellow jacket had been there and touched off a hallucination, that man couldn't have just disappeared off the beach. He could not have walked from the beach into the forest that fast, not even supposing the exact distances were deceptive.

He glanced at the kerosene stove and thought about lighting it. He cursed himself. This place reminded him of the *Lenore*. There was the kerosene heater. Here were the wooden walls, and outside was the wind and the sea. Suddenly he felt as if he had not really come ashore. There's no underestimating the forces of guilt or redemption, he thought. Wouldn't it be good to have Olson survive even if—Maggie didn't?

Maggie, he thought, was dead.

Rising slowly, he got up and squeezed his eyes closed. He leaned against the wall and wept silently in the shadow. The morning light filtered through the dusty plastic of the window onto the floor. He watched the light, his eyes brimming, remembering Maggie's soft features, then Erica's smile, knowing that whatever difficulties they'd encountered, these things were what anchored his life and gave it meaning. But it was as if Maggie's depressions had reached a tragic, cruel, and logical end. There had been that part of her he couldn't reach, couldn't understand. This time she *knew* what was wrong but couldn't tell him. Why? He lay down on top of the slick green sleeping bag, wiped the moisture from his eyes, cupped his hands behind his stiff neck, and let the weight of time bring him back to a functioning state.

Sanity returned but seemed diminished.

Forcing himself to go outside, he walked slowly up to the diggings.

"You missed my big find of the day," said Kallabush, looking up from the trench. "I found a coin here this morning, an old English penny right at this level in the clay layer." He pointed to a cross-section of strata with his muddy rubber glove. He turned to Matsamura who was hunched down next to him. "I was kind of hoping it might be one of the old Spanish coins from the late 1700s. It's there on that flat board," said Kallabush, pointing a few feet away.

Mark bent down to a board with several small objects. He picked up the coin and read the barely discernible date: 1912. On the reverse side was the corroded portrait of George V. He felt the cold copper between his fingers.

"That's typical," said Kallabush. "Stuff from near the turn of the century. I like the older things, though: fishhooks, mussel shell and stone blades, and here," he said, nodding to his right, "is part of a whale jawbone."

"Maggie implied that you'd found something genuinely significant."

Matsamura answered instead of Kallabush. "Well . . . I don't know what she may have meant. We've uncovered a few things. We think there was, in fact, a small village here."

"What about that big circular excavation?" Mark pointed to the shallower pit.

Matsamura glanced at Kallabush, then up from the trench. "That was when we started doing sample digs. The midden looked promising. We kept digging outward hoping to find a major pocket of artifacts. I think we were a little optimistic, not as methodical as we could have been. Basically, it didn't turn out as we expected."

"These guys started this while I was gone," said Kallabush, "otherwise I'd have found several old smokehouses by now."

"We can't fight the rain and mud much longer," said Matsamura. "This place has the highest rainfall of anywhere in the U.S. and it won't be long before our trench is nothing but a mud hole no matter how carefully we drain it. We're shutting down in two weeks for the season."

After a minute, Mark asked: "Do you guys know anything about the effects of hypothermia?"

Matsamura leaned against the trench wall. "Nothing much. Why?"

"A few minutes ago . . ." He paused. "I had a hallucination. I thought I saw the man who was with me, who was missing after the accident."

The two others stared at him.

"Where was this?" asked Kallabush.

"South toward the rock outcropping."

"Well, I guess you must have seen someone who looked like him," said Kallabush. "The boat sank way up near Sandra's."

"He couldn't have drifted this far south and be alive and just walking around, but in my mind I saw him. It's got to be because of the hypothermia. I felt very sick. I almost blacked out. I think I should see a doctor."

Matsamura looked at him intently, saying nothing. He frowned, perhaps working at some hidden question. Finally he said: "On the other hand, maybe we'd better go down there and take a look. Maybe you blanked out for a few seconds, long enough for him to walk into the woods."

"Take my word for it, he couldn't have done that."

Kallabush leaned back against the edge of the trench. His expression was one of skepticism. "After Richard and Judy yesterday, I wasn't prepared for this."

"Nobody has to go looking down there," said Mark. "It's not going to do any good. It's plain I didn't really see anyone, but it seemed very real and it scared the hell out of me."

"That's not what Kallabush meant," said Matsamura. "I don't really want to get into this—"

"Oh, man," said Kallabush.

"—but do you remember when Judy said the baby-sitter would be frightened of being alone?"

"I wondered about it."

"The reason is because your wife and shipmates aren't alone."

"What do you mean?" Mark asked.

"A Neah Bay man was presumed drowned in a fishing accident about a week before your wife disappeared. He owned a small fishing boat. The boat was found floating in the bay, empty. The man was gone and his body hasn't been found."

"Who was he?"

"A guy named Bill Ennis. No one knew him very well. I understand he was part Indian, but not a Makah, and he lived alone. He often took his boat out around the Cape to fish. His disappearance, and then your wife's, had people talking. I suppose it's why Richard and Judy's baby-sitter was nervous about being alone. There's been some worry in Neah Bay about this—and about other things."

"Are you going to start on all that old Indian bullshit?" said Kallabush.

"What makes you so intolerant?" Matsamura delivered the question with a quick, simple directness, and Kallabush did not answer. Matsamura's demeanor intensified.

"Mark thought he saw Olson," he said.

Kallabush put his hand out in a stopping gesture. "Doesn't know what he saw. Thinks he saw Olson. Everybody thinks too goddamn much around here."

Matsamura turned his head sideways as if wanting to bow out of the whole thing.

"The man here's got enough trouble," said Kallabush.

"Does it relate or doesn't it?" asked Matsamura.

"Relate to what? The town?"

"Of course, the town."

"It's the town that's bothering you. Who has lived in the town all his life? You or me?"

"All right."

"Nothing weird is happening in town," said Kallabush. "I've heard this kind of thing since I was a kid, and I've never seen anything or experienced anything except this right here." He put his hand up in front of his face and spread his fingers apart. "And I have an open mind," he added emphatically.

"What for Christssake are you two talking about?" Mark asked irritably.

"I'll tell you. Bill Ennis was seen again the day after they found his boat out in the bay," said Matsamura.

"OK, OK," said Kallabush cynically. "Before Maggie disappeared people were talking about Ennis and his boat. Ennis never came home, but all his stuff is there. So he must have drowned, right? Then your wife disappears. Rick Hermann, the deputy county sheriff, comes to Neah Bay. Now we get the story about your sailboat accident and two other drowned people—see what I mean? Pretty soon, you know, every superstitious person in Neah Bay starts connecting these things together."

"What happened to you is yet another coincidence," said Matsamura, looking at Mark. "I don't understand . . ."

"It was in my mind and that's the extent of it."

"The Native American way of thinking does not discount your experience because it was in your mind." Matsamura glanced at Kallabush. "We don't know what's going on in Neah Bay with the Makahs."

Kallabush put down his pick and shook his head in frustration.

Mark recognized the tension and for the first time saw the anguish connected to Maggie's disappearance, which was not an isolated event.

"Your wife's disappearance is not something we wanted to relate to these other things," continued Matsamura. "But up here, there's a strong tradition surrounding events like this—the dead being seen again and that sort of thing. I don't know all the circumstances of the other missing man. Logically, these things are disconnected incidents—coincidences. But with other people missing, it creates a nervous atmosphere. I didn't want to load that onto you yet, because it won't help to get too involved in other people's thinking. Yet, what happened to you is damn coincidental."

Kallabush shook his head. "You sound like Richard Walker."

Matsamura gestured toward Kallabush. "There's another reason I didn't say anything."

"Look, my wife is missing or dead," said Mark with irritation, "and two men I was with have drowned. I'm lucky to be alive myself. I don't understand what happened to me on the beach just now, but I felt ill and dizzy. I feel like I've been beaten with a club, and right now I'm getting more than a little annoyed with this whole conversation."

Matsamura turned to Mark with a beleaguered look on his face. "We spent three days and nights looking for her. This hasn't been easy for any of us. Everyone was extremely upset, and they worked like hell trying to figure out what happened."

"Let me level with you," said Mark. "I don't want to think about *anything* but Maggie. I came up here to talk to her because I thought something was wrong. Apparently you don't have the answer to that. Why would she have sounded frightened last week?"

Matsamura had a crushed look on his face. "I don't know."

"Now she's gone, and in some half-assed way I may not be over the trauma of the accident the other night. I fell down a couple of times on the yacht. Maybe I hit my head, got a small concussion. I don't know what. But I'd probably be smart to see a doctor. And I want to ask some questions of the tribal police. Whatever supernatural non-sense people are talking about up here is not my problem."

"All right, then," said Kallabush.

Matsamura was apologetic. "I'm sorry. You've had a hard time and I wish there was something we could do."

"The sheriff's deputy doesn't think the disappearances are con-nected," said Kallabush. "He thinks the sightings afterward are mis-identifications, and I'll guarantee you won't find anything in Neah Bay except gossip."

"My only business is Maggie," said Mark.

Matsamura was staring at the forest, perhaps to avoid Kallabush's gaze. Then he turned and said, "I'll drive you into town. There's a doc-tor who can check you out, and you can also talk to the tribal police, let them know you're staying here."

"OK," said Mark.

"You are not going to find out anything in town about your wife," said Kallabush.

Chapter Six

I n the gray noon, the village of Neah Bay had the dismal atmosphere
of an abandoned amusement park. Curbless streets faded into the
misty air, and no one could be seen on the few sidewalks by the bay or
behind the windows of the small, silent houses. The bay, which faced
north toward the straits and British Columbia, seemed about a mile
wide; there was an industrial-looking wooden building at the end of a
long pier, a marina with fishing boats, a rocky beach, and a breakwater
in the foggy distance. Driving with Ken Matsamura, Mark noticed the
fishing fleet, and with a mildly ill feeling reminded himself that this was
where the *Lenore* would have anchored overnight on its way to Victoria.

Matsamura had taken a short detour to show Mark the town, but
he now guided the S.U.V. away from the waterfront while a light drizzle
began to spot the windshield. The flat, main residential area was like an
old blue-collar neighborhood, with small, boxy houses, dull lawns, dog-
houses in back yards, and no sidewalks.

They parked in front of a health clinic that looked like a small
1950s elementary school. "The health center is for the Makahs," said
Matsamura, "but if the doc's not busy, we'll smuggle you in and get him
to check you out." He walked up the wheelchair ramp and into the central entrance. In a few minutes, he motioned Mark inside.

Dr. Roland Veress was a Makah of medium-height, dark complexioned, with medium-length black hair and an inflection that sounded
somewhat east-coast academic. In an examining room, he questioned
Mark about the events of the last couple of days and did a brief physical
exam while listening to Mark's descriptions. Then he folded the black

fabric of his blood pressure gauge, put it on his desk and stood looking at Mark as if staring at a strange insect. His voice was calm and precise.

"There's nothing physically wrong with you that I can find, aside from a couple of bruises. There's no special connection between hypothermia or minor concussion and hallucination. You seem to have come through a rough couple of days in pretty good shape."

Mark stood next to the examining table and buttoned his shirt. "Do you know what has been happening in town concerning the kind of thing I've described?"

The doctor continued to stare at him curiously. "What do you mean?"

"I was told that someone from town disappeared, and he was seen *after* being reported missing, just as my wife was."

"Yes, I heard that."

"Any idea what happened?"

The doctor shrugged his shoulders. "I don't know. I heard he'd fallen off his boat and drowned. Ordinarily, the body would have come to the surface, but who knows, the tide might have carried it out."

"Was he seen after his boat was found?"

Veress smiled obtusely and offered an inconclusive answer. "That's what I heard." But when he looked at Mark, he seemed to weigh his answer carefully. "Seeing the dead and missing is . . . well, it's kind of a tradition around here for certain people—and rumors dart around like sparrows in this town. There's always been talk of the supernatural in Neah Bay; but for now we have a perfect right to assume your experience this morning was the result of post-traumatic stress."

Mark nodded.

"I wouldn't worry unless it happens again," said Veress.

"Thanks for seeing me," said Mark.

"We aim to please. Let me know if you have any more problems."

They both walked down the hall to the waiting room.

"Did the doctor butcher you in there?" asked Matsamura.

"Not too badly."

"No lawsuits today," said Veress.

"That's good."

Mark asked if he could use the phone. He went into an office and called the county police. No progress had been made in finding Maggie. Then he called the Makah Police. Next, he used his calling card to call Maggie's mother and tell her there was no news. She was inconsolable. There was nothing he could do. He told her not to give up hope.

When Mark was finished, Matsamura said, "If it's all right with you, I'd like to go over to the general store."

"Fine," said Mark.

"Do you need anything, or any money? I'd be able to make a small loan."

"Thanks. But my wallet and credit card made it through the shipwreck. I'll look for a change of clothes and a few things."

They walked to Matsamura's car, got in, and drove back onto the street.

"What did the doctor say?"

"He mentioned post-traumatic stress."

"Makes sense."

"Yeah."

They drove in the drizzle back along the waterfront, then east along the main road past some storefronts and a couple of motels.

In a few minutes, they pulled into a large parking lot. The big general store carried a combination of groceries, hardware, plumbing supplies, and miscellaneous items like wall thermometers and coffee mugs with pictures of whales on them. In one area were some clothes— mostly rain parkas, sweatshirts, and T-shirts. Mark found three pairs of boxer shorts, three pairs of gray wool socks, a thick blue work shirt, and, among others, a T-shirt with a Native American drawing that said "Raven captures the sun." They didn't sell pants, so he'd have to make due with his jeans. The simple act of choosing clothes and a few other simple things had consumed his attention, and he thought it odd that in the midst of a crisis he could do something ordinary. But the narrow back aisles of the store pressed in on him, and the hope of finding Maggie was fading. The emptiness seemed intolerable, and the life that now lay ahead would contain unending loss. "What happened, Maggie? What happened to you?" he whispered to himself.

Matsamura was near the checkout stand. He held a plastic basket of groceries by a thin metal handle. Feeling emotionally drained, Mark got in line, and they went through the checkout. They carried their purchases outside past a couple of Coke machines into the parking lot, got into the car, and drove across the street to a cafe overlooking the east end of the bay.

While they ate hamburgers, Matsamura explained his interest in Makah history. "My grandparents were sent to one of the Japanese American internment camps during World War II," he said. "That's one reason I'm studying these people. Their ancestors were treated badly and I guess I can identify. You can't turn the clock back, but you can learn."

"Kallabush seems hostile to traditional ways of thinking," Mark noted.

"Yeah. Well, he's not a politically correct Indian," said Matsamura, chuckling. "I don't know the whole story of Jim Kallabush, but he can be pretty unpredictable. He's not easy to get to know, but he cares about his tribe and its history, that I can tell you. He helped with the last whale hunt. He puts on an attitude, but I think he's serious about his people's past. I think he mainly cares about the truth. At least he mingles well with a bunch of interfering scientists."

As they finished eating, a police siren sounded in the distance. In a couple of minutes, another siren could be heard coming from the other direction. Mark recognized the deputy sheriff's dark green S.U.V. as it raced down the street past the cafe. It could be heard heading southwest into the residential heart of town, then the sound stopped.

They paid their bill at the cash register, went outside, and got into the Nissan. "It'll be getting dark in another couple of hours," said Matsamura. "We'd better head over to the tribal police station if you want to let them know where you'll be."

The main road bordered the waterfront, but they drove through an area of small houses to get to the police station. As they drove, they looked down a street where, oddly, a crowd of people was gathered in the drizzle.

"That's where the siren ended up, I guess," said Matsamura. He stopped and backed up to get a better look.

From this distance, the backs of the people in the street blocked the view of what was happening. What did this peculiar gathering mean? Matsamura turned and drove part way down the street. One or two older people walked past carrying umbrellas. A man and woman folded their arms against the cold and hurried in the direction of the crowd, having come outdoors without their coats.

Mark felt a flash of dread. The crowd seemed ominously still. Near the first row of people, he saw the sheriff's vehicle positioned at an odd angle.

"Weird," said Matsamura.

"Let's check it out," Mark said.

They parked and got out. All Mark could see was a wide gap in the middle of the block, and on the other side, another, more modest crowd of people formed around another police vehicle. Something was going on in the middle of the street between the two groups of onlookers.

They walked toward the crowd almost reluctantly. Now, one or two people could be heard shouting something. A Makah woman turned away with tears in her eyes. New arrivals talked among themselves, then became watchful and silent. Expressions of shock or fear could be heard. The majority endured the chill, their faces dark and motionless, as if waiting for something to happen.

Making his way into the crowd now, Mark imagined he'd see some bullet-riddled body lying in the street.

"Give it up, Hanley!" someone yelled.

The name was familiar. Mark got to the front of the crowd, with Matsamura behind him, but he didn't immediately understand what he was seeing. He looked first at a bearded man kneeling in the street. Yes, he had recognized the name. It was the man who was at Sandra Torrel's house, Reverend Garman Hanley, thin and middle-aged, dressed in slacks and a partially unbuttoned white shirt. Reverend Hanley crouched attentively over a boy lying face up on what seemed to be a large sack of fertilizer.

Mark knew the boy. It was Hanley's son Michael, the boy who'd found him on the beach.

With a sick feeling in his stomach, Mark thought Michael must be hurt or dead. Was Reverend Hanley stunned? Why wasn't anyone helping them?

Mark leaned toward Matsamura and spoke with great intensity. "I don't believe it. That's the little boy who found me the other night. Michael Hanley. What the hell's going on here?"

Deputy Sheriff Hermann stood in front of a row of people, a small megaphone in his hand. Across the way, a Jeep Patriot had an emblem on the side that read "Neah Bay Police"—apparently the tribal police. A woman who came to the front of the crowd next to Mark put her hand over her mouth.

The reason for the woman's shock became clear as Hanley shifted position.

Nothing could have prepared Mark for what so malevolently unfolded—like a whip snapping in his brain.

Garman Hanley held a knife, somewhat concealed, at the boy's throat. Nor was the boy just lying on the big sack. He was lashed to it with a thin black cord.

As Mark confronted this horror, a short, dark-haired woman pushed him aside and guided her child quickly away. Mark grabbed Matsamura by the arm.

"This is crazy."

"Take it easy," said Matsamura.

"He said he was a church minister, the First something-or-other church."

A shuffling of people interrupted them. In the street, Hanley looked at one side of the crowd, then the other.

"You can all leave!" he yelled. "None of you belong here!" His voice was angry, rasping, anguished.

Hermann raised the megaphone, then lowered it when Hanley shifted from one knee to the other, looking back down at the child. He did not move or shift his hand from its threatening placement. His face was white and intense, cruelly hardened. Every motion he made caused the crowd to shudder, as if at any moment the knife would plunge. He looked from the boy to the crowd and back again.

A woman nearby cried "Oh God!" and a tall, pale man near the Makah police on the other side loudly said, "Reverend . . . !" but said nothing more.

Mark could not believe what he was seeing. That's right, he thought, not believe, and he felt a horrible disorientation, as if the fabric of reality were being torn away. He wiped the sky's moisture from his face and neck and remembered what Kallabush had said: *Pretty soon, you know, every superstitious person in Neah Bay starts connecting these things together.*

"He's from the First Missionary Church," said Matsamura soberly. "I know him well."

"That's it," said Mark irritably.

The crowd stood in silent turmoil. Some were visibly shaken, some holding onto one another in the drizzle. Little Michael Hanley was crying, terrified, and a dense wave of fear and anger overcame Mark as he thought of his own child Erica. What this man was doing was the ultimate betrayal, the ripping away of a child's life.

And the man had seemed so fond of his son.

Deputy Hermann raised the megaphone, which shook slightly in his hand. Yet his voice was controlled.

"Reverend Hanley, these Makah officers here have requested that I have a talk with you. We're a little stuck here for ideas. This is a hard situation, and I'd hate to, ah, just stand around and not know something more about it."

Garman Hanley paid no attention and kept looking the other way, which made the Makah officers on the other side visibly nervous.

"Reverend Hanley? I've never known a little conversation to hurt anyone."

The minister turned quickly, which jolted the onlookers. Then he focused on Hermann, eyes blazing—was it with anger, fear, or what? "No. You are from around here," he said. "I have seen you on the roads."

Michael made a gagging sound, Hermann flinched, and the megaphone lowered. "Don't hurt that boy, now," said Hermann as calmly as he could without the megaphone.

This set off a quick stroke of temper in Hanley. "You are wrong! This is not my doing but the Lord's doing, the Lord's commandment!" His voice rose to a high shattering pitch, then trailed off, and he again looked down at the boy. He whispered crazily to himself in an incomprehensible rush, which started the crowd talking.

"Lay down the knife, you crazy bastard!" a man yelled.

"Yes!" several shouted.

Someone nearby said, "I've gone to his church, over there to his church."

Hermann turned around, searched for the source of the loudest voices and said, "Back up, all of you. And shut yourselves up." He looked again at Hanley, who hadn't moved.

An old Indian man whispered loudly to Hermann, "Can't take a chance on shooting him." Hermann nodded and again raised the little yellow megaphone.

"I know you're getting tired out here." Hermann lowered the megaphone as if having second thoughts, then put it to his mouth again. "If the boy did something wrong, I'm sure we can find a way to handle it. Wouldn't it be worth a little talk?"

Hanley rested his arm across the child's small heaving chest. "I've seen you driving around here," he said.

Hermann seemed to mark time. "Well, yes, I do that now and then."

Hanley said, "Everyone here knows I wouldn't do this unless I had good reason!" He brought himself to smile defensively at the crowd. "It is the Lord's will!"

A hollow terror filled Mark. This guy thinks God is instructing him and he's really going to kill his son. Hanley waited for a response from the crowd, and when none came, removed the forced smile that had crossed his face like a disease; after a moment, he bent down again, shook his head, and began to sob.

One of the Makah officers moved slowly forward, but Hanley looked up.

He virtually screamed, "You doubt that the Lord has ordered me, yet many of you come to my church! You know me! But I tell you . . ." He wiped his eyes and swept back his thinning wet hair. ". . . the Lord's holy emissary has commanded it. Today the Lord's commandment must be obeyed, and the Lord will not forsake me." He looked down again at his son.

Whispers raged in the crowd on both sides. Deputy Hermann said, "Reverend Hanley, would the Lord have told you to do this?"

Several in the crowd responded emotionally. "No!" they yelled.

Hanley shifted moods. "I say to you that an *emissary* of the Lord came to me last night! He came to me out of the wind and rain!" He paused again, with that same shaky smile. "The man came out of the rain into my mind, and spoke unto me, and yes, instructed me as you see now, and I will obey the Angel of the Lord."

Hermann lowered the megaphone, shaking his head.

"Everyone here is a doubter," Hanley repeated. "The Lord is my shepherd, I shall not want, He maketh me to lie down in green pastures . . ."

Mark stared at Hanley and wondered if *something* had happened last night to force him to do this terrible thing. Then, with dread, he made another observation: Here's a man who keeps saying that everyone he knows doubts him.

Mark moved to the front of the crowd. That boy had saved his life, and he would not let him die if there was the slightest chance of doing anything about it.

Hermann recognized Mark, but said nothing—gave no indication of whether it was all right to interrupt.

"The man says you live around here," said Mark quietly. "He's seen you on the roads. Get it? Maybe I'm wrong, but I think he means that you live here, so you can't be trusted. I don't know why he thinks that, but I'm guessing it's what he means. In a way, he knows me too, and yet he knows I don't live here. He knows I'm not from here." He stared with a determined expression at Hermann.

Hermann looked steadily and breathed deeply. After a moment he said, "I don't know. You want to talk to the guy?"

Mark nodded slowly.

Hermann wiped the drizzle off his face with his sleeve. All he could do was shake his head. Then he said, "All right, go ahead."

In the street, Hanley shifted back to the other knee, keeping the knife poised.

Mark hesitated, struggling with his anger, uncertain of his logic. He forced himself to think of something that might break the ice. The discomfort of involvement unsettled him. He was an alien here. Whether or not he could talk to this man was anyone's guess, but it wasn't hard to see that no one here had better ideas.

Mark took a short step on the concrete. "Reverend Hanley," he said quietly. He carefully thought out his sentence, slyly trying to interpret what Hanley had uttered. "You can't trust people from around here."

Hanley didn't respond, and Mark felt as though he were falling down a huge hole. "You . . . can't trust people who live around here, is that right? Well, look, you remember me? You know me from the other night. I don't live around here, so you weren't warned about me." Mark flinched at the insane logic, and felt the impending anguish of failure. The crowd was silent and focused on him. Then he looked at the child and forced himself to continue. "You say you know everyone here—but I'm a stranger. So you can explain it to me. You can tell me about it."

He waited while Hanley stared at him from the kneeling position. The Reverend said nothing.

"I'll come over a little way and you can explain. That will help, won't it? For you to tell someone *exactly* what's going on." Mark desperately wanted to glance at Hermann for support, but dared not. He was committed. He had to separate himself from both Hermann and the crowd. He felt like a madman, for all he had was the outward appearance of control. "Reverend Hanley, I'm walking forward a little so you don't have to yell."

Hanley said nothing, but shifted his eyes to the left as if watching someone else. Each step Mark took felt like the spin of a roulette wheel. He stopped only about six feet from the big sack that said "Rosemary's Weed & Feed." Michael's eyes, wide and glazed, blinked up at the drizzle from the sky. Here was a flesh-and-blood child. The skin of his neck was white and soft near the cruel blade. His small T-shirt and pants were drenched from the mist. Once every few seconds his whole body shook with cold and terror. Not only was the sight of the child more sobering from this distance, so too was the Reverend more imposing, his demeanor untempered by the short expanse of concrete. He was almost within reaching distance, the narrow lines on his forehead clearly drawn, his white face wet and pale, his blue eyes ironically serene within their widening sockets, his long, narrow face distorted with tension. Any notion of sympathy toward this man was impossible, especially for a parent. The knife was of the kitchen variety, well used, perversely clutched by tremulous bony fingers.

The minister turned, and Mark stared into the pale eyes. What had this man specifically seen or heard? No clue, not of sanity or insanity, was written on his face—only killing determination.

"Remember me?" said Mark. "I had one hell of a night before last. Your son found me on the beach after my boat went down. I've experienced some strange things too." He maintained a neutral expression. "If I could just sit here for a while, we could talk."

Hanley breathed ponderously and seemed to stare at the ground in front of Mark; he rocked forward a little, then back, a slight whimpering coming from inside his throat. Mark knelt down slowly on the wet pavement. A subtle thought came to him: This man does not really want to kill his son or I wouldn't have made it this far.

"It's God's commandment!" Hanley burst out. "God will not forsake me!"

Mark's heart jumped and he cursed himself for thinking. Then he said, "Maybe your friends are right. Whatever happened to you, they are saying that God wouldn't ask such a thing."

Hanley looked directly at him, saying firmly and carefully, "I am not the only one who has been put to the test. God tested Abraham likewise, did he not, and said unto him, 'Take your son, your only son Isaac, whom you love, and go to the land of Moriah, and offer him there as a burnt offering upon one of the mountains of which I will tell you.' It comes now that God will test another of his servants."

At this, Hanley bent down more closely to the boy, as if ready to lunge. "It's God's test." Several in the crowd recoiled. Mark tensed, ready to spring forward. He was caught between having to act and having to stay frozen in case it was a false alarm. He didn't dare precipitate the very thing he had come to stop. He put both hands out in front of him. "Please wait," he begged. "No hurry. No need to hurry. It's your son, isn't it? You don't want to hurry."

"No matter," said Hanley, his voice cracking. "The Lord will not let me kill my son."

Mark paused for a moment. "No, of course not."

"No sir, no sir, *the Lord will stop the knife*. I am His servant."

Mark felt himself on the verge of panic. Hanley believed God wouldn't let him kill his son, but he had to *try*. This lunatic was just not the same man he'd met the other night.

Hanley was waiting for an acknowledgment from God, ready to slash the soft flesh under his blade.

Mark tried to kick his mind into gear. The story of Abraham and Isaac flashed through his memory.

"God," said Mark, "will stop you when you try to kill your son?" It was all he could think to say. He had never thought much of a God who demanded such jealous, cruel, and uncompromising respect.

Hanley nodded.

It's not good enough, thought Mark to himself. The Bible teaches unquestioning obedience. I can't question God. I lose. Thinking of what the doctor said about his own hallucination that morning, he asked, "Have you ever been fooled?"

"What?"

"I said, have you ever been fooled?"

Hanley stared at the damp concrete. Whether he was pondering the question, Mark couldn't tell, so he said: "We've all been fooled once or twice, haven't we? Haven't we all been lied to once or twice?"

Hanley kept silent.

"I mean, let's say the devil wanted to do some mischief, and he found your house, and looked in and saw your son and decided he'd like to have a recruit from the clergy. How would he go about it?"

"It was not the devil who spoke inside my head, it was God's minion!"

"How do you know? Listen, this morning I hallucinated . . ."

"You're an atheist. I can see that. You're an unbeliever just like everyone here."

Mark was losing. He felt hopelessly stupid for getting into this. Now he wanted to use every skill at his disposal to get out of it. But he was so damn close to the knife. Hanley turned his attention back to the child, who struggled in the bindings.

"No, you're wrong," Mark said slowly. "The devil is tricky, very tricky. He made me think I saw Olson this morning. Remember? Olson was lost. There were three of us on the boat. You were there the other night and you had to drag me up from the beach."

Hanley said nothing.

"So, you know I'm not from around here. There are other things the devil can do, and you'd better believe one thing the devil can do is a first-class impersonation of an emissary from God."

Hanley's expression narrowed, and Mark thought he might be getting somewhere. But then the expression changed. "Atheist!" he screamed. "Get away from me!"

Hanley spread his left hand on his son's chest. Mark saw the Makah officer in the police Jeep huddling behind the rim of the door, aiming a gun. Yet he couldn't possibly fire. Would he try?

"What did he say? What exactly did *it* tell you? To kill your son? Doesn't it sound more like Satan than God?"

"God spoke to Abraham likewise," said Hanley.

"Maybe that was *also* the devil speaking," said Mark.

Hanley smiled sarcastically, and Mark knew he'd trapped himself into questioning the Bible. You don't question the Bible to a fanatic. Logic had reached a dead end. This man had thrown away his questioning intellect years ago. I can't argue with him any more, Mark thought, and right now I need to get up and walk away and get out of this. He knows what he knows. Mark looked at Michael, pictured his own child Erica, then flashed back to the sailing accident. He searched his memory for something to grasp onto, some hint or clue. If he didn't get up and walk, he'd have to give Hanley the benefit of the doubt. And he knew one thing: He hated this man for what he was doing, and most especially for his cowardly religious rationalizations.

"Reverend Hanley, God will stop you from killing your son, but you must try to kill your son to obey God, to prove your obedience to God, just as Abraham did."

"Of course," said Hanley, not looking up.

"God will not let you kill your son because God is good."

"God The Almighty is good. He would not have let Abraham kill his son."

"You don't *know* that. God can do anything he wants. God commanded thousands of people to death at the hands of the Israelites. Do you remember the people that God ordered Saul to kill? Every man, woman and child was murdered on God's order, and when Saul saved some of the animals, God condemned Saul to a living hell. You think you're not going to kill this kid if you thrust that knife? Read your Bible, man. Don't count on it!"

"God's judgment was on those people who were killed."

"Judgment on children and babies."

"God's judgment, because times were different."

"They died on the ends of swords, crying and bleeding to death. They suffered horribly. Their mothers were raped and murdered because they happened to be living on land that the Israelites wanted. What kind of a God would *order* this?" Mark's fists had become two white knots resting on his legs.

"It's in the Bible! Why would God want me to kill my son?!"

"Your son's a sinner. We're all sinners. It's in the Bible. God's judgment was on those people . . . and now it's on your son."

"Then it's God's will!"

"You can't! Just put the knife down!"

Hanley raised the knife high into the air and looked upward into the mist. "Oh Heavenly Father, speak to me again so that I may hear your word!"

Mark stared in horror: If he hallucinates . . .

"Oh, Heavenly Father, I commit myself to you!"

Feeling a savage bolt of adrenaline, Mark launched himself forward. He caught the man violently by the throat and slammed him backwards. Hanley was caught off guard. His head smashed onto the concrete. The knife, still in his hand, flashed in mid air. Mark grabbed for it, missed, and felt the edge slice into the top of his hand. He caught a blow on his forearm. They struggled. There was the sound of shoes on pavement. Mark pinned Hanley down by the wrists. Now, the man's damp white face stared upward, and something like insanity lodged in his expression—a dull, unfathomable malignancy. Just before the other men grabbed them, Hanley looked into Mark's eyes and rapidly whispered something that was impossible, something that the shock of adrenaline must have translated incorrectly, for it couldn't make sense.

"Go forward and help Craig with the heads'l."

The blood drained from Mark's face. Stunned, he released his grip on Hanley's wrists. The other men were upon them. Hands pulled them away from each other, rolling Mark off, grabbing and bending Hanley's wrist, forcing the knife out of his hand. Weakly, Mark held onto his cut hand and lay back on the pavement. Hermann and the two

Makah officers pulled Hanley up, handcuffed him, and took him away.

Mark continued to lay on the pavement, breathless, barely able to think. He must have heard wrong. That was something Horn had said. Hanley must have merely cursed at him incoherently.

A large man in a wet Stetson hat cut away the cords from young Michael. He lifted the boy up, hugged him tightly and held him in his arms as people surrounded them.

Mark was helped to his feet. People were congratulating him, shaking him, patting him on the back. He looked over at Michael and the man with the hat, then down at the bleeding slash across his hand. He felt someone next to him gently grab his arm.

"You did a hell of a job, cowboy."

It was Richard Walker, Judy Roundtree's husband.

Mark was breathing hard, too shocked to respond. Someone handed him a handkerchief to wrap his hand. Matsamura came across the pavement through the crowd.

Walker said, "That hand doesn't look so good. Better see a doctor."

There were too many voices, and Mark did have a sharp pain. He couldn't shake Hanley's words from his mind—but he must have been mistaken, must have misheard what the words were. Hanley had said *something*, but he'd heard him say something else. So he decided to forget about it. He looked for the man who'd picked up Michael, saw the Stetson hat, and went to where several people were comforting the boy. Walker and Matsamura followed him.

For a moment, he leaned down, tried to get further control of his breathing, and put his uninjured hand softly on the boy's shoulder. "Are you going to be all right now?"

Michael nodded.

"You remember me?" asked Mark gently, now resting on one knee in front of him.

Michael looked, blue eyes moist, as if they'd soaked up all the ocean's mist. His eyes widened.

"Yeah," he said. "I found you on the beach. You weren't dead."

Chapter Seven

Instead of going back to the doctor, Mark decided to go to Judy Roundtree's and Richard Walker's. It was a small, clapboard house with a good view near the west end of the bay.

". . . so bandage this man well," said Walker, standing in the kitchen watching Mark's hand. "We've got a hero in the house. A bunch of people are coming over later. Thought it would be a good idea. Mark can meet some of the people who helped search for his wife. Judy, can you make some snacks?"

Roundtree gave him a burning glance. "First, Reverend Hanley going crazy in the street, then a bandage job, then a party? Why not invite the whole town and we'll have an old potlatch, give away the furniture. How about you have a little patience?"

"All right, all right. Can you make fry bread?"

Judy shook her head as if trying to clear water from her ear. "You get this man?" she asked Mark. "Demand this, demand that. Certain people have no patience." She finished wrapping the bandage. "What do you make of Hanley?"

"I don't know," said Mark.

"Well, there's your hand fixed up. We'll change the bandage in the morning. OK, OK," she said to Walker, leaning against the doorjamb. "I'll make fry bread. Now get lost."

Mark and Richard retreated to the living room. It was a small room spanning the width of the house, with a few pieces of modest furniture standing on a light-green carpet. Several intricately woven Native American baskets hung on the wall over the sofa. Mark had been invited to stay for the night while Matsamura returned to the dig.

The phone rang.

Judy Roundtree came into the living room. "The minute I start something I get interrupted. Anyway, it's for you," she said, looking at Mark.

"Me?" asked Mark.

Judy raised an eyebrow. "You can take the call in the kitchen while I talk to Richard."

"The deputy sheriff?"

"No, not the sheriff."

He went down the short hall into the kitchen and picked up the receiver. "This is Mark Sayres."

"This is Sandra Torrel. I heard about Hanley. Are you all right?"

"I'm fine."

Although Sandra's voice sounded anxious, its timbre came over the line like a warm sound from a distant island. "Kallabush drove over here again. He likes to gossip, you know. He told me you saw your missing friend on the beach this morning. I told him about Hanley. He hadn't heard about that yet."

Mark started to speak, but didn't get the chance.

"I need to talk to you," said Sandra.

"Sure."

"There is something you should know. I need to talk to you in person. I guess I should have said something while you were here, but I wasn't sure I wanted to, or that it would make any difference."

"How did you know where I was?" he asked.

"Cindy Morgan, a friend of mine in town, told me about Hanley and knew you'd gone to Richard Walker's."

"I'm a little lacking in transportation. I don't see how I can get out there."

"Can I meet you in town about a half mile away?" she said. "There's a cafe on the waterfront."

"Yes, I know the place, but Richard and Judy are having a party and they expect me to be here tonight. Have you heard from the sheriff?"

"No . . . just Cindy, and then Jim."

"Is there anything wrong?"

"It's just that there are things you don't know."

"What things?"

Her words were delivered with a chilling evenness of emotion. "My husband Gregory is missing. He hasn't called since the day before you arrived. He'd gone south on the logging roads and was supposed to be back yesterday morning. I kept hoping he'd turn up, and that's why I didn't say anything to you yesterday."

Mark turned toward the kitchen cupboard with the receiver close to his ear.

"Gregory was supposed to come back from the mill. We own a ce dar mill near Forks. He's not at the mill. He never got there. This isn't a coincidence, Mark. Something terrible may be happening. I have to get out of here because I'm frightened. I'm staying with my friend Cindy in town tonight, and I want to meet with you."

"Certainly."

"I'll meet you at the cafe near the east end of the waterfront in one hour. That'll still give you time to get back to Walker's before nightfall. Will you meet me?"

"Yes, of course. Ken and I had lunch there earlier. I'll be there."

She hung up the phone.

At that moment, Richard and Judy's children, Kathy and Franklin, came running into the kitchen, poking at each other with cardboard swords. They dashed around the room until Franklin pretended to be mortally wounded and fell with a pitiful shriek on the vinyl floor.

Judy came back into the kitchen. "What are you two kids doing?"

"We're just playing," said Kathy.

Judy said something in Makah: "hakʔuẋaqaˑk." She frowned, wrin kling the skin on her forehead. "If you're not hungry, anybody found in my kitchen after I count three, starts washing the dishes."

Franklin opened one eye. He rolled over and began crawling for the door. Kathy stumbled over him and they both headed for the living room. Mark followed, saying nothing about the phone call. He watched Richard and the kids play a video game for a while, then made an excuse about needing to get out for some air.

He made his exit into the early evening. The darkening sky was clearing, the sun was low behind a bank of clouds, and the small houses lining the streets were glazed in blue evening light. As he approached the waterfront, he saw the wharves and the fishing boats. It was the Pa cific Northwest Indian version of a tiny New England coastal town, he thought. He walked past a patch of grass no larger than an ordinary yard, with a totem pole in the center and a sign that said Dakwas Park/Place of Rest. He passed some one-story buildings, one of which had a rotting boat hull next to it. A couple of blocks later he spotted the cafe at the water's edge.

The place was empty. It was typical of most American cafes, but with a small dining room and big plate glass windows overlooking the bay. Sandra Torrel wasn't there yet.

He found a table by the window and asked if they had any wine. The waitress, a small, plump, dark woman, told him they didn't sell alcohol. He settled for coffee. On the walls were framed photographs of early days at Neah Bay, with a novelty sign near the cash register that said: "People who believe the dead don't come back to life should be here at quitting time!"

The joke seemed to mock him. He felt powerless. What was he supposed to do? What had happened to Hanley? Even if Hanley *had* said what John Horn said on the yacht, it meant little. Hanley had helped with the rescue from the beach the other night. Under the influence of hypothermia, Mark could have been babbling about anything—repeated things Horn had said. Then Hanley had spouted back something he'd heard just to rattle him. It had been a singular, unconnected event.

Sandra came into the cafe. She peeked into the dining room, and he greeted her with a tired wave of his hand. It was a slow weeknight, early, and they were the only people there. She sat down, folded her hands on the table and looked out at the bay as if reconsidering her decision to talk to him.

"I don't know how to begin," she said.

"It's OK. I'm glad to see you."

She kept her voice low. "I should have said something before, but I had no reason to confide in you and it was only that Gregory hadn't shown up at the cedar mill."

Mark studied her lovely face and tried not to feel guilty. Ordinarily, even Maggie had understood these natural attractions on his part, but with her gone he felt ashamed and disloyal. Furthermore, Sandra was offering him confidence and friendship.

"Did you report your husband's disappearance to Sheriff Hermann?" he asked.

"Officially this morning, but I told him yesterday when he came to see you that I hadn't heard from Gregory the night before."

When the waitress arrived, Mark ordered soup, Sandra a slice of pie.

"Was there anything that might have caused your husband to go somewhere without telling you? I doubt he ran off with my wife. She left her suitcase behind."

Sandra stared at him blankly.

"I'm sorry," he said. "That was a dumb remark. I'm just tired. Hermann asked me if I knew anything that would account for Maggie's disappearance. I told him no, which wasn't a lie, but the reason I came up here was because Maggie sounded nervous on the phone, and she'd gone back on her word to come home at the end of summer. I thought she was hiding something. She's had bouts of depression. But this time something else was wrong. I'm sure of it, and I feel like a stupid son-of-a-bitch for not flying up here immediately. Now she's gone and maybe something more can be done. But I believe these guys up here searched every inch of ground for her and are doing their best."

Sandra quietly looked at him with the gray eyes that reminded him of the sea and sky of the coast.

"I'm sorry about her," she said.

"I'm exhausted," he replied, "and this whole thing has turned into a nightmare."

"And you don't know what the nightmare is about."

"If you think our spouses have been murdered or something, well, after what I've been through today I've got a pretty good idea who it might be."

"You mean Garman Hanley?"

"Yes."

"That's certainly on the police's mind by now."

The waitress served the pie and soup. Sandra took off her jacket. Under it she wore a finely ribbed beige sweater. She folded the jacket on the seat next to her.

"What I wanted to tell you concerns Gregory, my husband. You may not understand."

"Nothing new."

"You said your wife sounded strange on the phone."

"Yes."

"Were you having problems in your relationship with her?"

He didn't quite know how to respond. It was, in part, a difficult question. "No. I think she came up here to sort of get away from things and pursue her interests."

Sandra calmly stared at him.

"I suppose we had an ordinary amount of conflict and disagreement. Maggie had become somewhat remote. For Christssake, how do you measure that sort of thing? What are you getting at?"

"I guess I'm wondering how much you and I have in common. I met Gregory in Seattle just under two years ago. He was a lot older than I, and after we were married we didn't get along very well, but there were no serious problems until we moved up here."

"What do you mean?"

"He'd inherited the house and a small mill that produces cedar shakes just outside of Forks, both leftovers from his grandfather's lumber baron days in the 1920s. Gregory sold everything back east and came out here to restore the old ancestral house, live by the sea, and manage the mill. He put a lot of money into the house, which had been rented out and neglected. That was fine, but I noticed something curious, something I'd ignored as we were getting to know one another. Whenever I mentioned his family, he changed the subject or said he didn't know much about it. He told me that after his parents died— when he was sixteen—he'd moved out to Baltimore to live with his aunt. I began to think he really *didn't* know much about his family, or that something had been kept from him, because he began to go through a lot of old documents that he demanded his aunt ship out to us after we were married—three trunks' worth.

"He told me that since he was now managing the mill first hand, he wanted to know more about the history of his parents' and grandparents' business dealings. There is a manager at the mill, Justin Carroll, who's been there since Gregory's father Kendrick ran the business. Gregory had taken out what's called 'key man insurance' on this guy, but when Gregory took over he wanted to know more about the business, including the way things worked in the old days. He made trips to Port Angeles and Seattle to search out records about the early lumbering days on the Olympic Peninsula, and he photocopied anything that might have a bearing on his family's business dealings, especially his grandfather Joseph's."

"Kallabush mentioned Joseph," said Mark.

"There's a lot of rotten history mixed into this that I don't need to go into now, except that people around here shut up whenever I mentioned the name Joseph Torrel. Apparently he was a racist who exploited the Indians. And from what I gather, he worked closely with the government Indian agent to suppress Makah culture. His plan was that the whole tribe would work for Torrel Lumber—which fit right into the government's plan of indoctrinating the Indians into white ways. But aside from learning about history, Gregory got increasingly distant. It got so bad I didn't know if I could live with him anymore. He'd go for long periods of time hardly saying a word . . . but I'm getting ahead of myself." She looked out at the bay. It was nearing sunset.

"Can I ask you something?" said Mark.

"Sure."

"What was Garman Hanley doing at your house the night I came ashore?"

"He'd wanted to see Gregory. I've *no* idea what for, and I didn't know they'd ever met. Apparently, Hanley had bumped into Kallabush that evening, who was coming out to return some tools he'd borrowed from Gregory to fix his car. When they arrived, I told them Gregory was gone, but invited them to stay for tea. We visited for quite a while, but Hanley didn't say much. We'd gotten to know Kallabush pretty well, and Ken Matsamura, and Paul Radwick." A serious look came over her face. "What do you know about Paul Radwick?"

"Not a damn thing, except that he's in charge of the dig."

"You must have known *something* about him," she said.

"Only that he teaches archaeology at the U.W., that he was Maggie's professor ten years ago, and that he needed a summer assistant to help with the volunteers. Maggie had a graduate degree in archaeology."

"Did Maggie seem normal during your previous talks on the

phone—I mean when she first got here?"

"Normal enough, I suppose. She was down at the beach and could only call me a couple of times on a satellite cell phone the archaeologists use."

"When Paul Radwick came out here to start the dig," said Sandra, "Gregory got to know him quite well and invited him to the house. Gregory became interested in the dig, but after our first couple of visits to the beach, he told me not to come along with him. We had a hell of a fight about it. Something was going on, and I didn't know what to do. Kallabush told me you'd come up here because you thought Maggie was upset about something."

"And you're telling me there's a connection of some kind between Maggie's disappearance and your husband's."

"I doubt they'd even met, but I think they both found out something about the dig they couldn't talk about." Sandra slowly took a bite of pie. She was suddenly quiet.

"Something Radwick was doing?" Mark asked. "Like what?"

A peculiar expression came over Sandra's face. "I don't know. But my husband, your wife, and the archaeological dig are a common denominator. What's scaring the hell out of me is the town itself. Look what happened today. They were talking about unexplained disappearances. Now about Hanley and my husband. Some are saying your friends from the boat are related to the other disappearances. Others aren't talking openly. I've also heard that something like this happened a long time ago. They say there was a rash of disappearances like this many, many years ago during the time Joseph Torrel was here, and that a lot of people died—including Joseph and his wife Lucy. The people who might know about it—old people—are keeping their mouths shut." She paused and glanced around to see if the waitress might be nearby, then continued slowly. "The disappearances of the last several days aren't coincidental, Mark. I feel like I'm looking at the pieces of a bizarre puzzle. I don't know what the hell to do." She looked out at the water, then back again.

"I'll tell you this, too," she said. "One night, Gregory was at his desk upstairs looking through some family papers. I heard a noise as if something had fallen or he'd smashed his fist down on the desk. The door was unlocked and I found him sitting there shaking his head. He'd been drinking. He told me that something bad was going to happen—not only bad, but unbelievable. I've never seen a look like that on anyone's face."

"Do you think he was murdered?"

"Oh God . . . I wanted to tell you this because of what happened today."

"How can Hanley be connected?"

"I don't know, but I think your wife knew. I think Gregory knew. And Gregory said something else. He said that on the reservation, the past is more important than the future. Then he said he was afraid to stay here any longer."

Mark rotated his empty cup. He felt surrounded by darkness, unable to move in a decisive direction.

"Too many people are missing," said Sandra, "all within three weeks. Gregory, your wife, your companions, and the man from town. That man's disappearance is another remarkable coincidence, isn't it?"

Mark didn't know what to say.

"Look," Sandra continued, "you and I—and your wife, too—are intruders here, and so is Gregory. Many people are scared to death, including Makahs. What's happening is hard to explain. These events can't be a coincidence."

"Listen," said Mark. "You talked to Jim Kallabush, and you know something happened to me this morning that *I* can't explain. I thought I saw my dead companion, Craig Olson. But beyond my own mental health, it doesn't mean a damn thing, and I'm not going to give in to hysteria, which is what I think this mostly is. The men I sailed up here with undoubtedly *drowned*. I don't know what happened to Maggie or your husband, but if Maggie was murdered, or if someone here knows any more about it, I'm going to find out." He stared at her quietly, but felt himself growing angry at how the conversation had become less and less rational. His voice was prudently soft, but firm. "If anyone thinks I'm going to just walk away without my wife because of a few weird circumstances, or God help me, without recovering her dead body, they'd better think again. If she was frightened, maybe it was something concerning the dig or maybe it wasn't. She came up here for her own reasons. I don't know exactly why she wanted to stay here, or why she got nervous, or even why I saw a missing man walking on the beach, but I'm sure as hell not going to start believing in the supernatural, in the event that's what you're driving at—and I think it is."

Two people entered the cafe and came into the dining room, making it hard to converse any longer. Mark got up from the table, took a ten dollar bill out of his wallet and put it next to his plate. This bizarre conversation, he thought, was over. One normal clue or theory about what had happened would suffice. He stood there awkwardly, knowing how poorly he was behaving but unable to stop himself. Sandra could only gaze at him.

"I'm going back to Walker's," he said as quietly as possible. "You have someone to stay with tonight. I'm sorry I can't talk any longer. I'll see you tomorrow."

"Yes, of course," she said.

Chapter Eight

A pale moon drifted over the Olympic Mountains as Mark walked down the short path toward Richard and Judy's bungalow near the bay. Judy let him in. It was warm and comfortable inside the sparsely furnished house, but the living room had begun to fill with people. Walker seemed to detect Mark's disturbed mood and introduced him around without making a fuss. Food and beverages were plentiful. Judy Roundtree had made her delicious fry bread ornamented with butter and cinnamon sugar. B. B. King blasted away on the stereo, and a lot of people were talking about the big event of the afternoon. Now and then Mark received a nod from a stranger—yet to his relief no one made a big deal of his role in subduing Garman Hanley.

Aside from ethnic diversity, the party might have been anywhere, in any small town, but Mark felt detached. He wanted to go back to the restaurant to apologize, but of course it was too late, so he immersed himself in the party atmosphere as best he could. A Makah named Leonard, an Iraq War vet, told him stories about mistreatment of Native Americans, controversies about fishing rights, treaties, land, schools, and the limited resumption of whaling.

"To understand the history of this place, you have to imagine the U.S. Government taking it over by force, back in the late 1800s," said Leonard. "That's the first thing. Pretend you've lived here all your life, then they move in and outlaw everything you know—your religion, parties, dances, holidays—and if that isn't enough, change all the ways you work and live. It's a fishing community, but they think farming is better for you, so they force you to start farming in soil that won't support farming. OK, so they'll let you fish again. Then they take your children to boarding schools to assimilate them and forbid them from speaking your language. If you don't like it, you're in jail or dead. Being overpowered, many give up resisting in order to survive. You can't teach your children or pass on your traditions except in secret. In a generation or two, except for those who resisted, your culture is almost destroyed. The old people die off, then eventually you die, and all the Indian ways of doing things die. What you see up here, good and bad, has a lot to do with the past—trying to rediscover the past and still live now, in the present." He also told Mark it wasn't always easy to tell Makahs from their white-skinned brethren, much intermarriage having taken place on "The Res" in the last hundred years.

When more people arrived at nine o'clock, the news broke out that Gregory Torrel had disappeared. (Mark reflected on how accurately Dr. Veress had described the speed at which news travels in Neah Bay.) But Leonard was explaining that "to be a Makah, you only need trace your lineage directly to a member of the tribe, and many tribes are being as- similated into the surrounding culture over time. Soon it'll be difficult to find a full-blooded Native American."

Mark eventually excused himself. He went into the kitchen where he found Kathy and Franklin playing a board game. "It's called 'The Farming Game,'" said Kathy. "You see, I have all these fruit trees here, and Franklin's got a bunch of wheat, and I make more money off the fruit trees. You've got to get $250,000 to win. It's like Monopoly only better."

"Looks like fun," said Mark, pouring himself a beer.

He heard the doorbell ring. A commotion broke out in the living room, so he went back. A man whom Richard introduced as Sam Fuller had arrived with a surprise guest. It was little Michael Hanley. Fuller apparently had custody, and Mark recognized him as the man who'd lifted Michael off the fertilizer sack. Judy brought Michael into the middle of the room, took his coat, and made a fuss over him. Michael seemed in good shape, but the look on his face was a bit vacant. Judy whispered something in his ear, then led him away from the crowd and into the kitchen. Fuller shook Mark's hand. "Thanks again. My wife is the boy's aunt."

"I'm glad someone can take care of him."

"That's one hell of a thing you did this afternoon. They got Hanley over in Port Angeles, prob'ly in the nut house. I always thought he was crazy . . . well, in certain ways. I don't know, I guess we're all a little crazy in certain ways. I thought it best to bring the boy with me. They got anything to eat around here?"

"Kitchen's that way," said Mark. "I'll come with you."

Mark and Fuller got a piece of fry bread and stood looking over the game on the kitchen table. Franklin let Michael sit down and roll the dice for him.

Michael looked up at Mark and gave him a weak smile.

"First time I seen the boy smile since what happened," said Fuller, leaning against the door frame with a beer in his hand.

Judy pushed past Fuller into the kitchen. "What you guys doing in here?"

"Nothin'. Well, I guess we better head back to the living room," said Fuller. "You goin' to be all right?" he asked Michael.

Michael nodded.

"Yes, you're going to be all right," said Judy.

In the living room, Walker was repeating some of the things he'd complained about at the archaeological dig. A man with a pony tail came up to him. "The sooner white men learn Native American ways, the safer we'll all be," he said. "It's their turn to learn from us, before the whole earth goes to hell in a hand basket. Say, Richard, I heard Paul Radwick was coming back. Some guy told me."

"No way. They're done down there."

"Should be here at the end of the week."

"No way," said another man.

"Can't say as I care," said Richard.

"They found somethin' down there," said the man with the pony tail.

"Maybe," said Walker.

"You hear about Torrel?" the first man interrupted.

"Yeah."

"Sheee-it."

"Are they going looking tomorrow?"

"Beats me. I think it's got to be bullshit. I think the guy's just run off."

"Hey, man, you did OK today," said the pony-tail man to Mark. "I want you to know that. And also that we're all sorry about your wife. Some of us here went looking for her. I want you to know that."

"Thanks," said Mark. "You said they found something at the dig. What did you mean?"

"Hell, I don't know. Must have found somethin' or they'd be gone by now. What do you think happened to Hanley?"

Mark shrugged.

"Where are you from?"

"San Diego."

"Oh, hey, I got a cousin down there who lives right near Mission Bay. You know where that is?"

"Yes."

"This cousin of mine, he goes to the Unlimited hydroplane races every year in September. I went down there once. You know about the hydroplane races on Mission Bay?"

"Yeah," said Mark.

Whether these people were hiding something, he couldn't tell; but after a second beer, the bits and pieces of conversation echoed like a disorganized concerto in his mind, and he worried again about leaving Sandra so abruptly. He had rudely left her in that restaurant. And her husband was gone. He felt more and more ashamed of himself. Skepticism had led to unforgivable behavior toward someone he liked, and who had helped him.

Long after the last guest left, he found himself trying to sleep on the sofa in the Walker's living room, still thinking of Sandra.

The night passed. Deep, oppressive sleep, needed sleep, mercifully came to him. But in a dream he saw Olson floating helplessly by his life jacket in the sea, waving for help. He struggled to get to him, but the harder he swam the farther Olson drifted—until everything was swallowed by darkness.

Chapter Nine

After he awoke in the morning, Mark went into the bathroom to change his bandage. Then Judy served him cereal, toast, and coffee in the kitchen. While he ate, there was a knock on the front door. He heard Richard answer it. A man was asking for volunteers to help search for Gregory Torrel. He could hear the man say: "They need all the help they can get to search the logging roads."

He thought of Ken Matsamura and wondered again if the archaeologist was keeping something from him. Maybe it was Matsamura's unwillingness to pass along rumors, or did he really know what had been bothering Maggie? Mark knew he should have flown here right away. He now believed Maggie was dead, but she had come here to get away; and whatever was to blame for that, whether his own unprofitable pursuits or just life itself, nothing counted now more than answers.

When Judy came back to the kitchen, he thanked her for her hospitality. Then he got his jacket from the hall closet and went outside. Richard had left with the man who'd knocked on the door, and it was a short walk to the tribal police station. Mark prepared to join the search for Gregory.

Before he got half a block, he watched Sandra Torrel pull up to the curb in her black Land Rover. He was glad to see her. She rolled down the passenger window and leaned toward him. "I was just on my way to find you. They've opened the security gate and I'm going south on the logging roads. The county police are covering all the main roads he might have traveled. Do you want to go with me?"

"Sure."

They drove in silence southwest until they crossed the Waatch

River, then south, traveling on a primitive road of hard earth spotted with potholes.

"Look, I'm sorry about last night," said Mark.

"No, it's all right. I understand."

"A week ago I was home designing a new gymnasium for an elementary school and going to the bus stop once a day to meet my daughter."

"I understand."

"Any ideas about your husband?"

"No news. I keep remembering what you said about your wife. Something was bothering her. Well, something was sure bothering Gregory. We have to help each other."

"I'll help if I can. I see why you think these things are connected. I just don't want to jump to weird, unacceptable conclusions."

"Nor do I."

"What's going on this morning?"

"The police are checking along the main roads from Neah Bay, Forks, and Ozette. Our mill is near Forks. It's a long way from here. Gregory took great pride in knowing how to get to Forks by the logging roads, but he usually didn't try it at night. Maybe he made a wrong turn in the dark. The forest covers thousands of acres, and the logging roads are like a maze, especially farther south. If the police don't find his truck broken down along the paved roads, and we can't find him, he could be lost for days unless the truck is visible from the air. Right now, there's too much fog south of Ozette for a helicopter. I've been hoping Gregory just had too much to drink and ran out of gas or something. Kallabush and the rest are rounding up some people, and they'll follow soon. There are hundreds of logging roads. They're going to need a lot of help if he got off the normal route."

"What was he driving?"

"Our blue Toyota pickup."

The road was now straight as an arrow, and above the forest the sky formed a wide gray path between the trees. Soon they passed a large, tubular metal gate that had been swung aside.

"That was the south gate to the reservation," said Sandra. "The lumber company has been more cooperative lately about letting certain people use it. Gregory's mill is leasing some of the land, so we have keys. So do the archaeologists. And the police have access for emergencies." She paused. "Do you remember I said I didn't know that my husband knew Garman Hanley?"

"Yes."

"Well, I found out something this morning. A month ago, the archaeologists moved their lab from a borrowed garage into a larger space—the basement of Garman Hanley's church."

Mark turned to her.

"So," she said, "there's a serious connection between Reverend Hanley and the dig."

Mark wondered what this new information meant.

Sandra drove at a relentless pace. The road was getting bumpy, and in a few minutes they would be inland adjacent to the Torrel house, when they would normally have turned west. Sandra continued south.

"I shouldn't have walked out on you last night," Mark said emphatically.

"Don't worry, I didn't take it personally."

"I was rude."

"It's all right," she said. "My story was unexpected."

"What can this basement lab have to do with Hanley's insanity?"

"I don't know."

A while later, after crossing the main road to Ozette, they followed the logging road south and approached the southern end of Ozette Lake where the maze began to get more complicated. Soon a decision had to be made. Sandra slowed. An intersection in the dense forest created the sensation of being lost. With nothing but trees, there were no good landmarks, and Mark could see how much know-how it took to find one's way.

"I went with him three times this far south," said Sandra. "I don't know if I can remember."

"Don't worry. I'd guess the police or one of the other searchers are bound to find it if we don't. Let's try not to get lost ourselves."

Sandra made a decision, stepped on the accelerator, and glanced at her passenger.

"I don't know what I'll do if he's gone," she said. "I mean that.

Most of my time was devoted to handling Gregory's life, his problems. We had great dreams when we came here, but our marriage began to collapse soon after Gregory's obsessions began."

"The first step is to find him," said Mark.

"Yes," she said tiredly, sincerely.

They drove into the dense forest along a southeasterly logging road.

Ten minutes later, they slowed down. Mark put his hand out on the dashboard and leaned forward for a better look while Sandra held securely onto the steering wheel. Ahead of them, at the side of the road, a vehicle was shaded by tall trees. Mark looked at it as they slowly drove by. It was the old rusted hulk of what appeared to be a '68 Camaro, and it lay in the ditch, half covered with brambles—one of those hollow automotive fossils that cause disturbing thoughts of mortality.

In a few minutes, they encountered the fog. Although it wasn't heavy, Sandra clicked on the headlights. She had a determined look on her face as she watched the particular way the road curved and then widened into an area of sparser forest. Although the trees were not as dense here, the fog diffused the light before it could illuminate the forest. The road was merely a narrow, partly visible band pressed in by tall evergreens. In a few minutes, they slowed again at the sight of something up ahead. Sandra smoothly increased pressure on the brake until they came to a stop.

"My God."

They sat staring.

"That's it, isn't it," said Mark.

Sandra nodded.

"OK, you don't have to do anything but sit here. I'll take a look."

Sandra tapped nervously on the steering wheel. "I'll go."

"Let me take care of it," said Mark. "He's a stranger to me. If by chance something's happened to him, it's best if I go first."

"OK," she said. "But maybe he just left the truck here and walked south."

"We'll see." Mark opened the passenger door, which groaned. He thought it might be corrosion from the salt air.

Feeling the soreness that still lingered in his muscles, he walked through the light fog toward the truck. The fog was cold, and he was aware of the pungent smell of the green forest and of the hard, moist dirt under his boots.

The blue truck looked abandoned, like a lonely prop on a stage. The forest was utterly silent. Mark licked his lips.

In a few more steps he reached the truck, and for a moment he hesitated with the ordinary childish fear of what might be around a strange corner. If Gregory Torrel *was* in the truck, sleeping or unconscious, Mark was going to be a bit surprised, so he took it slowly before coming up to the window.

At the last moment he expected nothing.

Before he could peer through the window, the door of the truck moved in front of him, and with shocking fluidity, it swung open.

Maggie . . .

His wife, her hand clutching the door handle, her blond hair falling in a graceful curve, her somber white face expressionless, stared at him from the driver's seat. . . .

An incoherent sound came from his throat as he staggered back.

Maggie, in abnormal slowness, slid off the driver's seat and stepped out of the truck onto the hard earth. Mark began to speak, but was paralyzed—because he could not accept what was happening. It seemed an impossibility.

With a look of subtle surprise, the realistic image of his wife stared back at him silently. Then, in a detailed unreality that seemed outside the realm of normal motion, her expression changed, as if her attention was being pulled toward the distance. Her gaze transformed from a blank stare into an incomprehensible sadness. As if distracted by an inner voice, she turned and looked into the offshore fog that enveloped the forest.

Mark fought just to continue watching, but as he was overwhelmingly certain this was *not* Maggie in the flesh, but a cruel manifestation in his mind, he turned away as he had done on the beach. Nausea overcame him as it had before and he went down on one knee in the road. Then he looked again.

Nothing but the fog, the calm forest, and the silent truck remained. He put his head in his hands, squeezing his temples. This delusion was worse than before, worse than anything he could imagine. He was as frightened of the idea that it *was* in his mind as he was of its potential reality. To be assaulted like this was unbearable. Then he heard footsteps coming toward him from the Land Rover. Sandra ... The footsteps came nearer, like thudding hammers, exaggerated, like the breakers on the beach after he saw Olson.

He shifted to the other knee and turned toward her.

"Oh God ..." he slurred, because it was not Sandra at all. It was *Maggie again*, walking toward him. She came purposefully, stopped near him, almost over him, and then, nightmarishly, an inexplicable look of profound fear momentarily contorted her features.

A terrible expression of despondency came over her face—as if she had discovered something tragically conclusive—but that expression faded with an anguish such as he'd never seen on anyone's face, and it was this visible changing emotion, this terror of *hers* that caused him to shrink back.

She looked at him as tears began to roll down her cheeks.

She said, "What did we do to the children?"

Before he could form another thought, his vision blurred in a scattering of grainy light, he looked away, and just as he felt about to black out, he found himself looking up into someone else's eyes.

"Mark! My God! Mark! Goddamn it, talk to me!"

In the mix of faintness and images, he was aware of someone pulling at his shoulder. He waited, and refused to look again until the ounce of sanity remaining caused him to put his hand out and touch the person shaking him. Sandra was crying to him hysterically, and it was *Sandra's* voice. He managed to raise himself up, slowly, then stand and look. She had a wild, determined, but uncomprehending glare in her eyes. "Who was it?!" she asked.

He stared at her.

"That was Maggie—*Maggie*, wasn't it," she cried.

He nodded. They grabbed onto each other, moved away from Gregory's truck and held each another. The nausea began to leave. Nothing was more reassuring than the feel of Sandra's solid form.

It was a full minute before they let go. "At first I couldn't move," she said in the tone of a person condemned.

"For God's sake, what can this be?"

"I don't know, I don't know," she said. "I got out of the car . . . I couldn't move. I thought I saw someone get out of the truck, but my vision . . . It was a person, though, a woman. Then I saw your face quite clearly, and your reaction, and I just . . . I tried to move, but I couldn't see again. I couldn't move because I couldn't see her clearly."

He took her and they quickly moved farther away from the Toyota. The door still gaped open. They went back to the Rover and got in.

It took a full thirty minutes for them to regain a semblance of composure. They sat unmoving. Mark focused on one thing only: Sandra had seen what *he* had seen. That was his redemption from sickness or hallucination—but also a key to unfathomable terror. Because if she had seen what he'd taken as a hallucination, then there was nowhere to go except down an untraveled road into the supernatural abyss.

*   *   *

They sat numbly in the Land Rover for another ten minutes. Then a car approached from behind. It was filled with three laughing Makah teenagers. They pulled up alongside. A young man rolled down the window.

"My name's Jamie. You found the guy yet?"

"That's his truck up ahead," said Sandra. "We were just about to look."

"Is that right . . . ? You want us to do it?"

Sandra turned fearfully to Mark. "What do you think?" she whispered.

Mark still didn't know if Gregory was in the truck or not. "Might as well," he said.

"Sure, thanks," said Sandra, turning back to the teenagers.

The three volunteers parked their car about fifty feet away, got out, and went to look inside Gregory's truck. They were casual about it, talking, chuckling among themselves as they went. From their slightly distant vantage point, Mark and Sandra saw two of them lean close and look into the windows of the truck. But they suddenly backed away. One of them—a tall, skinny kid in a white T-shirt—almost fell backwards, then turned and walked off the road where he went down on all fours and started to vomit on the ground. Mark gripped the dashboard, let out a short gasp, then put his hand on the door handle and started to get out.

"Wait!" said Sandra.

The third, shortest of the three teenagers came running. He came up to the Rover, and his face was pale white. He put his hand on the fender. Mark got out. Then Sandra.

"He's in there," said the young man.

Mark quickly came around front and took the kid by the shoulder. "Goddamn it, I'm sorry. I should have gone instead. Can you get your friends back into the car?"

"Ah . . . yes."

"Do it now."

He and the young man went back toward the Toyota. The kid who'd gone down on all fours got up slowly, and he and the other member of the threesome went back to their car and got in. The young man with Mark stayed outside, leaning against the car's fender, while Mark took a deep breath and went forward once again to look inside Gregory's truck. He turned to look over his shoulder at Sandra, who was standing by the Rover. Then he looked at the young man again, hesitating.

"Can you tell me anything?" he asked.

"I couldn't see him very well. Bobby was in front of me."

This time, Mark went around to the Toyota's passenger door. As he approached, he could see that the window was open. A spattering of blood could be seen on the dashboard and a few drops on the inside of the windshield. How do you prepare yourself for anything? he asked himself. He stopped. All these witnesses. . . . Could Maggie jump out of that truck again? No, no, he thought, if such things could happen twice, in front of five people, the world would be a whole different place. But maybe this territory *was* a different place. Goddamn it, he thought, just take a look. There is a dead man inside this truck. That's all it is. Whatever happened, that's all it is now.

His stomach tightened as he moved numbly, efficiently forward, and gazed into the pickup at who he assumed was Gregory Torrel.

Torrel was dead, sitting up in the passenger seat, eyes staring forward into the shadowy roadside under the trees. Blood had flowed out of his mouth and nose and in a torrent down the front of his shirt and into his lap. It wasn't unexpected, Mark thought callously as he turned away. Not the death. Not the blood. That wasn't what caused that kid to be sick. What was so unexpected was Gregory's right hand still firmly gripping the handle of a large hunting knife thrust deep into his own throat.

Chapter Ten

Mark and Sandra sat in the Rover numbly watching the scene of death as it steadily transformed from their private horror into a crossroads of public activity and conjecture. The number of townspeople and law-enforcement officers grew until the road was lined with more than a dozen vehicles.

After county police detectives had documented the scene, Gregory's body was discretely maneuvered onto a covered stretcher and lifted into the back of the coroner's van. Deputy Sheriff Hermann walked over and told Sandra he'd contacted Justin Carroll, the manager of the Torrel mill, who'd agreed to identify the body for legal purposes, if that would be more comfortable. Hermann said there were some details the detectives wanted to discuss. Sandra was pale and quiet, and she solemnly agreed to all the suggestions and procedures.

Two county detectives thoroughly questioned them. One of the detectives took notes. When the questioning was finished, Sandra started the Rover's engine, and with Mark still in the passenger seat, headed back along the logging road.

"I'll go back to Richard and Judy's if you like," said Mark.

"The hell you will," she said. "We're in the middle of this, both of us, I'm scared and I've made the decision to trust you. Don't think I'm going home alone."

"I wasn't trying to leave you alone."

"You can stop being polite. You told me you weren't going to walk away from this. And you weren't going to listen to supernatural bullshit. All that's a little lame now."

". . . Because we both saw her."

"Damn right. Damn right. And Gregory is dead." She was anguished and desperate.

Mark leaned back in the seat.

"I also think there's something you haven't told me," said Sandra. "There's something missing."

"What do you mean?"

"You told me you should have flown up here right away. I ignored that. But now I'm not sure. You haven't said anything much about her, and we've been together all morning. You're a stranger to me, but you're not afraid to talk about your feelings when it's appropriate."

"What are you getting at?"

"Let's try this. You didn't love her. You once loved her, but didn't love her anymore."

Mark watched the road. "Why are you saying this?"

"It's a feeling I have."

"Of course I loved her. I love her now."

Sandra looked at him, then back at the road.

"She had moods," Mark admitted. "She'd become distant. I didn't always understand her. I blamed myself for her depression. I was mad because she left me alone to take care of our daughter and wouldn't come home when she'd promised and wouldn't say why. What do you want from me?"

Sandra was silent. She glanced at him with her gray, yet piercing eyes.

*   *   *

When they drove up to the Torrel house, the wind had risen, but the firm spruce trees resisted the gusts. Seaward, the sun was hidden behind offshore clouds.

They parked in back and went inside through the kitchen. In the dark living room, sitting on the sofa, Sandra's accustomed stoicism broke down.

She began to cry, twice leaning forward and placing her forehead in her palms, then taking quick, gasping breaths. Mark got up from the chair opposite, sat next to her, put his arm around her, not knowing whether she wanted him closer, but held her near and tried to comfort her. In a minute, she began breathing more normally. He realized there was nothing he could do but be with her.

In a while, she calmed down enough to talk again. There was much pain and bitterness in her voice.

"What do you do when the closest person in your life turns into a stranger? Each day with him was so terrible and unpredictable. He knew his grandfather and father were hated and despised. Being part of this community was important to him. His first line of defense was anger, but there was something *else*—now we know that, don't we Mark? Something *else*. And he wouldn't tell me. Same as your wife—and she was in the truck with him—her spirit was there with him." Anger and fear glazed in her eyes. "Whatever's going on, it's terrible, and worst of all it may be something no one can understand. Gregory kept his thoughts to himself—like the older people in the town, the ones who pass you on the street and look at you out of the corner of their eye and say nothing. You haven't experienced it yet, but you will, and when your wife disappeared, the mood on the reservation got so weird it was like another planet."

Sandra stopped for a moment, and Mark could feel the intensity of the resentment she had been harboring. Her body became stiff and resolute.

"Gregory became angry, moody, insufferable, and I was supposed to put up with it and keep things calm without trying to understand. When he told me people were going to die, I asked him why, and all he said was, 'Because this is not like other places.'

"One day I insisted on going with him to the dig," she continued, "but he grabbed me so hard he sprained my wrist. It kind of snapped. I thought it might be fractured. I had Dr. Veress look at it. It was the most embarrassing moment of my life. I lied to Veress, but I think he knew. I couldn't get away from Gregory because I thought if I stuck by him just a little longer I could figure out some way to reach him. God—what was I supposed to do?" Sandra pulled away slightly, and Mark took his arm away from her. "He made life hell. I started to hate him. I didn't know I could do that. We had such dreams for this house. What am I going to do?" She began to cry again.

The room darkened with the movement of clouds outside. Mark sat close to her with his hand on the back of the sofa next to her head. He wanted to say something to her, comfort her. He offered her his hand; she grasped it and held it on the sofa next to her. It struck him how terribly isolated and alone she was. They sat for a long time, he staring sympathetically at her flushed profile, she leaning back, tears streaking her face.

Chapter Eleven

A small group of people stood on the open cemetery lawn and looked out from under their umbrellas and rain hoods as four workers, hand over hand, lowered Gregory Torrel's casket into the ground by ropes. The topsoil was soggy, but only a few inches down, the dirt was dry, changing from black to reddish brown. The surrounding stone markers at the Quillayute Prairie Cemetery represented a cross section of the area's residents, mostly from Forks. Gregory could not be buried on reservation land, so Sandra had chosen this small rural cemetery a few miles from the mill. To Mark, the many other gravestones seemed to symbolize the decisions and details that had ruthlessly descended upon them during the last week. With his help, and in a kind of resolute daze, Sandra had given permissions, signed documents, and answered questions in an endless ritual of civil and criminal bureaucracy. There had been no time to grapple with profound questions. Mark had driven to Richard and Judy's to retrieve the new clothes he'd bought, while Sandra struggled with more of her responsibilities; then he'd started to search through Gregory's study. He'd also cooked meals, answered the telephone, and helped with funeral arrangements. At night, he had been sleeping much-needed hours in the upstairs guest room.

Now, the quiet onlookers, the raw earth, the polished mahogany casket, and the ground's gaping hole reminded him of those flashing terrors that might have been dreams had they not been so vividly experienced. In general, he believed his experiences were broad enough, his perceptions accurate enough, to form a good picture of reality; and in the everyday world of light and shadow there was no reason to doubt that picture. But what if there were wavelengths one could not perceive? What if hidden variables existed that he could not accept?

As the casket continued its slow descent, Mark realized he had left a wide margin of space between himself and the other mourners. Sandra was closest—standing only a few feet from him on the grass. Though he had helped her deal with all the numbing duties of death, he felt unable to lend much support at the moment, for fear of what others might think. Sadly, she would pay this last debt to her mysterious husband alone.

Mark also looked across the grave toward a large, heavy-set man he'd been introduced to earlier—Justin Carroll, the manager of Gregory's cedar mill. He wondered if this man knew anything important, but today wasn't a good time for questions. No one else from the mill had shown up. Ken Matsamura was also absent. He had been evasive. Maybe it was understandable, and it was a long way out here. Yet Mark believed Ken was keeping something from him.

Sandra stepped toward him to get under the umbrella he had opened—Gregory's umbrella—while the volunteer workmen struggled with the ropes that lowered the casket its final few inches. He decided to gently put his arm around her shoulders. She was shaking slightly, though her eyes were dry and her gaze steady. He admired the way she had faced everything, and he felt guilty that emotional complications might be on the way. Whatever he, she, or others thought, he was staying at her house with a definite understanding that it was the right thing to do. They both shared the loss of their spouses. Who could blame them for wanting to help each other?

With his arm around her, he noticed a white Jeep Liberty pull up and park near the fence behind the row of other cars. A tall man got out, found the little metal gate, and began to cross the lawn. He looked about sixty years old, with white, receding hair and a short white beard. The medium-length jacket he wore and his leather hiking boots were appropriate for rainy weather, though his gray slacks were more formal, and when he arrived at the graveside he looked solemnly toward Sandra, stood off to one side and folded his thin hands in front of him. He remained motionless until the casket finally came to rest.

On cue, Jim Kallabush stepped forward and thanked everyone for coming. The silent ceremony was over. Several of the onlookers came up to Sandra to express their condolences, then the group broke up and began walking back to the road.

The short-bearded man came over and walked alongside Sandra. "I'm sorry I'm late. If there's anything I can do," he offered in a quick, authoritative voice, "please let me know. Gregory was interested in our work, as you know. I'm very sorry."

Sandra's response was swift. "It was nice of you to come all the way down here. And maybe you can come out to the house in the next two or three days. I'd be interested in talking to you."

He looked at her without expression. "Well, yes. This is a terrible tragedy. As I say, if there's anything you need, let me know."

Sandra then took Mark by the elbow, turning him toward the man. "Mark Sayres, I'd like you to meet Dr. Paul Radwick, director of the archaeological dig."

Mark shook Radwick's hand, which felt something like a cluster of coated twigs.

"Good to meet you," said Radwick. "I've heard of you. I'm sorry about Maggie. Have you learned anything new?"

A coldness went through Mark. "No, I'm afraid not. How long will you be around?"

"Only a couple of weeks until the dig is secured for the winter."

"I'm planning to visit there tomorrow or the next day. I'd like to speak with Ken Matsamura again."

Radwick took two or three steps before continuing. ". . . You should know we're closing it down—and the trail has gotten soggy in the last couple of days. But if there's anything I can do to help, feel free. Ken and I have our hands full. We're preparing to remove the remaining items we've located, secure the shacks, and block off the trail as best we can. I'm afraid we're going to be very busy."

Mark said nothing, but felt a rush of heat over his skin. Was this man saying, in so many words, that he was not welcome at the dig any longer? He thought he might make a mistake by trying to get a firm answer and decided to let it pass.

"Now that Gregory is gone," Sandra said, "I thought you might like to come by the house and clear up some things. I suppose you heard that Garman Hanley almost killed his son."

Radwick looked straight ahead. "Yes, I heard. We're pretty busy securing the dig," he said disconnectedly, "but I'll honestly try to stop by."

"Could you come for dinner this Friday at seven o'clock?"

As they arrived at the gate, Radwick said, "Well, sure, I suppose so."

"Bring Ken along with you."

"All right. I'll try."

Radwick went back to his vehicle. The automobiles drove off one by one into the drizzle, leaving Mark and Sandra in each other's company.

"Oh God," said Sandra. "I thought I'd explode."

"You handled that very well."

"Thanks. I didn't think I could be that forceful and diplomatic all at once." She turned and looked at the spindly population of rhododendrons that decorated the cemetery, while the workers began shoveling dirt into her husband's grave. Then she looked at the ground.

"I'll drive on the way back," said Mark as they left the cemetery.

"OK. I'd like to get back to the house." Her eyes were moist. She gently took the umbrella, folded it up, and walked around to the back of the Land Rover to let the dog out for a couple of minutes.

Once Barney was safely back in, Mark and Sandra drove the S.U.V. to the main highway and turned left toward Clallam Bay. While the wipers arched over the windshield, Mark imagined they'd be in Neah Bay in about an hour, before heading south toward Sandra's.

"I know you want to keep going through Gregory's papers," said Sandra. "Did you find anything yesterday?"

"I didn't find a diary, but there were a lot of notes on coastal mythology, and his reading focused on the supernatural."

"I've seen the books he bought," said Sandra. "He hunted them down through a used book store in Port Townsend."

"The one called *The Wolf Ritual* discussed some ghastly things that took place as late as the nineteenth century, some involving rituals for successful whale hunting. What he'd marked up the most was a photocopy of a manuscript called *Pacific Coast Myths and Secret Societies*. The original had been typewritten. It's pretty arcane. Gregory had marked some passages, but I don't know what they could mean to us."

"What were they?" she asked.

"Well, he seemed interested in secret rituals. Some parts talked about the Indian concept of 'power,' where someone gains certain abilities by going into the woods and engaging in traditional rituals."

"That's a well-known idea—and there's always been talk on The Res of secret societies, but nothing specific has ever come of it as far as I know."

"Anyway, the two lower drawers of his desk were locked, but I found the key. The surprise was a loaded .38 revolver. His main trunk is full of company records from Joseph Torrel's early days, just as you said, along with photocopies of historical material he'd collected about lumbering. I read through some of it, and it seems that his grandfather was always in the background."

"I'm sure that Hanley wanted to see Greg concerning the dig. Why else would he show up at my house? I can't believe there isn't more scandalous material on Gregory's ancestors somewhere in the house."

"Well, it's true that the Indian agent oversaw government repression of Makah culture, and it's true that Joseph Torrel worked closely with the agent."

"Gregory discovered that Joseph was bribing the Indian agent, as I said, and trying to arrange for cheap labor. The government was trying all kinds of schemes to get Native Americans to give up their traditions."

"Maybe Gregory threw that material away because he didn't need it, or maybe the information implicating his grandfather in bribery was merely reported to him. I feel like an intruder rummaging into someone else's business, incidentally."

"I told you I trust you," she said.

A few seconds went by. He glanced at her. ". . . Why did you let me stay that first night? I appreciated it, but I don't know if I understood."

"I don't know. Maybe I didn't want to be alone," she said, looking out the passenger window away from him while he concentrated on driving. When she turned, the light cast a soft glow through the windshield onto her face.

"I was afraid of being alone that night because along with everything else, Gregory had become an alcoholic, and there were times when he'd been abusive. It happened in stages, like it does I suppose. The whole thing took about six months, Mark. He stopped talking to me. He stopped sleeping with me. He excluded me from his life. Sometimes he'd go into Forks to visit the mill and to drink. When he came home, he was often bad tempered, though I wasn't afraid at first. There was a compelling reason to forgive, I thought—but it doesn't really matter, does it, in the long run." She watched the trees as they sped by.

When she turned back, her eyes were moist. "Whatever came to obsess him also destroyed him. Moving here was Gregory's dream, and for some terrible reason it dissolved. In a sense, he wanted to take up where his grandfather left off. But this time he wanted to *do* something for the Makahs. He was very liberal. He wanted to make up for his grandfather. He talked about starting a mill near Neah Bay, hiring the townspeople, that sort of thing. Then he changed—and I partly blame the town for that. But it didn't stop there. I told him it wasn't going to be easy. He laughed and said things had happened up here—things so absurd he wondered if he might be dreaming. What was I supposed to think, Mark? What kind of secrets do people keep like that?"

Sandra got some Kleenex out of the glove compartment and wiped her eyes. "Once when he was drunk I tried to bluff him into telling me what was wrong by saying I'd talked to some people about his grandfather. Another time, I lied to him that I'd gone to the dig and talked to Paul Radwick about him. He realized what I was trying to do. I told you the other day that he'd grabbed me by the wrist. That wasn't all, Mark. That night, he grabbed me by the throat. He squeezed so hard my neck turned black-and-blue. I hit him in the face so I could get loose, and he stumbled and fell on the floor. He didn't get up. He lay their crying. He stayed on the floor, sobbing. Then he got hold of himself and kept apologizing. He begged me to forgive him, but later I had trouble with my throat and I was forced to see Dr. Veress for the second time. God, it was horrible. There was no way to lie about what had happened this time. Veress became concerned, even angry, and asked if I wanted him to get personally involved. But I didn't.

"When I got home, Gregory had gone to Forks and was drunk when he called, raving about death and insanity. That was recent, Mark. On the night of your accident, I thought he might come back drunk again. I probably would have invited Jack the Ripper to my house rather than face Gregory alone. I'm sorry. I just thought, here's an emergency and maybe it will distract Gregory for a day or two—but of course he didn't come back at all."

Mark nodded.

"You try to keep this alcoholism thing quiet," she continued. "Gregory had his secret—and I had Gregory. I went back to see Veress. Nothing really came of it, though I had trouble convincing Veress to stay out of it."

"What kinds of things did Gregory say to you when he was drunk? Did he ever come close to hinting at what was wrong?"

"No. He finally told me that I should leave." Sandra was becoming exhausted, and her voice broke. "He said I'd have him committed to a mental institution. Sometimes he'd walk to the edge of the cliff and stare at the sea. I swear I thought he was going to jump."

"Did you tell this to Rick Hermann?"

"Yes." She ran her fingers through her hair. "I told him most of what I told you."

"Did you say anything about seeing Maggie?"

"On the logging road? No, I didn't."

"That's good. If the police or anyone else think we're crazy or insincere in some way, we'll not be able to do anything at all."

*   *   *

After a long, exhausting drive along the straits, they wound through Neah Bay, headed south, and used Gregory's key to the south logging gate. About twenty minutes later, Mark splashed the Land Rover onto the rutted drive leading to the Torrel house. The gate marked "Private Road" was only about thirty feet from the logging road. The rusty metal was wet and cold. He replaced the chain loop over the post. There was no lock. Getting back into the Rover, he released the brake and started down the muddy drive toward the house, wondering if there would ever be any news of Maggie's body being found.

Emerging from the forest into the clearing, he drove to the front of the detached garage on the other side of the house. After turning off the engine, he held the steering wheel for a moment and turned toward

Sandra. He wanted to bring her near, but the last several days intruded into the very air they breathed.

"I wish I could help you," he said at last.

She reached over and took his hand. Mark wanted to respond seriously, for she must have known he was drawn to her, but he held back, keeping her hand tightly in his. He wanted to kiss and embrace her, but if he made such a serious move—and on the very day of her husband's funeral—there would be a price to pay in guilt for the both of them. His life would be intertwined with Maggie's for a long time to come. Sandra waited, looked at him carefully, then gently released his hand when Barney got restless to get out. Opening the door and stepping onto the ground, Mark felt the cool outside breeze. Sandra let Barney out the back. Mark petted the dog vigorously while breathing the fine ocean air.

Sandra joined him, their eyes met again, then they walked with the dog across the worn lawn toward the back door.

Inside, Mark made coffee. Sandra sat at the kitchen table, sipping the coffee, now and then glancing out the window at the forest.

Mark sat down across from her. "Maggie used to stay up late at night in the living room," he said, "and play classical music on the stereo. One piece in particular she used to play; it was usually the last thing I'd hear as I fell asleep in the bedroom—*Veris Gratia* by Kenneth Leighton, an English composer—and it meant something important to her. There was great sadness in the last movement. But she said the title meant 'For the Sake of Spring.' It was heartbreaking, and I didn't know what to do."

"I'm sorry," said Sandra.

"Maybe I didn't take it as seriously as I should have. I didn't have a lot of time for analyzing Maggie. She wasn't happy, and I guess I wasn't happy—but was it us or the world at large? How can you separate these things and make sense of them?"

"You temper your expectations," said Sandra almost to herself.

The clock chimed like a death-knell.

Sandra said, "I want you to stay here for a while. Our lives are at a standstill. I can't be in this house alone yet."

"I have nowhere to go until I know what happened," said Mark.

"We *can* help each other."

"Yes."

"We owe it to ourselves."

Mark nodded.

Sandra finished her coffee, then went into the living room. She arranged some logs and kindling in the fireplace and lit it. She and Mark sat on the sofa as the flames began to warm the room. It was a romantic yet ironic scene, for the house was temporarily death-ridden—an isolated campsite in an infinite night. Sandra's face was beautiful but sober as she gazed at the fire.

"I want my future back," she said, turning to him. "Before Gregory."

He watched her eyes, the light on her cheeks, the gentle arch of her dark eyebrows.

"Mark, we've been through something together. It's an accident, and we're susceptible to a lot of mixed emotions."

"I know," said Mark.

"What are we going to do?"

They stared into the fire, feeling heat on their faces.

"We wait," said Mark.

"Are you saying nothing can happen between us until we've worked through this?" She didn't look at him.

He was glad she'd said it. Yes, regardless of Maggie's death, he wanted to move slowly ahead with Sandra, but felt the timing was grossly disloyal and might jeopardize their feelings for each other in the long run.

"We have time to think this through without making a mistake," he said.

She continued to stare at the fire. She had less to lose than he, Mark thought. Her husband had abused her. She wanted to regain some love in her life. He, on the other hand, couldn't move so fast, and he had his daughter and Maggie's parents to think of.

"Mark, we have to move on somehow, regardless."

"I realize that."

"Radwick implied we weren't welcome at the dig any longer," she said. "Remember, they were closing it down."

"If they were going to tell us anything more, they'd have done it."

"I understand that."

They let the silence linger.

"We have to assume that when Maggie was alive, she found out the same thing Gregory did," said Sandra.

"It always leads back to the dig."

"Yes."

"OK, then," he said. "Maybe there's a small, responsible thing we can do before Radwick comes."

"What do you mean?"

"They moved the lab to the church. It might be coincidental, but it might not. I think we should pay a visit to the lab."

Chapter Twelve

The First Missionary Church lay on its own piece of property where a street ended on the outskirts of town. The traditional white paint was in good condition, but the small, open bell tower needed repair where the siding was separating from the sill. It was a carpenter's church, thought Mark, nailed together in imitation of a finer New England specimen. Its primitive quality gave it a discomforting charm that suited the bleak character of the town.

"Why is the basement boarded up?" asked Sandra as they stopped.

Two daylight basement windows at ground level were covered with plywood sheets. A basement might be unusual to begin with, difficult to drain and waterproof, thought Mark. But that space was now being used as a scientific lab as well as a storage area.

"Why do they need to block light to the basement?" she asked.

"Vampires?" said Mark.

Sandra didn't laugh.

The unexpected sun reflected off the white siding and the plywood rectangles.

"Do you think anyone's inside?" Sandra wondered.

"Can't hurt to find out."

They got out and walked across the dirt lot toward the rear entrance.

"What will we say?"

"Just that we're interested in seeing the lab."

The rear entrance had a half-dozen wooden steps leading up to a small porch with a shallow courtesy roof and a windowless old door.

Mark stepped onto the porch and knocked. He waited for a minute, then knocked again as loud as he could. Sandra stood at the foot of the stairs with her hands in her coat pockets. Mark thought he heard something inside. Then the door opened.

Jim Kallabush peered out, holding the door half open.

"Hi," said Mark. "We thought we'd come by and look around. I thought Maggie might have worked in here."

"Oh, sure, it's possible she was here," said Kallabush. "Too bad I can't let you in."

Mark looked at him steadily.

Kallabush shifted uncomfortably. "They don't allow anyone in here except me and the scientists who are working on the artifacts. No one's allowed. And the only reason they allow me is because I'm guarding the place." He smiled.

Mark gave him a long look and did not smile back. "OK. But maybe you can ask Dr. Radwick if we can come back later."

"Sure, but I might as well tell you he hasn't let anyone in here except the scientists and some of the tribal council. He won't make exceptions. Quite a few important people have come to town, and not even they come into the lab. There are artifacts in chemical baths, and he don't want anything disturbed. He has a rule."

"Did he say anything about us in particular?"

"Ah . . . no," said Kallabush.

Maybe it was paranoia, but doubt arose in Mark's mind.

"We were just curious," said Mark.

"Sorry," said Kallabush.

Mark left the porch, Sandra smiled weakly at Kallabush before he shut the door, and they walked back to the Rover.

Inside the vehicle, Mark and Sandra looked at one another. "What do you think?" asked Sandra.

"You first."

"OK," said Sandra, "he's lying. I mean about us. I think Radwick told him not to let anyone in—not even us."

"Maybe."

"Now what?"

"Well, I'm not putting up with this."

"Those boarded up windows must be for security," said Sandra.

"Or they just don't want anyone seeing in."

*   *   *

At the Torrel house, Mark stood quietly in the big upstairs den. This room had been Gregory's office and had a large window facing west. On the varnished fir floor lay an oriental rug under a brown leather chair and sofa. Against one wall was an oak roll-top desk and a file cabinet, and on the other was a large oak computer desk with piles of books. In the corner was the old 1800s steamer trunk full of notebooks and file folders Mark had searched before the funeral. He'd opened the roll-top, too. Inside a drawer were a pair of wire-rimmed glasses, a scant reminder of Gregory's persona. Sandra had shown him a photograph of her husband. He was older than Mark had imagined, his hair brownish-blond and graying, his face scholarly and intelligent. Dressed in a waist-length leather jacket, he wore those same delicate glasses and held a cardboard box under his arm. But in the disorder of his things, no important answers emerged.

Sandra watched the clouds drift over the sea. The big, old-fashioned window had a good view—but the ocean seemed transformed. To Mark, it had become a mask. He couldn't analyze further. The day was nearly over.

Sandra turned to him. "Radwick is coming for dinner on Friday."

"*If* he comes," said Mark.

Sandra nodded. Then she said, "You know, I should have left months ago. Maybe there's nothing we can do. I'm having second thoughts, Mark. There's no one left to protect or fear or argue with. My husband—and your wife—are dead. And I don't want to suffer any more over Gregory."

Mark sat down on the sofa. "I'm not convinced anyone's going to handle this if we leave. The police don't have all the information. We've seen some strange things and haven't told them. Maggie is dead, but somehow, in some way, she reappeared on that logging road, just like Olson on the beach."

"Your daughter is your primary responsibility."

"Sure. But how do I just walk away from here without answers?

What do I *tell* my daughter?"

"Why didn't you come up here immediately?"

He paused, pursing his lips in frustration. "Because I wasn't sure it was necessary."

"Then you aren't to blame."

"I'm not trying to blame myself."

"But you feel guilty."

"This is my wife we are talking about. I'm trying to find out what happened. Does that seem unreasonable to you? I owe her that much. And you agreed."

Sandra turned away.

"We have to see this through," he said. "We're in the dark right now, but I'm not going to walk out. Our lives are going to be permanently affected by how we handle this."

She turned. "Gregory tried to answer *his* own questions, and he's dead."

"But it's not clear why. And Hanley almost killed his son. *Something* happened to him having to do with a presence or a voice of some kind. He interpreted that as an angel testing him. People might interpret the supernatural in a way that fits their own model of reality."

"Your wife was in Gregory's truck."

"You think she forced his suicide?"

"I don't know."

"Maybe she was drawn there afterwards."

"I can't leave until I find out what this is about." Harshness entered his voice. "How much I loved Maggie has nothing to do with it. You've accused and questioned me."

"I'm sorry," said Sandra.

"My daughter will want to know what happened to her mother. What am I going to tell her if I walk away?" He got up, put his hands in his pockets, and started pacing. "Maybe something *was* wrong between Maggie and me. Maybe I didn't have the nerve to admit it. I don't know how to assess that. But it doesn't matter now. Gregory told you something would happen, right? But he didn't say what. Maybe he was also thinking about his own suicide."

He ended up next to the computer table and tapped on the blank monitor. "Do you ever use this?"

"No. My computer is downstairs in the sewing room."

He breathed deeply. "Is this password protected?"

"Yes. He had his own user account. I found a folder with computer information in it: help numbers, settings, stuff like that. Would he have written his password in there?"

"Possibly."

Mark pulled out a lower drawer, found the folder, and sat down at the computer. "Mind if I turn it on? It's something I didn't check."

"Go right ahead."

He switched it on, and while it booted he looked through the manila file folder. "I know what you meant in the restaurant. It's a puzzle. Or a nightmare, maybe. But we have to keep it down to a practical level."

"What are we going to do? Go to the sheriff again?"

"No . . . OK, here. . . ." He pointed to a couple of random, handwritten words at the bottom of a page of computer and Internet server help numbers. "Maybe this is it," he said. "People often write passwords down where they can find them again."

He typed the first word, "crypto," into the password window and hit Enter. Nice work, he thought, as the desktop came up. He clicked the e-mail utility, but there was nothing of consequence in the Inbox or any other folder. Then he hit "Send and Receive" and two messages downloaded.

"We got something."

"This one's from a friend of his in Baltimore."

Mark opened it, but it was about baseball.

"I know this other name—from Neah Bay," said Sandra. "Bob Silvers. He used to be a member of the Tribal Council."

Mark opened the message, and they read it together. Silvers apparently hadn't known Gregory was missing at the time of the message.

Gregory:

Hanley tried to kill his son today. Remember what I told you. Water is everywhere, and the dead will be pulled into the whirlpool. The wanderers will take others. Much time has passed, but Sisiutl is ancient beyond years. Do not believe the myth of a twin-headed serpent. Come and visit me at home. As you know, my wife and I live on the outskirts of town.

—Bob S.

Mark read it for a second and third time. So did Sandra.

"This looks like gibberish—but after Maggie, who knows? The archaeologists may know what it refers to. Maybe they've been holding out on us because whatever the Indians are talking about is too weird."

"What are we going to do?"

"First, I want to make another unannounced visit to Hanley's church—tonight. The church is still the place to start. If no one's there, I'm going to break in. Then I'll go back to the dig and *tell* them I broke in."

"Why? I don't . . ."

"Because those guys are not criminals. They're just reluctant to discuss this seriously—especially with someone who's lost his wife. But if they realize I intend to go to any lengths—even breaking and entering—they'll have to tell us what Gregory thought he knew or why Maggie was frightened. And now we've got this e-mail to show them."

"I'm scared, Mark. Look what happened to Hanley. Something happened to his mind, and to Gregory's."

He studied her face; it seemed to hover softly in the late afternoon light.

"If we give up now," he said, "we'll never be at peace with ourselves."

Chapter Thirteen

On the far edge of town, the church was dark and silent, with only a single streetlight nearby. At the back and side of the church was a large patch of grassy ground used as a parking lot.

"We're committed," said Sandra, who had insisted on driving. She switched off the headlights, steered the Rover around to the back and shut off the engine.

Mark didn't know how they'd get in, but he'd brought some tools along in case he had to pry a lock. He wondered if there was any danger of finding someone working late.

After a minute, with no sign of life outside, they stepped onto the ground and closed the doors of the 4 × 4 as quietly as possible. A row of houses nearby was dark. It was almost midnight, and Mark was satisfied that he and Sandra were being unobtrusive. He felt for the flashlight in his jacket. The church's high first-floor windows had been completely black when they drove up.

Mark motioned Sandra to the rear entrance. They went up onto the small porch and took one more look at the surrounding area before Mark reached out and tried the knob. To his surprise, it turned. But then came resistance, and of course the door was locked—so the next thing was to knock and wait for an answer. When there was no response, he got the idea to simply kick the door in. He gambled that the archaeological team hadn't installed an alarm system, but even if they had, the point would be made that he was serious about finding out what was going on. After cautioning Sandra, he braced himself against the porch railing with his right hand and gave the door a single powerful kick. The lock gave way, the frame broke, and the door came open.

They both looked around again for signs that anyone had heard them.

Going through into the darkness, they closed the door as best they could, switched on their flashlights, and found themselves in some kind of utility room with another door across from them. They kept the flashlights on, crossed to the inside door, opened it, and stepped into the main part of the church, just behind the pulpit. They clicked off the flashlights; the glow of the distant streetlight was enough to dimly illuminate an interior of beamed ceilings and horizontal pews. The small church was divided by a central aisle, the far ends of the pews butting up against each wall under the windows. The floor was wooden planking. Looking around to his left, Mark saw another door.

"Keep the flashlights off," whispered Sandra. "There's a door over there."

"OK, we don't have to whisper. Yes, I see it. Might be the way to the basement."

He opened the door, clicked his flashlight back on and scanned the beam of light from wall to wall. It was Reverend Hanley's office, and it contained a writing desk, a five-foot metal file cabinet, a couple of odd-looking wooden chairs with guitar-shaped backs, a portrait of Jesus, and the inevitable framed print of an old gray-haired man praying with folded hands.

"I don't see any way into the basement," said Sandra.

In the dark, Mark's thoughts went back to Hanley's insanity.

"There's no way into the basement here," repeated Sandra. She gently gripped the slick fabric of his rain jacket.

They went back to the pulpit. There was a creaking noise overhead as if the building were settling. At Sandra's urging, they returned through the door they'd left open and stepped again into the utility room.

Sandra turned on her flashlight and pointed it to the broken back door. "There's nothing here. We'd better go."

Then Mark saw the other door. It was near the darkest corner of the room. "There it is," he said. "Hanley's office is on the other side of the wall over here, and this is a staircase on this side."

Sandra shone her light on him. "It's a closet," she said firmly.

Mark gazed into the bright light at her, shook his head, opened the door, and pointed his own flashlight down a set of wooden stairs descending to a landing, then left into the darkness.

Sandra followed him and they slowly went down the stairs until they emerged onto a concrete floor in the chilly basement. The cold penetrated their clothing, and there was a musty smell that mingled with a chemical odor. Although they pointed their flashlights into the gloom, the basement was too large to be totally scrutinized. Mark noted the covered windows—and now, as he searched around, he could not find a light switch.

"There must be a switch at the top of the stairs," Sandra said.

"Wait here for a second." Climbing back up, he located a metal switchbox, flicked on the switch, and went back down to join Sandra.

The room was now brightly illuminated by fluorescent tubes about six feet long. In the middle were long tables arranged between two rows of foundation posts, and along the concrete walls were shelves made from new, unfinished pine. The shelves held a variety of stones, pieces of dark wood, and sea mammal bones; also notebooks and clutter that was typical of the archaeological dig. Mark walked between the long tables into the middle of the room. Large, shallow, rectangular vats rested on the table in front of him, about eight inches deep, containing the chemical that he and Sandra had smelled. Submerged in the nearest vat were three thin, dark wooden objects. Mark looked under the table where he noticed a couple of space-heaters, then turned back to Sandra. "This basement is where Maggie must have helped with the artifacts."

He went to the shelves and glanced at the samples and specimens. Farther along the wall was a five-gallon container labeled "Polyethylene Glycol." On the table nearest were a couple of gallon containers labeled "50% Carbowax Sol. Approx." and several gallons of distilled water.

"Maybe Hanley got into some of these chemicals," he said jokingly.

Sandra went to the third table. "What discovery could Maggie have referred to in her letter to you?" She turned off her flashlight and put it in her coat.

"Nothing here looks significant. Or maybe it's right in front of us and we're too ignorant to see it."

"The chill is certainly significant."

"What was Hanley coming to see Gregory about that night? Maybe

I should try to talk to Hanley in the nut house. I've got to . . ." He was gazing past Sandra to the right of the wooden stairs that angled upward, and something about the wall was distinctly odd. It seemed too far forward compared to the stairs. In fact, what appeared to be a curtain of muslin covered nearly its whole length. ". . . Hold it . . . hold it . . . what's that about?" He walked around a table toward a place where the curtain was slightly parted, showing darkness behind.

"What's wrong?" asked Sandra. "Don't scare me."

Mark pulled the section of curtain to the side, moving it back along a cord overhead. He pulled for a length of about a dozen feet.

"Look at this," said Mark.

Sandra walked over and grabbed his arm.

"The curtain was hiding these shelves," he said. "My God, look."

From floor to ceiling, pine shelves were labeled with a numbering system that probably stretched between the underside of the stairs to the side of the basement wall. On the shelves were amassed and organized hundreds of bones—not sea mammal bones, but shelf upon shelf, row upon row of human bones. Each was tagged with a label attached with twine. The most recognizable were human skulls, about thirty of them, resting on the shelves amid apparently disassembled skeletons. The hideous skulls rested at different angles as if looking in various directions. Mark and Sandra stood in silence. They realized the significance. These remains had been discovered at the dig.

"Matsamura used to gaze out the little plastic window at that circular pit," said Mark.

"What pit?"

"When you visited the dig, did you see a large area that had been dug out further up on the shoreline?"

"I think so, but I don't really remember it."

"Matsamura said they'd given up on it. It was an early excavation that hadn't worked out, he said."

"It's been a long time since I was there."

"Clearly, Matsamura was minimizing that part of the excavation in his descriptions. And Kallabush kept quiet too."

"Then Maggie knew about this."

"Of course. Of course she did."

The recognition that this morbid white gallery had caused his wife to stay here made Mark aware of the extent of his misunderstanding and lack of information. This was the secret she was in on.

"It's unbelievable," said Sandra. "Gregory knew about this, and I wonder who else knows. The town's elders wouldn't allow this. If these are Indian bones."

"They were pulled out of that pit," Mark repeated.

Sandra gazed at the skulls. "How old are they?"

"I don't know."

"There are children here," she said. Slowly, she reached out for one of the small skulls, lifted it silently, felt the weight of it, then turned back to Mark. "It can't be recent," she said.

"You're right. If so, it would be a mass grave and everyone would know about it. Radwick and Matsamura didn't want *us* to know. Now we're one of the privileged few. I understand why Radwick wanted this hushed up. If these are Indian bones, and if I understand this sort of thing, then you're right—many Native Americans would not like this, however valuable these bones are." He bent down to examine the large lower shelves, which contained even more skeletal remains. "The tribe would want these folks buried. There could be hostile feelings surrounding this." He walked along the length of the shelving in front of Sandra toward the wall. Sandra returned the small white skull to its place, then picked up a larger skull from the shelf above. Mark kneeled down to examine the lower shelves at the end. Sandra turned to him with a horrified expression on her face. "Mark . . ."

"What?"

"This . . . there's a hole here," she said, turning the side of the skull toward him.

He came over and looked at it. In the side of the skull was a hole with radiating fractures.

Sandra stared at him in dismay. "Is this a bullet hole?"

The weight of these words was self-evident.

Sandra put the skull back. "Mark, for God's sake, *what* are we looking at here?"

"I'm not sure." He bent down and took another skull from the shelf, holding it up to the antiseptic light. No sign of anything wrong with it—but as he returned it to the shelf, he caught a glimpse of another skull with a hole in it. He lifted it from the shelf and turned it over in his hands. It was cold and dry. Here was a large bullet hole in the forehead and an exit hole in the rear. There could be little mistake. You didn't have to be a forensic expert, he thought. He put the skull back and picked up one of the smaller ones.

"Oh, God," said Sandra.

He wanted to say something intelligent, but could only stare. This bullet had apparently crashed through the back of the head, and a *very small* head it was. . . .

He put it back on its storage shelf and felt the basement chill enter his flesh anew.

"Mark," said Sandra quietly, "they . . . all of them were shot to death."

"Likely," he said. "All of them. Even children. Now it's time to leave."

"Should we put the curtain back?"

He shrugged. "We bashed the door in, we might as well leave the curtain open. We aren't going to tell the authorities about this, not before confronting Radwick. There are too many questions to answer. A number of people had to know about this. It wasn't a small operation. Radwick and Matsamura were being helped by all kinds of people at the dig itself, even students from the University of Washington. Maybe the bones were discovered at a very early point in the excavation, before the students arrived, and Maggie found out about it later. But it had to have been the discovery she'd referred to in her letter."

"Gregory knew," said Sandra.

"And it seems unlikely that Radwick could keep this from the tribal council. If he had, what would happen when he was through with these bones? He'd have to go to the tribal council at that time, and then what?—admit that they'd dug up people who'd been shot to death and hid them here in the basement of the church? Hell no. The tribal council knows."

Sandra drew another section of curtain aside for a couple of feet and examined some shallow bins on one of the shelves. "Mark, I've found some lead bullets. They're organized in these containers. Look, they've got bullets divided up and labeled to correspond with the shelves, but some aren't marked." She examined a container, then walked over to him and said, "Open up your hand." He did, and she dropped a bullet into it. "Put this in your pocket. It was their evidence, now it's ours. Let's go. I'm freezing. I don't want to be here any longer."

He put the iniquitous bit of metal into his pocket and took Sandra by the arm. They turned away from the shelves and went to the bottom of the stairs. The archaeologists were trying to avoid controversy, he thought, and the Makahs were cooperating. Radwick would be closing down the dig for the winter, but hadn't Maggie implied they'd be here, in this lab, studying what they'd found?

They ascended the stairs, shut off the lights, and used their flashlights to find the way back outside. Mark shut the back door as best he could and walked with Sandra quickly toward the truck. He was thinking of one person he'd like to talk to before going back to the dig, someone who wasn't officially connected to the archaeologists or to the tribe: Garman Hanley—a potential killer who'd come to see Gregory Torrel in the night, and whose church had become a repository for some sort of massacre.

Chapter Fourteen

A little before nine the next morning Mark left a message on Deputy Hermann's answering machine asking to visit Reverend Hanley at the state mental facility in Port Angeles, a city about sixty miles east. He borrowed Sandra's Rover and the key to the logging gate, went to Neah Bay, and started to drive the twisting road that skirted the straits. In his pocket was the bullet they'd taken from the lab. He had called a gun shop owner who might be able to identify it. Dr. Radwick was scheduled to arrive for dinner tomorrow night at seven, and Mark was anxious to learn as much as possible beforehand.

When Sandra handed him the keys to the Rover, she looked tired, and insisted on staying home. She had Gregory's loaded revolver, and it wasn't clear she was in danger anyway. She said she'd be all right.

The rolling, curving highway conformed to the harsh terrain and it was all he could do to stay on the right side of the painted line. It was not a pleasant journey, and the Makah reservation still lay behind him like a trap.

When he stopped at a McDonald's on the outskirts of Port Angeles, it had begun to rain, and he thought of his daughter. The ache of fatherly separation returned, and he yearned to pick her up, hold her in his arms, and comfort her. He imagined himself driving south along the west side of Puget Sound, connecting with Interstate 5 and continuing on and on toward San Diego, leaving everything else behind. He found coins in his pocket and headed toward a phone booth—but he remembered that Erica was in school. He'd been calling her often from Sandra's. Long before Gregory's funeral, he'd told her the only thing he could think to tell her: "Honey, mommy's lost, but we're looking for her." And she seemed to accept this with whatever understanding a six-year-old could muster; but eventually she'd have to know that Maggie was gone.

Across the parking lot, some kids with their parents went into the McDonald's, and he was glad he'd told Sam and Dorothy to keep Erica busy with as many friends as they could shuttle around. A child like Erica, in the short run, could be amazingly resilient to loss. On the other hand, she was so very young. He'd only just taught her to button up that little blue coat. She missed her mother. Yes, she'd gotten used to being without her this summer—but he reassured her that her mother would be back soon. That was one reason he'd been angry with Maggie when she'd broken her promise. But he'd never let Erica forget that her mother loved her as strongly as he did. What overcame him was the thought of the long summer that in a sense would never end.

At last he turned away from these thoughts, for they couldn't do him any good now. He slid open the phone booth door, put his coins in the slot, and called Sandra. Her voice was reassuring. This was another world entirely, and Sandra meant a great deal to him.

"I haven't heard from Hermann," she said. "Are you all right? I was a little worried."

"Sure. You?"

"Yes."

"I'm going to the gun shop."

"Hermann may call."

"That's OK. I'll see what I can do about visiting Hanley anyway."

"Watch that dangerous road on the way back."

"Yeah. I'll be careful."

"OK, see you."

"See you."

He hung up the phone, then got back in the Rover. He drove down the main street of Port Angeles looking for "Mettler's Gun Exchange." Finally the store came up on the left. He illegally made a U-turn in the middle of the block and then parked, not a maneuver he'd have routinely used in San Diego.

The store owner, Steve, a skinny guy with blond hair combed

straight back, placed Mark's bullet between his fingers and settled into attentiveness. ". . . Well, it's been fired of course, but you're asking what it is."

"And if there's any way to tell its age."

"Forty-five caliber, probably. A bit deteriorated. Where'd you find it?"

"In a layer of clay above the ocean tide line."

"I don't suppose you found any cases."

"No," answered Mark, thinking he might have looked further when he was in the lab.

"Wait here a minute." The man went into a back room. When he came out a few minutes later, he handed the bullet back to Mark. "I believe this is an old .45-70. Weighs a little over 26 grams, about 405 grains. I checked the computer for a match. 'Course, you can't tell when it was fired. Could have been fired yesterday. But it's deteriorated. That eliminates yesterday." He smiled.

"How old is it?"

"Not easy to be sure, but this bullet was manufactured mostly in the late 1800s and stayed in supply well into the 1900s. The army used it in Springfield rifles and carbines. It was replaced with longer-range ammunition. He held it up. "Big little sucker, ain't it? Some people still use this ammo for certain kinds of big game, but you don't see it often."

"So this thing was likely fired long ago, as early as 1900?"

"Probably, given where you found it. But there's no way to be sure. Besides, I'm not a true ballistics expert."

"Look, ah, thanks for your help."

"Glad to oblige. I'm having a sale next weekend. Stop by."

Mark left the gun shop and, wishing he had a cell phone, walked to a gas station with a phone booth. He called Sandra again.

"They won't let you see Hanley," Sandra said.

"Damn it, why not?"

"Too soon. They just won't take a chance on having you there, since you were the one who subdued him."

"What sort of condition is he in?"

"Hermann didn't say."

"Anyone else call?"

"No, that's it. What about that bullet?"

"It's probably quite old. That massacre must have taken place beyond recent memory. You'd think it would have been a well-known event, even so. It'll be up to Radwick to tell us. I don't see any point in searching newspaper records."

"OK," said Sandra. "Drive carefully on the way back. That's a treacherous road."

"I will. But it's early yet, I've come all this way, and I'm going to try to see Hanley anyway. Maybe it depends on who you talk to."

"I suppose it can't hurt to try," Sandra said.

"OK, I'll see you later this afternoon."

Mark spent a few minutes trying to find out how to get to the mental facility. Then he wound his way out of town. When he got to the hospital, he parked behind some cyclone fencing. The building, he noticed, was made of a lot of concrete and very little glass. He walked to the entrance. A black woman, about forty, sat behind a counter and told him he could not see an inmate without permission. Hanley was under tight security. Mark would need permission, so he filled out a form, waited for a half-hour, then was led by a guard through hallways until he arrived at Room 132 where an official told him Hanley could only be made available to his attorney at this time. Mark thanked him for his trouble.

Frustrated, but also relieved, he drove back downtown, bought a new shirt, shoes, socks, underwear, two pairs of pants, and a watch, then resumed his journey from the house of the insane back to the land of the dead.

*   *   *

It was cool inside the Torrel house when he returned. Going into the kitchen, he put down his bag with the new clothes, removed his jacket and hung it over a chair. For the moment, the house was silent, and as he called out to Sandra he walked through the living room to the entry hall. She wasn't in the parlor, opposite, so he went upstairs to check the office, then to her bedroom, knocked lightly, and peered in through the open door, hoping he would not seem like a curious predator. The green botanical wallpaper seemed lifelike and exotic. But the room was empty.

The two other bedrooms were empty, as well as the bathroom. He stepped back into the hallway and listened for sounds. He was indeed in a quiet, empty house by himself.

"Sandra!" His voice echoed down the stairway.

Either she was in the sewing room, the small downstairs bathroom next to it, or else gone. He'd have noticed if the outside trapdoor to the half-basement had been open. Sandra didn't have the Toyota truck, which had been temporarily impounded. He looked downstairs again, but she wasn't anywhere; then he went into the kitchen and looked out the north window. Barney was sniffing around the yard. Mark was growing anxious, rubbing his neck as he turned to gaze toward the garage where he'd parked the big Rover.

Thinking she might be walking on the beach, he plucked his jacket off the kitchen chair and walked to the front door. Stepping outside onto the porch, he looked north, then south along the cliff edge, appraising the empty green and gray landscape with its strikingly sparse trees. The same sinking fear he'd had over Maggie's disappearance threatened him, but he tried to stay calm. As he walked toward the sea cliff, he heard a car.

The blue Toyota pickup came out of the woods road, crossed in front of the house, and drove around the corner into the garage driveway. In a dreamlike instant, Mark knew the truck was Gregory's. Sandra had probably gotten a ride and had gone to get the truck. He walked along the right side of the house into the driveway. It was doubtful she'd seen him. The truck was parked in front of the garage, but walking toward it, he felt a sense of déjà vu. (Why wasn't Sandra getting out?) He approached from the left side where he could see a silhouette in the shadow behind the headrest, and his heart began to pump faster. Anxiously, almost without thinking, he decided to open the door. He came up to it purposefully, stopped, put his hand onto the handle, and squeezed. The door started to come open, but simultaneous with the motion of the latch and the movement of his arm came a scream from the cab.

He flung the door open.

Sandra stared at him, covering her mouth. Then she put her hand up to her forehead, her other hand on the steering wheel. "My God, you scared me to death," she said. "I was looking for my receipt."

"Receipt," repeated Mark awkwardly, trying to recover from the scream, wondering at his lack of sense.

"For the truck," she said. "Here it is on the floor."

"How can you just calmly drive this truck home?" he asked.

She took a deep breath and looked at him. "It's our truck. I . . . I don't know . . . they got all the evidence they needed, samples and things . . . they took out the seat that . . . they didn't need it any more." She seemed stricken.

"It's all right," said Mark, who was as upset as she. He peered into the cab and saw that the passenger seat was gone and the dash was clean. "Sorry. I was outside looking for you. I was worried. Come on, let's go inside."

She stepped out of the truck, gave him a misty-eyed look, briefly hugged him, and then walked with him into the house.

"Cindy Morgan drove me to Forks where they kept the truck. They'd taken pictures and gone over it for fingerprints and fibers and blood samples. They got me a fax of the medical examiner's report."

"You should have left a note for me," he said. "I thought you'd disappeared."

"I'm sorry."

"I was on the verge of going to look for you."

"Honestly, I'd have left a note, but I didn't think it would take this long."

"What did they find out?"

"Pretty much as expected. The medical examiner has no evidence of murder. But I was able to identify the knife—a large hunting knife with a Nuu-chah-nulth design. Gregory kept it in his glove compartment."

"Were there anyone else's fingerprints?"

"Nothing they could use. If he was murdered, his hand was put on the knife after the fact. Or maybe he tried to pull the knife out and wasn't able." Her voice became subdued. "But it's more likely he moved to the passenger seat to keep the truck more drivable afterwards. They said suicides are often courteous." She took off her coat, hung it over his own on the kitchen chair, and went through the dining room into the living room.

Mark followed her, checking to see if she was all right. She switched on an antique floor lamp on the far side of the sofa. He noticed she'd replaced her customary jeans with tan slacks but retained a customary black turtle-neck. Behind her, outside the big living-room bay window, the waning sun and low clouds made purplish-red streaks over the sea.

After a moment, she asked, "Did you see Reverend Hanley?"

"No."

"I guess he'd be the only murder suspect they'd have. But why would Hanley come to the house trying to visit a man he'd just killed? It doesn't seem plausible."

"It's about as plausible as anything else going on around here."

"It would be difficult to argue with that, Mark. After all, we saw Maggie."

"Maggie's ghost didn't stab your husband. That would be a bit too implausible."

"That's not what I meant."

"Of course not. I'm sorry. To be honest with you, I can take fear and pain and sadness, but not having answers is going to kill me."

"You wanted to stay and handle this."

He looked at her. "I wanted to stay because I thought we could find out what happened."

"And because I asked you to stay."

He took a deep breath. "Yes, that's true."

She said, "I feel better now. I don't know why."

"I'm glad you're all right."

"You must be hungry," she said. "I've got some spareribs in the refrigerator. Why don't we put on some music, make dinner, and pretend nothing's wrong just for tonight? Radwick's coming tomorrow. Let's not think about anything tonight."

"Fair enough."

*   *   *

Mark was impressed by how quickly she seemed to rebound from what must have been an unpleasant journey. In the kitchen, they prepared dinner. Night closed in. They felt more alone than ever before.

The days had provided an emotional buffer, and the discovery in the church was more an abstraction than an imminent threat. Mark put some romantic jazz on the little stereo in the living room.

At the dinner table, he and Sandra talked about their own past before their recent troubles, consciously avoiding anything about their spouses, recognizing the need to rediscover something of themselves as individuals. To Mark, this seemed a healthy, though undoubtedly temporary, transformation. They were also pleased with having made some progress, criminal though it may have been to break into the church.

"I am not a religious sort of guy," Mark said. "People come down on one side of that fence or the other. I'm not exactly the village atheist, but I think the world is just what one would expect if there was no God. Still, I can't conceive of time having a beginning. Where did time come from?"

"You mean why is there something instead of nothing?" asked Sandra. "I can't remember who asked that—some famous scientist."

"That's the wall we run up against. Existence itself, generated how? So I'm a fence sitter. An agnostic."

"How do appearances of the dead fit into this?"

"They don't, that I know of." said Mark.

Sandra nodded.

"Things here don't seem quite real, do they. Yet they are."

She smiled and told him about her lackadaisical Protestant background. Her goal had been to write poetry. A useless economic enterprise, she admitted, but one that fit into living away from the urban anthill. Her parents were wealthy enough to send her to Sarah Lawrence, and she'd taken a course from Billy Collins, a living poet Mark had actually heard of. When she returned to Seattle she'd worked for an oriental rug dealer. She'd collected a number of books about oriental rugs. She was thirty-four years old. Loved Pacific Northwest beaches. The rain. Wished there were fewer people in the world and wondered how to get rid of a few bad examples. At this, she laughed at the quizzical expression that crossed Mark's face.

After dinner, she said, "I'll light the fire. We can read or watch a movie in the parlor. Gregory collected quite a few DVDs. We hadn't installed a satellite dish yet. That's a big deal up here, of course, but we intellectuals are immune." She smiled, and he was glad to see her enjoy-ing herself. She could draw a line and escape for a while. Could he?

After clearing the dishes, they decided to just sit and talk some more. Kneeling down in front of the fireplace, Sandra put some paper and kindling onto the grate. She arranged a couple of logs on top of the kindling while Mark stood by, then struck a wooden match.

When the fire caught, she stood up, looked at the fire for a mo-ment, then started to walk past him. But she hesitated. Her face was lightly flushed from the heat, and when she turned slightly aside, a shadow fell across her cheek. She'd started to say something.

"What is it?" he asked.

"Mark," she said, still looking away from him, "I'm very attracted to you." She didn't say it in an overly emotional way.

They stood close to each other. She waited for him to speak, and in that instant Mark's resistance melted. Partly, he felt the guilt of his own intense attraction, but mostly the cumulative effect of long hours of be-ing near this woman but unable to touch her. Even if he wanted to, how could he reject someone like this who'd gambled on him so trust-ingly?

When she turned toward him, he gently held her by the upper part of her arms. She was uncertain of him, but it was that very uncertainty that endeared her to him even more. They were alone, and this was no longer the real world. She closed the gap between them, he felt the movement of her against him, and in another moment they were kiss-ing passionately. Propriety vanished. The room seemed to shrink and disappear. Neither of them could stop. Only Sandra's lips and the feel of her body entered into Mark's senses, and it was a desire fulfilled. No thoughts interfered, and if subtle misgivings remained, they were sub-merged by the spontaneity and intensity of her accommodation. They held each other, searched each other's eyes, then held hands tightly and went across the living room toward the stairs.

Chapter Fifteen

Sometime in the middle of the night, Mark awoke in the darkness of the bedroom. He slowed his breathing in order to listen, for he didn't know whether he'd actually heard his name spoken or whether he'd dreamed it. He rolled over on his right side toward Sandra. They had taken solace in each other's desires amid personal crises, and there would be guilt to share; but they'd also been accidentally thrown together and drawn toward one another during many difficult days. Sleeping apart inside the somewhat sinister ancestral house seemed less natural, and therefore less feasible, regardless of loyalty to their dead spouses. Unsure how he'd awakened, he felt for Sandra in the dark, but she was gone. He raised his head after noticing a bathrobed silhouette standing in the doorway.

"Mark," whispered Sandra.

He raised himself up on his elbows and stared at the door.

"What time is it?" he asked.

There was an odd anxiety in Sandra's voice. "It's two o'clock."

"What's wrong?"

"Someone is standing outside the house."

Now he came fully awake.

She stepped into the room. "I went down to the kitchen because I couldn't sleep, and when I came back into the living room I saw . . ."

"All right, take it easy." He got out of bed, walked awkwardly across the room in his boxer shorts and reached for the light switch. She grabbed his hand and held it tightly.

"Please leave the light off," she said urgently. "I've turned the lights off in the kitchen and the living room."

"It's probably someone from town," he said ... but thought to himself, why would someone come out here in the middle of the night?

"Are the floodlights on in the front and back?"

"Yes."

He went to the bedroom's front window, which had a view from the upper northwest corner of the house toward the cliff. The light from the front porch reached only about thirty feet into the fog that had drifted in during the night, and he couldn't see anything there at all. Sandra came to his side. Her worried face was illuminated as she moved close to the glass. Then, oddly, she bent her head down, causing her silky black hair to fall close to the window sill.

"Take it easy," said Mark. "Are you sure you saw someone?"

Almost inaudibly, she said, "Yes."

"How far from the house?"

She paused, not looking at him.

He put his arm around her shoulder, but she didn't say anything. Then she looked out the window again. Tears mysteriously streaked her cheeks, and her voice was trembling.

"Sandra, what's wrong?"

"They come back," she said.

"What do you mean?"

She looked at him, and her face was white. "I mean Maggie and Gregory."

Mark said nothing.

She looked with terror into his eyes, and her voice was weak. "Is that what happens?"

Mark turned from the window. The house was quiet and he could hear the pounding of the distant ocean. He pictured the downstairs and tried to think of what to do. Ironically, he felt for Gregory's borrowed bathrobe at the foot of the bed. The house was chilly; he'd let the fire burn in the living room after going to sleep but had left the furnace off.

Sandra's silhouette was outlined in front of the window. "It's my husband," she said.

"All right. You wait here."

Leaving Sandra, he went quietly down the stairway, emerged into the entry hall, then turned into the living room and stood a few feet away from the large, divided bay window. Outside, the fog continued to move slowly through the floodlight. The light cast an eerie arc from its strategic position under the porch roof. It was not particularly strong, and the view was primarily of a slowly drifting white opacity and the spotty darkness beyond. The distance one could see shifted in and out with the changing thickness of the fog. Anyone might have imagined seeing someone out there—some shifting of mist creating a temporary form.

Sandra came downstairs and stood next to him. Barney whined a little on the back porch. Now something moved in the distance to the left. Sandra fearfully took Mark's hand, tightened her grip, and tried to move him away from the window. He let himself be taken back into the room's shadow. This acknowledgment, at the moment of doubt, unnerved him, and even in the shadow he saw that Sandra's face was terror-stricken.

At the edge of the light from the porch, a dark figure seemed to materialize out of the fog. It appeared to be a man, and Mark hoped it was in fact someone coming to see them, and who, because of the hour, was reluctant to knock on the door. Unfortunately, there was no vehicle—and wouldn't a visitor have parked under the floodlight? Mark didn't feel fear, but a sense of fatalism. He had assumed a certain randomness in the ghostly appearances thus far, and in that lay an aberrant security, as if he faced an enemy without a plan. If this was Gregory Torrel, the pattern would be coherent. This wasn't just something that was happening. This was a dead man who'd come home. If it wasn't Gregory, who was it?

"What are we going to do?" whispered Sandra.

The figure seemed to wait at the edge of the light. Mark just couldn't give in to the idea it was Gregory, and if it was a criminal he was showing an incredible lack of caution. It had to be someone who'd come out here for a reason.

"I'm going outside to see who it is and what he wants."

"Oh, God, no." Sandra tightened her grip on him while continuing to look out the window.

"The only other thing is to call the police, but there isn't time for them to get here. Where's that damn gun I found upstairs?"

"Listen to me," said Sandra. She grasped his robe at the sides with both hands, and her low, frightened voice had a tone of stultifying authority. "I know how suggestible I might be, but think for a minute about what's happened. We are in the middle of something unnatural. Don't discount me. These encounters are dangerous. Something happened to Maggie and the others. And Hanley. Maybe we've been lucky until now, while others are dead or insane." Her eyes widened and her words came out in short bursts. "I know my husband. I know his form, his behavior, the way he hesitated like this when he was drunk and afraid to come into the house. I'm telling you that is him."

Mark stared toward the window. While Sandra had spoken, the figure had advanced halfway to the house. Sandra looked, then started as if caught by a seizure. She released her grip, moved back through the dining room archway and bumped into the table.

Mark had seen Gregory only once, and that was in the truck, in death, and in a photograph. Unfortunately, these memories weren't enough to reject the idea that this figure, who was now more clearly visible, was Gregory Torrel.

"Goddamn it," said Mark. He backed up toward Sandra, also wishing to stay in the shadows. They looked down the length of the dark living room, and then Mark began to feel a touch of that same nausea he'd experienced on the beach and the logging road. It was the same feeling, and he had to accept it. Would an apparition, whose body had been buried three days ago, try to come *into* the house? The idea was so absurd, and yet so terrifying, that he decided to act immediately to prevent the possibility.

He let Sandra go and went toward the door.

"No!" she yelled.

He motioned her to stay in the dining room, and with a jab of fear, realized he didn't know whether a locked door would act as a barrier, or whether his own proximity to the door would accomplish anything. An archway about six feet wide divided the living room longitudinally from the entry hall. From the entry hall, one could either go back into the living room, upstairs, down a short hall to the left of the stairs toward another entrance to the kitchen, or through an opposite door into the parlor. If he opened the front door immediately, he could pray that he and Sandra were victims of a little hysteria that would evaporate as they confronted a normal person who was perhaps lost. He looked back into the room for Sandra. Her frightened form remained next to the dining room table. Stepping into the entry hall, he was almost to the front door. He grasped the frame of the archway and told himself that his nausea might be a simple reaction to fear this time. Yet he should do something before whatever was out there decided to come to the door or retreat into the fog.

He made his right hand into a fist, then relaxed it and reached slowly out to open the lock.

"Mark!"

He turned. Sandra was standing in the middle of the living room, her face as fixed and pale as that of a statue.

"Mark, don't open it." Her voice was so completely in control that it sent a shiver through him. She was in a state of extreme terror, yet making a monumental attempt to sound unemotional.

He held back . . . and then, with a swift, almost invasive perversity, a strange thought came to him. Might the archaeologists be playing Sandra and him for fools? Trying to scare them? As the nausea grew and threatened him with incapacitation—as it had before—he knew his notion was wrong. But in his panic he felt he had to totally eliminate the idea, attack it head on—and the evidence was standing outside.

He turned to Sandra with those improbable thoughts on his mind, and as she looked at him, her expression collapsed when she saw some new form of reckless determination.

"If it's Gregory," he said, "and Gregory is dead, there is nothing to stop him from coming right inside, right into this room. If it's not Gregory, then who is it?"

"For God's sake."

Taking a quick breath, he reached out, unlocked the door, grabbed the doorknob, turned it and pulled, but the unaccounted-for chain kept the door from opening more than a wide crack, and he worked too furiously to get it off instantly. Then he felt Sandra behind him. Saying nothing, she violently grabbed him by the hair with both hands, and with great force pulled him painfully backwards. He fell hard to the floor, his fear diffusing into anger and surprise. She kept her grip, trying to keep him down and off balance.

"Let go!" He moved his hands to pry her fingers loose.

Breathing rapidly, she pleaded with a desperate voice, then paused for one unaffordable second and gave a painful cry as he cruelly pried her fingers away. A rapid expression of revelation crossed her face, her eyes were wide, and while she still lay on the floor she grabbed his robe with a clenched fist. "Goddamn it, listen to me! How do you know Gregory can come in? Maybe you've got to go *outside*." She stared at him, eyes blazing. "*Why* are you trying to go outside? For God's sake!"

He pulled free, but was so nauseous now that he could only stay on the bare wooden floor. He looked out through the partially open door as, without a doubt, Gregory Torrel appeared on the front porch.

Sandra struggled to her feet and rushed forward as the figure had come onto the porch. She stared at her husband, paralyzed—his form silhouetted in the fog. Then she slammed the door by shoving her full weight against it, leaned into the door, turned the lock and began to yell. "Greg, leave me alone! Leave me alone!"

Mark was ill. He got up, swaying, but had to go back and sit on the stairs. Sandra covered her mouth as if she was also ill, came to him, grabbed him with one hand and remained with him, staring with terrible anticipation at the front door, her body trembling. He waited also, held her tightly, and felt the sickness subside as they sat on the stairs, she clutching a railing post, he listening for movement on the porch.

They sat still, breathing heavily until the sickness left them.

Mark's physical exhaustion intermingled with shame and confusion. He looked at the front door and tried to understand why he'd reacted as he had. Suspicion had moved him, and he began to think he was becoming desperate to find a simple answer, whatever the cost. Or did his speculations have to make unfounded convolutions in order to save his rationality? These dreamlike experiences were real. Maggie was not alive. Olson was not alive. Gregory was not alive. Yet they had all returned.

After several minutes, he helped Sandra up. They went into the living room and cautiously approached the bay window, coming inside its perimeter, making sure they could see the whole empty porch and the empty, foggy halo of light beyond.

Chapter Sixteen

Candlelight from the center of the dining table illuminated Paul Radwick's thin, bearded face. The broad detachment he'd shown at the cemetery had withered away while Sandra described her husband's death. She didn't mention Gregory's reappearance outside the house, or Maggie's appearance on the logging road. The fog had lifted at 10 A.M., and she and Mark had agreed not to mention the apparitions to Radwick.

The dining room was warmly lit by the tall candles as Sandra, and now Mark, told what they knew about Gregory's apparent suicide and the circumstances of the last few days.

"Whatever your reasons," said Mark, "you've been withholding information from Sandra and me. Lives have been lost. Loved ones."

"You guys broke into our lab," said Matsamura evenly.

"We know what you've been through," Radwick said, "but you shouldn't have done that." His dry, unhappy face lost its intellectual resilience.

"The food is getting cold," said Sandra.

Matsamura took a bite of chicken, and they all began to eat without interrupting the conversation.

Mark addressed Matsamura about the lab. "As I said, Maggie had mentioned something being found at the dig, but when I asked about it, you said you didn't know what she meant. When we found out there was a lab in the church—that was after Hanley had gone crazy—we had to look. We assumed you were keeping something from us—and Sandra knew that Gregory was keeping something from her." He

glanced at Sandra, who was sitting at the head of the table, then back to
Radwick. "Also, Gregory was in bad shape. He'd become an alcoholic."

"When you came looking for Maggie," said Radwick, "Ken here
didn't see the need to say anything about the find, and you must understand it's a very sensitive issue. We have the complicity of the tribal
council and the county police only because of the extreme nature of it.
This was a massacre of an entire small village many decades ago, and
everyone agreed we needed to learn as much as possible. We promised
the tribal council to keep the remains only until the forensics could be
done, and then to arrange for reburial. My instructions to the volunteers—including your wife—were to keep it quiet. When you arrived, I
was gone. We just wanted to stay out of the news."

Matsamura seemed tense. "No one connected Maggie's disappearance with the bones, and that's why I didn't mention them to you. Now
you say Gregory's death might be connected. I don't get it."

Radwick looked at Sandra. "Gregory told us not to say anything to
you about the discovery after he began to help with some research. I
don't know why. He did a lot of leg-work, running back and forth to
the library in Port Angeles and Seattle. Roland Veress did forensics on
the bones, and the county lab did the ballistics on the bullets."

"How many people on the reservation know about the bones?"
asked Mark. "How could it be kept secret?"

Radwick smiled faintly. "I suspect most people have heard rumors.
The people understand there's a good reason for the way it's being
handled. The main thing is that we didn't want to have the media down
our necks—that means Seattle media, especially—because once this
thing got that far it would go all the way. We pulled thirty-six skeletons
out of that pit. If this hit CNN even for a second we'd be in the middle
of a huge controversy about a big massacre, the reburial issue, the digging up of Indian graves, and the whole thing."

"Aren't there Native American activists in Neah Bay?"

"You bet. And they want to know who killed their ancestors."

"And who did?"

Radwick's face took on an appearance of sadness and irony. "My
archaeology department doesn't encourage so-called educated guesses."

"We have a theory," said Matsamura, taking a bite of potatoes.

"What I try to drill into my students," Radwick explained, "is that assumptions are next to worthless. Any number of coincidences can intervene between an observation and an interpretation. At the U.W. we don't deal much in circumstantial evidence. We prefer to let others publish unverifiable theories about artifacts." He stopped himself. Then he shrugged his shoulders a little and gave a look of resignation. "OK, on the other hand, what we've got are bullets that were used in a certain type of weapon. Although we don't have the weapons, we've got historical material that shows who on the reservation owned such weapons—purchased from the U.S. Government. The rifles were part of a government armory that hadn't been used for two decades at the time of purchase, and the ammunition found among the remains was of the type used by these weapons. At this point I would tell my students that what they have is a bunch of data and that a description of that data concludes the find. There is no *scientific* way to connect these particular bullets with the rifles that were, in theory, capable of using these bullets, and certainly not to the owners of the rifles. Unfortunately, the few people up here who know about the bones and the bullets are *not* my students, and the circumstantial evidence we found fits perfectly into what has been rumored for decades."

"And that is what?"

"And that is that Gregory Torrel's grandfather, Joseph Torrel—who purchased the rifles—and some of his men, came down to the beach one night and slaughtered an entire village of men, women, and children because those people were rebelling against the government and impeding plans for cheaply harvesting trees."

Mark gazed at Radwick. Sandra continued to eat as if this revelation about Joseph Torrel wasn't a surprise. Indeed, it fit almost too logically into her traumatic experiences of the last few months—and into Gregory's habit of secrecy. So she continued to eat and look at her plate.

"When did this massacre take place?" Mark asked.

Radwick glanced from Sandra to Mark with a subtle, guilty look.

"In the late 1920s," he said, "just before Joseph Torrel's disappearance from the reservation and his wife's suicide."

Sandra now stopped eating.

Mark couldn't squelch his surprise. "You mean that Joseph Torrel disappeared and his wife killed herself, and we didn't know this—I mean, Sandra was never told about this?"

Radwick responded, "I would have assumed you knew." He looked at Sandra. "These are things that Gregory discovered after he moved here. The tribe's elders knew but never had cause to speak about it. You've got to remember that these things happened a long, long time ago, back in the late 1920s."

"But not forgotten."

"Not entirely."

Mark began to lightly tap the table next to his plate, as he sometimes did when irritated.

Radwick looked at him soberly.

Mark finally spoke. "I'm not the most 'politically correct' person around, but it looks like Gregory has been the victim of hatred—and by default, so has Sandra. Innocently moving back into this house—Joseph's house—symbolized an unforgivable tyranny to the Makahs."

"From the point of view of the tribe, or from anyone, you can easily see the enormity of this crime," said Matsamura. "Thirty-six men, women, and children."

"The enormity of it is clear," said Mark.

"Thirty-six . . ."

"A crime by a man living here more than eighty years ago who happened to be Gregory Torrel's grandfather."

"You can't expect an entire people to just brush off the past," countered Matsamura.

"And Gregory himself couldn't overcome that tragedy in several ways," said Mark, "at least one of which was emotional, because naively, and with a liberal mind, he'd invested his future in coming here to start where his grandfather had left off, without having been told by his relatives what had happened."

Matsamura gazed across the table. "His living relatives may not have known. His father, Kendrick, was taken away as a child after his mother's suicide. No one managed to come up with the linking evidence, particularly the sale of the rifles, until now."

"How were those villagers interfering?"

"They were encouraging others in the tribe to keep their children out of the boarding school, to continue their old ways, speak their native language, not cooperate with the government or with Torrel Lumber."

"They were having an effect," said Radwick. "These people moved south to the site of a earlier village to avoid white indoctrination. At that time, the government was virtually kidnapping children and sending them away. This new village was a subversive organization. They demanded to raise their children using their own language and in their own way. Cultural autonomy was something Joseph Torrel could not tolerate. And this was something the United States Government could not tolerate."

"Joseph Torrel had the authorities on his side," said Matsamura, "so there was no way this massacre was going to be investigated and solved in the 1920s by the U.S. Government. The bodies were buried and forgotten. And the blame was placed on intra-tribal conflicts. The Makahs, of course, knew what had happened."

"And they *disposed* of Joseph Torrel," Mark surmised.

"Probably. We don't know the exact circumstances. But several days later, Lucy Torrel, his wife, was found hanging from a makeshift noose upstairs in this house."

Sandra put her silverware down. Mark reached over and took her hand. She looked up, despondent but self-contained.

"My husband didn't trust me with this information," she said icily.

Radwick wiped his mouth with a blue cloth napkin, then spoke sympathetically. "I'm sorry. I don't know what was on your husband's mind, but I think he felt, up to the last, that the evidence might be kept secret and that he'd still have a chance to redress his grandfather's deeds."

"Now we learn that Lucy Torrel hanged herself upstairs in this house," said Mark, still holding Sandra's hand.

"But there is more to the story," said Radwick, pouring himself another glass of wine. "There's no trace of what happened to Joseph's or Lucy's bodies. Gregory couldn't locate any graves." He bent forward slightly and looked at Sandra as if through invisible bifocals. "He also found disturbing information about his father, Kendrick Torrel."

"Gregory didn't say much about his father," said Sandra, "only that he had come out here from Baltimore in the early 1960s."

"Gregory's father, Kendrick, returned to Neah Bay in 1964, at the age of forty-four. Gregory found this out, but withheld it from us until recently. Kendrick ran the mill near Forks just like Gregory."

"Excuse me," said Mark, "but I've searched Gregory's office upstairs and haven't found a single thing that pertains."

"Yes, well, Gregory kept his notes and copies of articles at our rented motel room. The records concerning the weapons, the bullets, and the forensic work on the remains are there, too. I managed to budget the motel room into the dig as a consideration for the people who stay here the longest, as a place where they can use a computer and a telephone and get a hot shower and that sort of thing. Anyway, decades after being taken away, Kendrick—your husband's father—came back to Neah Bay, not only to reopen the family lumber business, but to investigate the circumstances of his father's and mother's deaths. He became obsessed with reclaiming his father's empire—and you know that children can remember a lot of what happens to them, especially upsetting things. He wasn't satisfied with the knowledge that his father had disappeared and his mother had committed suicide."

"Like Gregory," said Matsamura, "Kendrick knew few details."

"He wasn't here very long," continued Radwick. "But before he left, he killed a tribal leader in a drunken argument."

"Gregory related this to us in very emotional terms, though there was no need for us to hear about it, except that it did relate to history and so forth."

"We knew Gregory had a drinking problem, too. His talk got less and less rational as he began alluding to old myths. We thought maybe he'd fallen under someone's influence."

Mark interrupted. "Have you ever heard the name Bob Silvers?"

"Yeah. Former tribal council member. Told us that digging up the bones would be dangerous."

"In what way?"

"He was rather cryptic, if I recall. He said that disturbing those at rest will awaken those who aren't. Something like that."

Radwick paused while he finished dinner.

"I don't know if I can take any more of this right now," said Sandra.

"Of course," said Radwick.

"Let's finish eating and go into the living room."

After finishing, Mark and Matsamura cleared the table while Radwick, thinking to himself, walked into the living room with his glass of wine.

Mark went out into the back yard to get more firewood. The cold wind bit through his shirt as the darkness seemed to press in upon the house. After picking up some split logs, he looked up at the steep rear gable. Like a broad spear, it pointed into the sky. In which room, he wondered, had Lucy Torrel hanged herself?

*   *   *

They gathered in front of the fireplace. Sandra turned the two chairs toward the sofa while Mark relit the fire. He could hear the wind in the flue as he bent down with the box of Diamond matches that were kept next to the hearth. Radwick sat in one of the chairs, Matsamura in the opposite.

"We wondered about Greg's drinking," Radwick said.

"Why?" asked Sandra.

"Well, he seemed emotionally distraught. He'd come down to the beach and pace around or stand there while we worked. We didn't take him too seriously after a while. He finally got rather antagonistic. He wanted us to bury the bones, and I think he finally asked a couple of tribal council members to have this done immediately—but of course his desires were rebuffed."

"I wonder if he wanted Hanley to take the bones out of the church," said Mark.

"Maybe," said Radwick.

"Sandra and I have been trying to understand why Hanley showed up here the night I came ashore."

"Hanley certainly wasn't interested in the dig. We offered him money to use the church."

"Greg might have tried to bribe him," Matsamura pointed out, looking at Radwick.

"This would have been a desperate move, then, out of touch with reality. We would have moved the lab elsewhere and not reburied the remains until we were finished."

"What happened to Kendrick?" asked Sandra. "Gregory never said anything about his father."

"As far as we know, he just rented out this house and left town. He didn't show up back in Forks. Eventually he was acquitted of manslaughter, but we don't know where he went after that."

"And years later Gregory naively returned to Neah Bay to manage the mill, which had always been in the family," said Mark, "with plans to lease more timber land south of the reservation."

"His life was centered around those plans," said Sandra. "He'd immersed himself in Indian history, studied the unfair treatment they'd received, and given up everything to come here."

"But Gregory was delving into other than purely historical matters," said Matsamura.

"He alluded to certain myths," said Radwick. "He wasn't very direct with me on this and I forgot about it."

"Just before he died," said Mark, "Gregory got a strange e-mail from this Bob Silvers guy. Something about a two-headed serpent and all sorts of other stuff."

"You mean Sisiutl?"

"I don't know."

"A Kwakiutl Indian myth," Radwick said. "The twin-headed serpent."

"Sounds like it. Silvers said not to believe the myth, or maybe he meant take it literally. But he also mentioned 'wanderers.'"

"What's it about?" asked Sandra.

Matsamura removed an unlit pipe from his mouth. "Well, according to the myth, Sisiutl is a two-headed sea serpent, but with a head at each end. And when the heads rise out of the water, you're supposed to stand still and maintain your courage. It's indescribably horrible, but as it comes closer, both heads come forward—and as they lean in to devour you, they see each other." Matsamura moved his arms and hands as if they were the two heads. "If you try and run, the heads will blow a fatal breath that will detach your soul, which will linger forever in the rain, mist, or sea. That's why Sisiutl is called the Soul Stealer. But if you stand your ground, the heads will see each other, and so the serpent sees the image of itself. This is a gift of self-knowledge you have bestowed upon it by standing firm."

"By facing down the serpent you are awarded the gift of enduring strength," said Radwick. "And the chips of mica found on the beaches are said to be the serpent's scales, which can bring good luck."

"The souls it steals exist in water," said Matsamura. "So, my children, better stay away from the sea on dark nights, and don't go out in the rain or get lost in the fog."

Radwick nodded to Matsamura. "I bow to your advice," he said. "But I'm afraid we aren't getting anywhere."

"I don't know," said Sandra. "Maybe in some strange way we are."

Mark knew what she meant. It was the mention of fog. Maggie had appeared in the mist on the road, Olson in the mist on the beach, and Gregory in the fog last night. It was crazy.

"The disappearances are related to water," said Sandra, "and Sisiutl may provide a metaphor."

Matsamura nodded and smiled. "Previously I'd have opted out of this conversation, but there have been a number of coincidences, as I've acknowledged—and which Kallabush refuses to acknowledge—not the least of which was your experience on the beach a few days ago."

Mark looked at Sandra on the opposite end of the sofa, a maybe-now's-the-time-to-confess sort of look. Sandra returned his look with a nearly imperceptible shrug that he took as permission.

"It's hard to admit, for me especially," said Mark, "that something supernatural is happening—not sea serpents—but something that this myth may indicate, like seeing the dead in the fog."

"Expectations can account for a great deal," said Radwick.

"One thing I want to say: We apologize for breaking into the lab, and I want to pay for the damages. But that's not all I want to say." Mark paused and looked down at the carpet. He couldn't really check with Sandra on their promise to each other, but he had to find a way of entering into forbidden territory with these two scientists.

"Would you care to hear about a dream?" he said.

"Why not?" said Radwick.

"Well, before Gregory died, I dreamed I had an encounter with my wife on that same logging road." He checked his audience as the crackling of the fire and the mantel clock seemed to grow louder. He was surprised at the serious faces of the scientists, and a wave of inappropriate mirth interlaced his thoughts, for he realized how funny it was to communicate by such an awkward deception. Maybe he'd had too much wine.

Sandra looked at him. "Are you all right?"

"Yes, yes. I'm just caught up in the moment here, in this strange moment." But if I'm going to continue this half-truth, he thought, I want to be accurate. "Well, in the dream, Maggie spoke to me. Her spirit or image spoke to me. She said—or to be precise, said to herself—'What have we done to the children?'" He smiled slightly and repeated: "'What have we done to the children?'"

The words seemed disproportionately significant. It *might* have been a dream. Indeed, the horror of last night seemed like a dream, too—but would its significance disappear?

The others were silent and contemplative.

"Children," said Mark, "children taken from their parents, children sent to boarding school, and finally, children massacred." The thread wove its way through the words, and the words remained in a kind of suspended animation.

Matsamura stared at the fire, his unlit pipe back in his mouth.

Paul Radwick sat with a puzzled, depleted look, as if not knowing what to make of Mark's "dream."

For Mark, the evening itself seemed to merge into something consistent. *They've discovered something up here.* That's what she'd said.

"I regret that you've both been left out of the loop," said Radwick. "I don't know what we can do to help."

Mark wondered whether or not the appearances of the dead would coalesce into anything comprehensible. He could barely understand his own behavior, his own failings, thinking how unhappy he'd been, how quickly he'd wanted to move on to another woman, Sandra, in the most guilty of circumstances, and how he'd managed to pile up one questionable decision on another until he could break into a sweat merely by contemplating the last few weeks. Maybe it was just the way things seemed in hindsight; yet now, again, he felt a guilty despair. He hadn't admitted to himself how his marriage had changed, perhaps how dissatisfied he'd become with Maggie, and she with him. And it was partly anger that had brought him up here.

He looked at Radwick, who leaned back, put his hands on the arms of the chair, and tilted his head as if wanting to say something else, but his tight lips assumed a crooked shape, his eyes focused on the flickering light on the walls.

"Maybe this Silvers guy knows something," said Mark.

"Perhaps," said Radwick. "But now it's getting late. We're going back to the motel tonight." He got up. "Kallabush may try to question more of the elders."

"Good," said Mark.

"We're all agreed about cooperating?" Sandra asked.

"Of course," said Radwick.

"Well, thanks for coming. I kept trying to find reasons for what was happening to Gregory."

"A terrible shame for him to get so depressed about these things," said Radwick. "It was very personal for him."

"Remember that the bones are a secret until they are reburied," said Matsamura, "which will be next month."

"We'll keep it quiet," said Mark.

"Your wife's suitcase is still down at the dig," said Radwick. "You forgot to take it with you. We should have transferred it to the motel room and given it back to you."

"Is anyone going to be at the dig tomorrow? I'll come and get it," said Mark, feeling a twinge of guilt.

"I'll be down there tomorrow afternoon, " said Radwick. "And incidentally, thanks for sharing your—dream." He looked at Mark with an indecipherable expression.

"Sure," said Mark, wondering if Radwick suspected the truth.

The archaeologists got their coats off the rack in the entry hall and put them on. They thanked Sandra for dinner again and said goodbye. Mark watched as the two men went out into the fog toward their car.

Chapter Seventeen

After the guests had driven away, the fire continued to glow with yellow flames beneath the varnished mantelpiece and its ticking clock. But Mark had trouble keeping his eyes off the front window. Outside, the fog was drifting in the floodlight, and he and Sandra were too nervous to go upstairs.

"I'd sleep with you," she said, "but my husband might show up at any minute."

Her black humor broke the spell. They laughed briefly, talked about other things, made a pot of tea, but for the sake of vigilance decided to spend the night in the living room. She would take the sofa, he a sleeping bag on the floor. They also knew they couldn't stay trapped or isolated in the house forever. Maybe even the risk of staying on the reservation was too great. Within the next day or so they should pack some belongings and leave.

Sandra went upstairs, put on pajamas and a long white bathrobe, got some blankets, then came back down and made her bed on the sofa. As he watched her, Mark knew how much he loved her, though he wondered how much of her love for him was reactionary, partly the result of her bad marriage. Yet, in the nearly twenty-four hours since Gregory's appearance, he again saw the doom of delayed grief in her eyes. Sandra had expected to retreat from her husband; but she had loved him, perhaps could better sympathize with him now, and the only thing that might lessen her guilt was to get away. For himself, he doubted he could find out the truth about Maggie's disappearance.

The mat under the sleeping bag wasn't very soft, but regardless of wishing to be alert, he had trouble staying awake, and when the wind came up, carrying the fog away, he nodded off.

* * *

He awoke as the sun broke over the ocean. Sandra was gazing out the front window, a coffee cup in her hand. She turned, and seeing Mark, came back and sat on the sofa. "I didn't want to wake you," she said.

A long silence occupied them.

"You mentioned Seattle. Do you know anyone you could stay with?" asked Mark.

"My parents."

"I don't want to lose you."

"No, Mark, you won't lose me."

"Gregory is more understandable now."

"Gregory wanted to live here in this house. He was confident and idealistic, and I believed in his plans. But I couldn't help when it counted."

"He wouldn't *allow* you to help him, Sandra."

"Why couldn't he just tell me?"

Mark didn't answer, but he realized that if Gregory believed the dead would come back, it would be difficult to tell anyone without seeming crazy.

"I made a mistake," said Sandra. "Perhaps it was my fault, but over . . ."

The phone rang.

Sandra started, then let out a sigh and picked up the receiver. "Hello? Oh, yes, he's here." She wiped the moisture from her eyes and seemed to erase her thoughts with a wave of her other hand. As she handed him the phone, she gave him an affectionate squeeze on the arm. It felt good. He stood by the sofa while she lay back down, her white bathrobe parting at the ankles.

"Hello?"

"Is that you, Mark?" Mark recognized Maggie's father's voice.

"Hello, Sam. Yes, this is Mark."

"I wasn't sure whether to call you at that number; we didn't hear from you yesterday."

"I'm still here. I'm sorry I didn't call."

"It's all right, and I guess nothing more's happened up there." His voice ascended a half-octave or so, then there was a pause of resignation. He and his wife were waiting to hear about their daughter, and Mark knew there was nothing worse than waiting. But what could he tell them? He didn't want to hurt them, and the experiences of the last few days would sound like lies.

"Nothing new, Sam. I'm sorry. There's nothing I can do. How's Erica?"

"She's fine. She cries, of course. She wants to know about her mother. She'd even begun to worry about you until day before yesterday when you talked to her. This morning Dorothy drove her to school. Thank God we don't live too far. Have they come up with anything at all?" His voice had begun to quiver. It was the voice of a man struggling to accept his daughter's death.

Mark fought off his own emotions. "No, Sam. I'm so damn sorry."

"We know it's not your fault. We've sent you some money to the P.O. box number you gave us—a thousand dollars—a bank check that should arrive day after tomorrow. Please use it for whatever you need. Mark, we have to know . . . you understand that, don't you? If she's gone . . ."

"Sam, I'm doing my best, but Erica . . ."

"Erica's fine. She's waiting too. She's in school today. Is there anything more you can do? Anything to get them to do more?"

Mark couldn't respond. He felt terrible.

"OK, son, we know you're doing your best. We're just waiting now. Have you called your own parents lately? We talked to them day before yesterday. They called us from Long Beach."

"I'll call them today."

"Mark, let us know if there's anything more we can do."

"I will, Sam."

"Take care."

He replaced the receiver in its cradle, but then stared at it.

"Maggie's father?" asked Sandra.

"Yes."

She shook her head. "It's so sad, so hard."

Mark said, "I know what her father's going through, but we can't even explain what we know, let alone what we don't. We have to protect ourselves, too. I have to think of you, myself, and my daughter."

A firmness entered Sandra's voice. "How are you going to tell your wife's parents that you came up here to see Maggie, found her missing, and oh, incidentally, met someone else and are now leaving with her? We want each other, don't we, Mark? Do I just move into your wife's house in San Diego? Or will you bring your daughter up to Seattle, perhaps, and introduce us?"

Mark tried to maintain mental equilibrium.

Sandra moved her hand up and brushed her hair back. "This isn't so simple. You are in a different situation than I am, because your in-laws are involved. Gregory's parents are dead. And my parents didn't think much of Gregory."

At that point he got up from the chair. "What are you saying?"

"I'm trying to tell you that you can't just come up here to find your wife, fall in love with me, and leave."

He was amazed at her bluntness. "You guessed I didn't love her."

"A guess."

She raised her knees, and the bathrobe fell away from her legs; she covered them again and leaned up against the pillow. "You have to wait until her parents are satisfied and you are satisfied with the story you're going to tell."

"She's dead."

"Is she?"

"She's dead."

"Like Gregory."

"Yes."

"And she comes back from the dead . . ."

"Goddamn it. What makes you so cool and difficult all of a sudden?"

But she was doing what she'd done before—analyzing her way out and burying her emotions. As he looked at her, he could see she was pale again, though the room was hot, and the look on her face was meditative.

He stepped closer, bent down, put his hand on her robed knee, and carefully looked at her face. If he hadn't been in love the first morning of his arrival, he was in love now. It had *just happened*, and he would not lose her.

"I'm going to tell Radwick we're leaving."

She didn't protest any more, but instead reached up and touched his face. He bent down to kiss her, then slowly untied her robe, slipped it off of her smooth shoulders as she sat up, and in a moment they were making love.

Chapter Eighteen

At about four P.M., Mark parked the Rover at the trailhead to the dig and shut off the engine. The only other car was Radwick's Jeep, whose glossy white paint reflected the light filtering through the trees. A clearing in the west created a long blue streak across the gray sky. Mark hiked anxiously into the forest, walking quickly amid the long shadows and abundant sword ferns beneath the evergreens. He tried to concentrate on the trail—the packed earth and glistening dampness. He'd promised to return to Sandra before sunset. The narrow trail curved, the light diminished, and it appeared that a fog bank was already forming offshore. The trail wound vaguely into the light mist that augmented the gloom. He had to tell himself not to imagine anything. There hadn't been a sign of fog at Sandra's house, but he knew the weather could vary considerably along short stretches of coast. He was determined to retrieve Maggie's suitcase and leave quickly.

By the time he climbed down to the beach, the sky was completely overcast. The tide was advancing, and its waves created a tremendous roar.

The boxy wooden cabins lay ahead past the pit. He had no desire to examine the place from which the skeletons had been removed, but was anxious to find Radwick and get away from the fog.

The fresh smell of the sea surrounded him as he knocked on the cabin door. But the door swung inward with his knock. It had been left open. The cabin was empty. The makeshift shelf of books and objects was gone, but the kerosene heater was glowing. A black camcorder sat affixed to a tripod and was pointed out the window toward the northern part of the beach. The window of clear, stretched plastic, was propped open, and Mark went over to close it so the heat wouldn't escape. He looked out, wondering what the camcorder was for. On the beach, a few seagulls walked on the sand. Beyond the driftwood, the dark bluffs disappeared into the mist. Where was Radwick? Maggie's suitcase rested upright in the corner. Radwick ought to be back any minute, Mark thought. The archaeologist's coat was hanging over a chair, while a blue-knit watch cap and a cell phone lay on the table.

Mark picked up the phone to see if he could switch it on and then call Sandra if he could remember the number. He tried it and it worked.

"Hello? Sandra, are you okay?"

"Yes, I'm fine. Where are you?"

"I'm calling on their cell phone at the shack. Radwick's gone. But his coat and hat are here."

"Where's Ken?"

"I don't know."

"Are you going to wait?"

"For a bit."

"What's the weather like?"

"Foggy and damp." He went to the window. "How about yours?"

"Gray, but the fog is still offshore. I don't like being alone."

"I've got the suitcase. I'll leave shortly."

"What about Radwick?"

"He's got to be around someplace."

"The fog, Mark."

"Goddamn, it's a *myth*."

"Don't go out."

"Now, Sandra, I obviously have to go out to get back to the car."

She sighed. "Yes, of course."

Mark looked south. Not a sign of Radwick. Then he went to the other window, moved the camcorder aside and looked out again. "There isn't a sign of him, and I didn't pass him on the trail."

"Don't go looking for him."

"OK. I'll call you back before I leave."

"Good."

He hung up. Just as he did, the door swung open.

Radwick stood in the doorway. He started when he saw Mark.

"You frightened me," he said. "When did you get here?"

"Just now," Mark said. "I came for Maggie's suitcase."

"Oh, yes."

"Where's Ken?"

"He had to drive back to Seattle for a day. Jim Kallabush is coming down to keep me company tonight. I'm goddamn nervous here."

Mark decided to sit down. It was cold outside, and the heat felt good. "Didn't mean to scare you. Any particular reason to be nervous?"

Radwick had a peculiar look on his face. "Not really. It's just that I don't like being here alone. It's hard not to be affected by the disappearances and deaths."

"I was out at sea when this stuff began, so you don't have to worry about *me*. Anyway, Sandra and I are leaving the reservation as soon as possible."

"Oh? Why?"

"For reasons we could have told you last night. We weren't being a hundred percent straight." Mark glanced at the camcorder near the north window. "Taking video?"

"Not yet, but please continue. I'm interested."

"Remember the dream I mentioned?"

"Yes."

"Well, I think you guessed the truth—that I was lying about it being a dream."

Radwick smiled. "Some people can't lie very well. You may be one of them."

"I'd like to explain it away. But mentally, at least, Sandra and I have shared some strange experiences. It's time for us to leave. What I didn't mention was that the night before you came to dinner, something pretty awful happened."

Radwick listened while Mark told him about Gregory's two A.M. visit. The older man remained expressionless, though at the end there was acquiescence on his face. He said nothing, but went to the window, propped it open again, and re-positioned the camcorder.

"What are you trying to tape?" asked Mark.

"Just your friend."

"What do you mean?"

"Olson."

Mark was stunned. He stared at the camcorder, then at Radwick.

"That's why I came down here today," said Radwick. "For the fog." He smiled gently and raised his eyebrows. "We weren't exactly straight with *you*, either. Your friend in yellow showed up again after you left here the other day. He appears up that way now."

"My God. . . ."

"This kind of thing has always been a lot of crap to me. But we've all seen him. And our physiological experience was similar to yours."

Mark rose, put his hands in his jeans pockets, and looked toward the window. "You've *taped* him?"

"Well, no. I thought I'd taped him. It was the third and last time he appeared. I was alone. Nothing showed up on the tape. The beach was on the tape, but not the man. Interesting, isn't it. Do the appearances depend on our conscious minds? That's the only explanation I can think of. That videotape isn't conscious. Maybe that's the nature of ghosts—images that are somehow encoded in the past and recon-structed by us, up here," he said, pointing to his temple.

Mark had no idea.

"There was something else," Radwick continued seriously. "A cou-ple of days ago, when the fog was thick, I was away from the cabin. I got anxious. The tide was high and the waves were crashing. You know how we often hear things amid 'white noise,' like when you're in the shower and you think the phone is ringing? Surf is white noise. And I imagined I heard a voice calling for help."

"Olson . . ."

Radwick went on. "The fog will thicken soon, and the light will be low. This thing will record in very low light, and this figure . . . well, I'm not giving up quite yet." He flipped a switch on the camera, looked at the viewfinder, then turned the switch off. "It doesn't do any good unless the phenomenon repeats itself often enough to be testable. As a scientist I have to live with that."

He stepped over to the table, sat down and paused at the sound of a large breaking wave. "Frankly, I've told the others to keep this to themselves."

"I understand," said Mark. "And I'm beginning to understand Sandra's husband. The question is, what else was he privy to?"

"I asked Kallabush to question the elders. He said he'd give me a report. But Kallabush has been very disgruntled. He won't admit anything. The only thing we know is that people are staying indoors. Apparently you don't want to come into close contact with the dead."

"Did Kallabush see Olson?"

"He saw him all right. He was here during the second appearance. He tried to go outside, but he stopped at the side of the cabin, came back mad as hell, cursing and swearing, and refused to speak to us. Your man was standing in the rain, and when Kallabush tried to go outside we experienced some nausea and visual impairment, like a migraine headache. We checked this with each other, Ken and I, immediately after the event. Kallabush refused to say what he experienced. He doesn't want to face this—whatever it is—and we'd rather forget about it ourselves, but the tribal council is going to have a closed-door meeting about the massacre, and they might put other things on the agenda. We don't know why these encounters are dangerous—but we do know a couple of things: Your wife is gone without a trace and Reverend Hanley is in a mental institution."

"I tried to get in to question him, but they wouldn't allow it."

"Something odd happened to Hanley."

"He said an angel told him to kill his son."

Radwick shook his head. "The man was an alcoholic. If he had an encounter of some kind that night, we don't know what state of mind he was in. It may have been a ghost, but it was no angel."

Mark thought about this as the archaeologist looked toward the window. The waves—white noise, thought Mark—were loud, for the tide was almost in. He thought of Sandra.

"Sandra is alone," he said.

"Then you'd better go back to her. I'll be fine."

Outside, the light was beginning to dim.

"Why don't you come with me?" said Mark. "Gregory was convinced something terrible was going to happen. We don't know how far this can go."

"No, I'm going to stay. Can't miss any opportunities."

Mark looked at him, not knowing whether to insist. He felt partly responsible, and he did not want to lose this man, too.

"Kallabush will be here soon," said Radwick.

"What if he doesn't come?"

"Look, I won't go outside except to relieve myself." He smiled.

"Well . . . it's up to you."

"What *is* happening around here, Mr. Sayres?"

"I don't know. Maybe Gregory knew. Or maybe Silvers."

Radwick shook his head. "I don't believe in ghosts." He smiled. "But what if they are shared hallucinations of some kind? What triggers them?"

The tide was high, the sound of the waves at their loudest.

"I'd better go," said Mark. "Oh, I used your phone, and I told Sandra I'd call her before I left."

"Go ahead."

He called and told Sandra he was leaving.

Zipping his jacket, he said goodbye to Radwick, went out, and walked back along the narrow path. Before starting to climb the rocky trail from the beach, he glanced at the pit. Then he looked toward the ocean. The four cabins lay on shore like a lonely outpost amid a sea of increasing fog. At least the man has a cell phone, he thought.

Chapter Nineteen

When Mark got back, the sky was darkening and the fog was drifting in cloudy veils through the forest. He left Maggie's suitcase in the Rover, crossed the back yard, and went into the house.

Sandra was in the kitchen putting dishes into the cupboard. He wanted to put his arm around her, kiss her. But the kitchen was too utilitarian, too domestic, and she wasn't his wife—not just yet. He removed his jacket and hung it over the chair.

"Thank God you're back. How's Radwick?"

"Fine. But it'll be dark soon."

She turned with questioning eyes as he sat down at the kitchen table.

"I'm glad you're here," she said, slightly perplexed.

He couldn't keep the frustration, or the irony, out of his voice. "Sorry, I'm new at adultery." He smiled half-heartedly.

"I have my own guilt feelings," she said.

"I often think she's watching me from a distance."

Sandra closed the cupboard door. "I understand. Sometimes when I go into a room, I expect Gregory to be there."

"I've never experienced anything close to what I've seen in this damnable place. I've never known anything that wasn't part of the everyday world. I move pencils around and draw lines on paper. There just isn't anything I do that isn't ordinary. Now, nothing is even comprehensible. What kind of place is this?"

"That's why Gregory wouldn't talk about it. It's like living on the tip of an iceberg with a great chill rising from below."

"Or out of the fog."

"So I've heard."

"Sandra, I came up here to help Maggie, whatever else is true. I wasn't jealous of her interests or need to get away, just mad that she didn't care enough to come back as we'd agreed. I took the slow way up here because I feared some kind of a confrontation, but now she's never coming back." He squelched a sudden wave of emotion. "I'd begun to resent her damnable depressions. I'm an ordinary man, Sandra. I want things to go smoothly. I don't like compromises, but you can't avoid that in a marriage. I used to think that once I was married, I wouldn't ever be lonely; but it doesn't work that way. And she may have had her reasons for wanting to escape."

"Mark, stop feeling guilty."

"I'm not in control of that."

"We have come together out of love, Mark."

"Maybe there's too much focus on love and not enough on loyalty."

She gave him a pained look. They'd been over it before. "We didn't intend to fall in love with each other," she said. "I want you. I didn't ask for it. My husband is dead, but the loneliness came before."

"And we're getting out of here, whatever emotional baggage we have to take along."

Sandra took a deep breath. Now she seemed hesitant.

"It isn't going to be that easy," she said.

"What do you mean?"

"I mean necessities. For one thing, there's the mill. I own the mill."

"The mill."

"Justin Carroll wants to buy it, but he says it'll take time. Then there's this house. I directed the restoration, and everything I own is here. I don't know if I can just walk away. I put more work into this house than Gregory ever did. He was at the mill most of the time. What can I do? You can't leave a house full of valuables out here. Anyone might break in. Mark, this just isn't going to work for me. A few days ago I wanted to leave. But I think I have to stick this out a little longer."

"Find someone to baby-sit the goddamn house. Stay in San Diego—or Seattle if you want—and deal with it from there."

She crossed her arms and looked at the floor.

He said, "Look, your husband did not die of a heart attack, and my wife is never coming home. This is a dangerous situation and I can't let you stay here alone. It's enough that I lost Maggie. I'm going to get you out of here. You can pack enough stuff in the Rover to get along until we can figure out what to do in general."

"What about Maggie's parents and the thousand dollars they're sending? What are you going to tell them? How many of the grotesque details?"

"I don't know."

The phone rang in the living room.

She took a deep breath. "Maybe that's them again." Mark followed her into the room.

"Hello? This is Sandra." She listened to whoever was on the other end of the line.

"Yes," she said. "He just got back. . . . No, I don't know . . . Yes, Mark's right here." She handed him the phone. "It's Kallabush. He's calling from the dig."

He took the receiver. "Hi. What's up?"

"Ah, not much. I'm sittin' here kind of wondering where Dr. Radwick is. I got here about thirty minutes ago. I noticed your wife's suitcase was gone, so I guessed you were here earlier."

"That's right."

"He didn't go back with you?"

"No. He was there when I left."

"I figured. His Jeep's still at the trailhead."

"He promised to stay in the cabin."

"Well, I've been here about thirty minutes."

"Great. Maybe I'd better come down there."

"Nothing much to do down here. Sun's gettin' low. You can barely find the trail in the fog. No sense *everyone* getting lost."

"You think he's lost?"

"Well . . ."

"You'd better stay there. Give it another fifteen minutes. What's your number?"

Sandra got a pen and note pad. Mark wrote down the number.

"OK, Jim. Better wait a bit longer."

"Man, I don't know what to do if he doesn't come back. Too god-damn many people disappearing around here."

"Are you sure he couldn't have passed you on the trail in the fog?"

"He'd have to have been way off the trail. Plus he wouldn't have left the phone here. I don't like it. No reason for him to be gone, and nowhere *to* go."

"Give it another few minutes and then call us back."

"Tell you what," Kallabush said. "I'll take the flashlight, go back up to the trailhead and make *sure* his Jeep's still there. Maybe somehow I did miss him. It'll take me a while to check and come back. Anyway, maybe he'll be here by then."

Mark didn't want to start talking about apparitions to Kallabush, but he had to respect the danger of going outside. "I don't think that's such a good idea. Just wait there—until morning."

"Naw, shit, man, I'll leave the cell phone. You can call to see if he's gotten back in the meantime. I'll call you when I get back."

"I don't think you should go out."

"The hell with that shit. I'll call you in about an hour."

Kallabush hung up.

Mark looked at Sandra. "Paul has left the cabin and he's nowhere to be found."

"Where would he go?"

"That's just the point. Kallabush is going to see if his Jeep is still at the trailhead in case they crossed paths."

Sandra glanced at the front window. "It must be the same down there."

The drifting fog was thick again. Only a single tree, the nearest to the house, was visible. The sea had disappeared. The house was sur-rounded by nothingness.

Sandra took him gently by the arm.

"I feel safe inside the house," she said. "I don't think they can come inside."

Mark looked at her smooth white forehead. She was about four inches shorter than he. She looked up at him with those unusual gray eyes, eyes he'd noticed were not quite gray, but had intricate blue facets. But it was her warmth and intelligence he admired most, even if the latter often cooled the former. What if she decided to stay here? It would be an impossible dilemma.

"Paul Radwick saw Olson," he said calmly.

Sandra's eyes widened.

"I didn't want to frighten you any further. But Paul was down at the dig with a camcorder waiting for *Olson* to appear."

Sandra bent down and picked up a hardcover book from the oval mahogany coffee table in front of the sofa, walked over to the bookcase near the fireplace and put it back on the shelf. "There's nothing to do," she said. "It's time to build a fire and listen to some music. You build the fire. Here's a CD. It's good music. . . ."

"Yeah, but our trouble is about as bad as we can imagine."

"You build the fire while I make dinner. I've got some chicken thawing in the refrigerator."

Mark didn't know how to react, gave out with a sigh, and decided to give her some space. Nothing would be decided by only one of them. He walked over and put the CD in the bookshelf stereo system, then to the hearth to prepare the kindling and arrange the logs in the fireplace. The music was Prokofiev's second piano concerto.

While dinner was cooking, he called the dig's cell phone. There was no answer. After dinner he tried again. Still no answer. All he could get was the messaging service. Now it was dark. No possible help could be given. The floodlight had come on at the front of the house. Another nervous evening was taking shape. Sandra moved from table to kitchen to living room, a silent enigma, her smooth black hair shining from the firelight as she settled down on the sofa, another book in her hand. With no television available, the news came through the Internet, so he went upstairs to Gregory's study to peer at the rest of the world. Afterwards, he checked Gregory's e-mail. Nothing. It was nightmarishly quiet. No music played downstairs now. Where the hell was Kallabush?

He went back down and began pacing.

"Why hasn't he called, damn it? He said it'd be only a while. It's none of my affair. But we know the kinds of things that have happened."

Sandra put down her book. "Maybe he found him up at the trailhead and they both left."

"Yeah, maybe. There'd be no point in going back just for the cell phone. We're going to have to assume everything's OK or we'll go nuts here."

"What are you going to do?"

"Well, are you going to leave your house or not? We can always come back later."

She lay back on the pillow and looked at the ceiling. "I don't know. I don't know. I don't know."

"You'll have to pack some things."

She sat up. "Maybe it's all over. Radwick or Kallabush will call and explain what happened tonight. No more manifestations. No more disappearances."

"Or suicides," he said.

She lay back down.

"You keep forgetting," he said, "that your husband did not disappear, he killed himself."

"Don't be sarcastic."

"I'm sorry. I just hate waiting for a damn phone to ring."

"It won't ring. And I'm tired. Will you come to bed? Just sleep with me. That's all. We can sleep together. We don't need to feel guilty. Is that all right?" She looked at him so painfully, yet with such charm, that he couldn't help reaching out for her hand and pulling her off the sofa.

"This will be a quiet night," she said. "A refined night. We'll pay slight attention to our guilt, and if we pay slight attention, our guilt may vanish. We'll talk about things more seriously in the morning. I don't want to be alone. If I stay, you will stay. If you go, I'll go. Let's decide tomorrow, and then give it at least another day." She hugged him, kissed him, and it was no ploy. Time is what she needed. A little more time. A day to decide. A day he would certainly give her. He looked at the clock on the mantel—the clock that ticked so serenely throughout the enigmatic night.

Chapter Twenty

In the morning, they awoke to the sound of a car pulling up in front of the house. Mark went to the window and looked down on Deputy Sheriff Hermann's dark green Chevy S.U.V. Sandra sat up in bed. Mark quickly dressed and made it downstairs just as the doorbell rang.

Hermann may have expected Sandra to answer, for he looked at Mark suspiciously. With a clipboard in one hand and a pen in the other, he came into the living room. "I heard you were still here," he said.

"Yes."

Hermann wrote something on the clipboard paper. "I wonder if you'd answer a few questions. I have this report to fill out."

"Sure. What's it about?"

Hermann's expression was sober. "Dr. Radwick was found wandering in the woods near the dig last night. He's at the clinic in Neah Bay."

"Kallabush must have found him. What happened? Is he all right?"

"When did you last see him?"

"Yesterday afternoon. I'd like to know if he's all right. I was waiting to hear back from Kallabush last night. Radwick wasn't at the cabin."

"He just comes in and out of consciousness. That's all I know. Do you want to tell me about last night?" he asked bluntly. "Did you have an argument with him?"

"Was he hurt? Did he fall or something?"

"The doctor couldn't find any injuries."

"OK, I'll tell you what I know, and it isn't much."

Mark recalled aloud his trip to the dig, but without reference to Olson. Hermann already knew of the strange events at Neah Bay, and he'd witnessed Reverend Hanley's insanity. That was one thing, but visions of the dead were another. Could it be construed as withholding important information? It seemed ludicrous.

"Why had you taken so long to get your wife's suitcase?"

Simple question. But a worthless vacuum of alternatives presented themselves. He wondered if he was in trouble, and began to resent the deputy's suspicious tone.

"Dr. Radwick was here for dinner the night before, and he reminded me about Maggie's suitcase."

"You'd forgotten about your wife's things?"

"Yes, temporarily."

The deputy looked at him and nodded.

"And you're staying here."

"Sandra's husband is dead."

"Yes."

"You are staying with Mrs. Torrel, you've been here since her husband died, but also since the night of your boating accident."

"That's right."

"Radwick reminded you of your wife's suitcase."

"Yes."

Hermann again looked up from the clipboard.

Mark continued. "Radwick said he'd be at the dig, and I could come get the suitcase. They were closing down the dig for the winter."

"Had you had any sort of argument with Radwick?"

"No. I barely knew him."

"You barely knew him."

"Yes."

"And Sandra?"

"I don't understand."

Hermann stood silently for about a minute, writing on the clipboard. Then he said: "My intuition tells me you're being evasive. I don't know what you're hiding from me, but you're hiding something. I understand you had a strange vision on the beach of one of the men who'd drowned, and this relates to other things I've heard. The investigation of Gregory Torrel's death isn't closed, Mr. Sayres. And I've got a lot of drowned or missing people around here. You're going to have to tell me what you know or what you think you know about what's been happening."

"I'm trying."

"I want to ask you again: Have you ever been to Neah Bay previous to your being found on the beach two weeks ago?"

"No."

"Did you know that your wife had previously been associated with Dr. Radwick at the University of Washington?"

"He was a professor of hers. That's one reason she came to the dig this summer."

"Had you ever talked with your wife about Dr. Radwick?"

"Not really. Nothing specific."

"Had you ever met Gregory or Sandra Torrel before coming here the other night?"

"No."

"You are a stranger, then, as you say. In a way, Gregory Torrel was a stranger, too." He looked down at the clipboard. "But you are the only genuine stranger, and you are not telling me all you know." He seemed as if he were talking to himself now, but never lost the professional inflection of voice that was characteristic of him. "And you have visions." He looked up again.

Mark felt a growing frustration. "If there were anything at all I could say that would help you, I would." The response was deceptive and they both knew it; but it was also sincere. Nothing Mark could say would help, and that was the truth. No one was going to force him to admit seeing Gregory the night before last. Or Maggie on the logging road. None of the weird experiences could do other than incriminate him or appear to taint tragic events.

"What did Kallabush say?" Mark asked quietly.

"Kallabush found Radwick wandering aimlessly in the woods near the trail." Hermann held the clipboard at his hip, and although the expression on his face was unchanged, a subtle irritation was apparent. "I haven't been able to question Radwick because Dr. Veress has him under strict observation."

Mark tried to think. He wondered what outline of events had pre-ceded this and what Kallabush had seen—or would admit.

"That was a good thing you did the other day with Reverend Han-ley. You get credit. But your relationship to it gets more complicated by the minute. I don't want you to leave the area. If you should try, I'll have you picked up on suspicion."

"Suspicion of what?"

"I'll think of something. I've got plenty to choose from. And I'd advise you and Mrs. Torrel to get a firearm."

"She has one . . ."

"Do you both know how to use it?" asked Hermann.

"Maybe. Until now, we were planning to leave soon. Why do you ask?"

"I guess you haven't heard. Reverend Hanley escaped from the Olympic State Mental Hospital last night." Hermann walked to the front door. He opened it, then turned. "Have a nice day," he said, shut-ting the door behind him.

Chapter Twenty-One

The parking lot at the clinic was empty. Mark got out of the Rover, and when he went to the clinic's front door, he found it open, yet no one was in the waiting room, no receptionist was behind the counter. The building seemed abandoned. Had they moved Radwick to another location? He hoped not, because he didn't want to take longer than necessary. Sandra had insisted on staying home. Though she had the revolver, Mark was still worried. He'd also decided to stop at Kallabush's on the way back.

He went past the reception area and down a hallway partly painted with childlike renditions of zoo animals. Dying in here, he thought, would feel like being gunned down on Sesame Street. The lights hummed softly above, and as he approached the end of the corridor, he heard someone muttering aloud in the last room. Another man spoke, and as he got nearer, he heard Dr. Veress ask a question in the professional tone of an examination. In the bright emptiness of the hallway, Veress's voice evoked anxiety as well as a sense of privacy. But Mark was too curious to return to the waiting area.

He shyly looked into a room at the far left of the hall. Veress was in a white lab coat, his back to the door. He was leaning over a bed with a patient in it whose face was out of view. Mark knocked lightly on the wall so as not to alarm anyone. Veress turned quickly with a look of consternation. He motioned Mark to come in—then moved aside to reveal Paul Radwick lying on the bed, head propped up on pillows, eyes staring at the ceiling.

Mark walked to the bed. Veress said nothing.

Radwick looked calm but peaked, his face thinner.

Mark leaned over him. "Paul, it's me, Mark Sayres."

Without moving his head, Radwick turned alert blue eyes in the direction of the voice.

Mark glanced at Veress, but the doctor remained expressionless. Looking down into Radwick's eyes, Mark said, "Do you remember my visit yesterday at the cabin?"

"Sayres . . ." said Radwick. "Still sorry about your wife. God, we're sorry that happened." He spoke slowly and calmly. "Yesterday. Don't know what happened to me."

Dr. Veress abruptly became animated and went to the other side of the bed. Radwick turned his head in that direction, and there was an odd exchange that Mark didn't understand.

"Paul Radwick?"

"Yes."

Veress then went through a brief check-up procedure, causing Mark to wonder whether or not Radwick had been unconscious.

"Has he had a stroke or something?"

"Possibly," said Veress. "But in general, he seems fine. Go ahead and talk. Maybe it's a good idea."

Mark leaned down and tried to keep his voice calm and easy. "Paul, did you see anyone outside the cabin last night after I left?"

"A figure. But it was getting dark. I couldn't help myself. I took the flashlight. It was cold, you know, and I wanted to just hurry. Everything was dark and foggy. I can't remember. . . ." He stopped, and a worried expression crossed his face. "I went . . . out sssside alone."

"Paul?"

"Alone."

"Is he all right?"

Veress nodded doubtfully.

A strange expression came over Radwick's face, and he stared at what seemed to be an imaginary point over Mark's shoulder. It almost made Mark turn in that direction, but he resisted the urge.

Now Radwick spoke dryly and evenly, as if he'd been in the middle of a conversation other than the one he was having. "We have to reboot the server at five o'clock this evening. Can you handle it? The I.T. manager is sick, and I've got to leave early."

Mark looked at Veress.

Radwick, perturbed, rolled to one side, then back again. "The I.T. manager is sick." He looked at, or nearly at, Mark for the second time, then said: ". . . He's gone home, so be sure everyone is logged off the system by five o'clock."

Veress leaned down and spoke in a calm, professional voice that sent an icy chill through Mark.

"Paul?" asked the doctor.

Radwick stared in perplexity.

"Where are you?" asked Veress.

"In the I.T. Department. I'm a systems analyst here."

This exchange caused a sinking sensation in Mark's stomach and he felt a mild sweat beginning.

Radwick looked up again, not to the side, and his expression changed again. Veress stood straight and put his hands in the pockets of his lab coat.

Radwick's brow wrinkled with confusion. ". . . Something happened again just now, didn't it?"

"Yes, Paul."

Veress came around and tugged secretly at Mark's sleeve, then said to Radwick, "Paul, we're going to step outside for a minute. I want to ask Mr. Sayres some questions and take care of some things in my office."

"Sure."

"Bye, Paul," said Mark. "Take it easy, now. I'll be back."

Veress led Mark to his office.

"What's wrong with him?" asked Mark.

"I don't know. I ought to get him moved to a hospital."

Mark wondered for a moment why Veress had kept Radwick here at all, but decided to withhold the question. "You don't think he's had a stroke? Doesn't this happen to people who've had strokes?"

"Maybe, if what you mean is disorientation, or memory loss of some sort, but I've been on the phone to a couple of colleagues, and this personality shift is odd."

"What's it about? It's damn frightening. He suddenly seemed to be in another conversation."

"Well, yes."

"I want you to know something confidential. Paul saw Olson, my drowned companion, just as I did, and Paul went out in the fog last night. He might have had an encounter."

Veress gave him a look of rapid assessment, but said nothing.

"You said he didn't have a stroke."

"I said maybe. He does become disoriented."

"All at once. Then he snaps out of it, right? And you've been asking who he is during these lapses."

"Mr. Sayres, you've had an anomalous experience."

"You don't know the half of it."

"You've got to calm down. There are strange reports, and the town is buzzing. I know that. And I know that stuff about not going outside in the fog. But I have a patient here, and he hasn't floated up to the ceiling yet, so let's look at it with a little reason, a little caution."

"What's Paul talking about?"

"He's probably recalling some place from his past. Maybe he does, or did, computer programming of some kind. If he's had a mild stroke, it wouldn't be surprising that this comes back to him."

"He was speaking very professionally of computer operations, but he's been an archaeologist for decades."

"What's odd, I admit, is the way he moves in and out of it so spontaneously, as if a switch is turned off and on. A stroke victim wouldn't behave with that kind of volatility."

Tired though he was, Mark felt his mind churning with half-insane ideas. "Something happened to Paul when he went outside. We know *that*, don't we, basically, and now he speaks as if he might be possessed." He gazed at the doctor, and something he'd almost forgotten blazed in his mind. "It's weird. Hanley repeated something to me in the street after I'd pinned him down on the ground—something John Horn, the owner of the yacht, said. I thought Hanley must have heard me mutter it while I was half conscious the night I arrived, but that's very unlikely. Why would I mutter something Horn had said?"

"What was it?"

"Hanley said: 'Go forward and help Craig with the heads'l.' The same thing Horn told me on the boat—to go forward and help Craig."

"What are you trying to tell me? That my patient was possessed last night by your companion, Olson?" Veress's expression was calm, but his skin was pale, perhaps giving away a little self-doubt. Then he became objective. "OK, was Olson a computer programmer?"

"I don't recall. He sailed some, and that's all I remember."

"You say Hanley acted like this."

"Not exactly like this, obviously. It was just a brief moment. At the time, I thought I had an explanation."

Veress now looked Mark in the eye with a penetrating but agitated gaze. "Unless we are going to believe in nonsense, we might ask ourselves what else could cause someone to change personalities," he said, "*if* that is what is happening. We also have to ask ourselves about the public impression that may be created, juxtaposed to other events or reported events."

"I understand," said Mark almost harshly.

"I'm not going to leap off the pier, Mr. Sayres."

Mark could only sympathize.

"There are a lot of other things we should talk about," Veress went on. "First of all, the assumption that Hanley and Radwick exhibited similar symptoms for exactly the same reasons. You understand me, don't you? You understand what an assumption of cause is."

"Yes."

"So we need to look at what might cause someone to seem to shift personalities or recall memories." Veress forced a thin smile. "We can keep this down to earth if we try, can't we?"

Mark took a deep breath and fixed his gaze on a child's painting on the wall. There was much to tell, but not now.

"Do you know anything about Radwick's behavior in the last few days?" asked Dr. Veress.

"Some."

"Anything out of character? Unusual? Any symptoms of pain or illness?"

"I haven't been around him that much. Listen, I have to get back out to Sandra's house. She's alone out there."

Veress shifted to one side. He looked confused, suspicious at

Mark's sudden withdrawal. He nodded reluctantly. "OK."

They went down the hall toward the front. Mark's thoughts were spinning. He had to find out more, had to investigate this personality phenomenon. Did Gregory's secret involve possession?

They walked into the waiting room. "Where is everyone today?" Mark asked.

"A slow afternoon, that's all. I told them to go home."

"I see."

"Try to calm down. Try not to think too hard. You're probably suffering from post-traumatic stress."

"I'll do my best. Listen, can I visit Dr. Radwick tomorrow?"

"Sure. If he's still here. I can't make that decision on my own. His wife is on her way from Seattle."

"I understand."

"Stop by if you find out anything, or have any more questions."

"Thanks. I will."

Mark went out the door and got into the Rover. He reached into the glove box and examined Sandra's instructions for finding Kallabush's place. She'd been there once with Gregory. Then he considered going straight back to her, instead, but he'd planned to visit Kallabush—only a few miles south at the most, and a detour in Sandra's general direction.

Chapter Twenty-Two

In a clearing at the end of a weed-infested road stood Jim Kallabush's long, oxidized aluminum mobile home. A big blue-plastic tarp had been drawn tightly over half the roof by ropes pulled through eyelets and attached to stakes in the ground, apparently to temporarily protect some deteriorating metal. Thin vines grew up along one end near the propane tank, windows were fogged with condensation, and a trail of smoke issued from a small pipe poking through the roof. Over the clearing in the evergreens, the sky was cloudy. Kallabush's Plymouth was parked on the remnants of a lawn.

Mark shut off the Rover's engine. He walked across the scrubby ground and knocked on the door. After a moment, Kallabush appeared. He wore a green-plaid flannel shirt and looked out from the doorway with a sly smile. "Come on in," he said. "You know, I should have called you last night no matter what, but I got back late. Should have called you this morning, too, but I only got up a couple hours ago. The deputy sheriff said he was going to talk to you. Here, sit down." He pointed to a beige cloth sofa that looked like it had been torn up by ravenous dogs. "Sorry about the furniture. I just sort of get along out here."

"It's fine," said Mark.

"Get you somethin'?"

"No thanks."

Kallabush sat in a brown leather recliner. "This trailer is my little outpost at the end of the world." He chuckled.

Mark mentally reassured himself it was necessary to be here.

"How's Sandy doin'?" Kallabush asked. "She's really somethin', isn't she? Too bad she's having such a tough time."

Mark smiled. "She's OK. She's a little nervous, but insisted on staying home. She's got a gun. I guess you must have heard about Hanley's escape."

"Yeah, I heard. Hell, no reason he should go to the Torrel house. Besides, he didn't kill Gregory. He came out to see him the night *after* he had left for the mill. Doesn't seem likely the Reverend would do that if he knew the man was dead." Kallabush retained his smile a little too long, which made him look uncomfortable.

"Or unless he was pretending," said Mark.

"Yeah."

"The coroner thinks Gregory committed suicide, but I don't like leaving Sandra alone."

"Can't say I blame you. So what are you doing out here?"

"On my way back from visiting Radwick."

"How's the guy doin'?"

"Well, I thought maybe you could tell *me.*"

"What do you mean?"

"Could be Paul had a stroke, but that doesn't account for all his symptoms."

"Well, man, I just found him walking around in a daze. At first I thought he was sleep-walking or something."

"In the fog near the cabin?"

"He'd gone into the woods."

"He went outside. I wonder why."

"Don't know."

"You know, it's funny how many people like to wander around in the fog down there."

Kallabush looked at him warily. "Yeah."

Mark gazed back. "People of *all* kinds."

"I guess."

"Even people who are not people."

Kallabush looked toward the window.

"In the fog."

"Yeah, yeah, yeah," said Kallabush.

"You saw Olson a few days ago."

"I saw *someone.*"

"What did you see last night?"

"Nothing. Not one damn thing."

Mark pursued it while he had the chance. "But you saw Olson—a drowned man—a few days ago. You, Paul, and Ken all saw him, and when you went outside the cabin you got too sick to stay outside, or too scared."

"Must be it."

"Come on, Kallabush. . . ."

The Makah went from distraction to annoyance, but Mark continued to press. "You know more than you let on. You're having doubts. Those needling innuendoes hurt. Richard Walker, especially, has been needling you. But you don't care about tradition, or what the old people say. Right?"

Kallabush sat back and put his hands in his jeans pockets. "Some wise ol' cowboy I got here, huh? How about you go back to Sandra?"

"Is that a personal barb?"

"Old cowboy who's lost his wife and has already found someone else."

"Oh, no you don't. Just isn't going to work."

Kallabush shifted his feet and now held the arms of his chair.

"You might as well level with me," said Mark. "What happened to Radwick?"

"Shit, I don't know. He was zoned out. Couldn't talk. By the time we got to the clinic, he was unconscious."

"Because he went out in the fog."

"We talked that over, didn't we?"

"Not really."

"Why pick on me?"

"Why not? We're friends."

"I sure am that, I guess."

"People are afraid to go outside because they don't want to come into contact with the dead," said Mark.

Kallabush shrugged again. "Not everyone believes this stuff."

"*You* might be having second thoughts, however."

"Hey man, that's pretty good, because you know I *still* think it's a lot of bullshit."

"If there's one thing I know, it's that you care about what's going on, one way or another."

"Don't be so sure."

Now, like two cranky people having a bad day at the office, they sat in silence. The daylight illuminated only part of the inside of the trailer so that its farthest reaches were dark. Kallabush began to tap his foot silently on the carpet.

"What I want to know," said Mark matter-of-factly, "is what is supposed to happen when someone *does* come into contact with the dead."

Kallabush continued tapping his foot. "Why should I tell you stuff I don't believe?"

"Can't hurt," said Mark. "I don't see what the big deal is."

"Man, what you're finding out is that you can't just come onto an Indian reservation, poke around, and learn everything."

"You make your lack of pride in the beliefs of your people fairly apparent."

Kallabush glared at him.

Mark continued: "You've rejected and criticized your people's beliefs, but *neither* are you the tribe's gate-keeper."

"I won't repeat nonsense."

"I don't care what you think, I want to know what you've heard. Ever since I've come here you've been writing everything off as superstition. So did I." He pointed toward the little window behind him. "But what we don't believe in is out there. Paul, Sandra, and I aren't members of the tribe, nor are we Native Americans, but we are hit with this where it hurts, really hurts, and you sit around worrying about the image of your people."

"They turned their back on me." Kallabush poked his finger rapidly into his chest. "I'm protecting myself. *My* image. Because I'm a member of the tribe and because I am proud."

"Then tell us what you know."

"They turned their back on me, now I turn my back on their fear."

"I don't care who turns his back on who," said Mark. "I want to know what happened to Paul Radwick last night, because maybe something like it happened to my wife if she wandered off."

Kallabush became angry. "I saw a man outside that cabin. You come here and see things, but maybe you were hallucinating after you almost drown . . . so there isn't a goddamn bit that's worth anything."

"Tell it to Paul. He's lying in the clinic because he went outside in the fog. That at least is true. Something happened to him. This reservation has got things going on under the surface that make your skin crawl. And goddamn it, I need your help. You know people here. I don't."

Kallabush angrily thrust his fist through the air. "I don't believe in superstitious bullshit!" he exploded. Then he fell silent. He sat back down in the chair. His eyes were watery.

Mark felt a throbbing in his temples.

Kallabush took a couple of deep breaths. "Damn white men."

"That's right," said Mark.

"Come here and get themselves killed on the reservation."

"That's right."

Kallabush turned one way, then another. He shook his head. "Let me tell you something. My father was a shaman. He used to bring me to see people who were possessed with spirits. Some of these people, they died. Dr. Radwick, he's been a friend to the tribe and to the heritage of the people. I'm not saying nothin' more."

"We're talking about *possession*," said Mark.

". . . My father and his father and his father," Kallabush said, sitting back, "won't leave me alone. I don't need *you* to pester me, too—or Walker." He took another deep breath, but his admission caused Mark to realize there was an ounce of friendship here. And this Makah had helped save his life.

They sat in silence again.

"You got time to hear a sob story?" Kallabush finally asked.

Mark looked at him soberly. "Sure."

Kallabush put his hands on his knees. "A long time ago, my father told me I could inherit a big secret. It had been passed down from generations because he came from the old school—'the ancestral ways-and-means committee,' he used to say. I don't expect you to understand. But what it is, is hitÁktÁkˣe, an old Makah word for 'Power.' Ours was a family secret that let us Kallabushes 'doctor' people, as shamans, including helping people who were haunted by their dead relatives, because maybe those people didn't give away their relatives' belongings when they died or bury their belongings with them—and the dead, they supposedly haunted families who kept those possessions. Well, don't that beat all. My father, he believed it!"

Kallabush looked away. "Well, man," he continued, "I used to believe it too, a long time ago. I went to the special place my father told me about so I could gain the Power that had been in my family, and I washed myself in the icy stream by the shelf of big rock until I was numb. That river, it was deep and green and it came out of the darkest forest and flowed over the big rock, and when I looked upstream into the shadows of the woods I knew this stream carried something from a forest where no one had been. In the back country are places no one has been, or maybe someone passed through once. I knew this. And I went to the place of my forefathers near that stream and waited in the clearing for three days and three nights without food, to get Power, and I tried and tried, but I couldn't. The thing I was supposed to see, the secret thing, did not happen, and so how could I do what my father wanted? I failed him. People told me how he had helped them, how he had removed bad spirits. These were mostly old people, you know, because a lot of people now, they don't accept these things anymore. But my father, he said, see, *they* get sick and die too, and the spirits make them miserable too, so why can't they try something they don't understand? But for me, I could not receive the Power of my forefathers and that hurt me—and you know, I decided it was all bullshit, and once you got that figured out, you don't need to worry." He glanced at the floor.

"What do the elders say?"

"The elders think they know what's going on. But they don't like to talk to me too much." Kallabush's voice cracked.

Mark shifted on the sofa, and the worn springs creaked.

"I had all this supernatural shit figured out," said Kallabush. "Like you."

Mark nodded.

"And here's something I don't tell anyone. After I failed to get Power, I decided I'd been made a fool of by my father. I stopped trusting him and everyone else old." He looked pained. "My father, he got drunk a lot as time went on. And times changed. He and my mother didn't get along any more, and then he moved away and died in Seattle down near Pioneer Square where the drunks would hang out. I've been to see this place."

"Is your mother still alive?"

"Yes, but she can't talk no more. Her eyes, they are wild though! They move around and around now, since all this stuff started. She says on those scratchy notes she writes that many people will die."

"What else does she say?"

"She says the moon is red." Kallabush paused as Mark looked at him. "She's in a rest home, you know, down in Hoquiam."

"Oh."

"The bones, I gotta tell you, were no big secret. Most people wanted to know what had happened to that poor village."

"Massacred by Joseph Torrel."

"Looks like."

"Did the elders you talked to say anything more?"

Kallabush smiled, but to himself. "Yes. They told me to stay out of the rain."

They looked at each other, and Kallabush's voice was low.

"The old people are inside their houses, waiting. Some say Sisiutl will rise from the sea and take many souls. They say there is great danger while the bones are unburied. Some of the old women, they sit in their rocking chairs and hum to themselves." Kallabush looked toward the door. "I've watched them sit in the senior center. Rocking. Thinking. Waiting for something to happen. No, I sure as hell don't talk to the elders much."

After a pause, Kallabush said, "Are you sure I can't get you something? Got some beer in the refrigerator."

"No, really. I ought to get back to Sandra."

"Yeah, sure."

Kallabush looked at Mark as if mulling something over. "I'll tell you what. I'll swallow my pride and talk to some of the elders and tell them what happened to Radwick. Fill in some gaps. I'm going into town. I have to make sure the lab is secure. Besides, Hanley might show up back there. It's *his* damn church."

"Why don't I come with you? I'd like to know as much as I can."

"I better talk to the elders myself. They won't open up with an outsider around."

"Do you know a guy named Bob Silvers?"

"Former tribal council member."

"Gregory got a strange e-mail from him. He seems to know something."

"OK, I'll pay him a visit. But I tell you, man, I'm out of the loop. Silvers, he's connected to some strange people."

"Will he talk to you?"

"Maybe. You can hang around in town and then meet me at the church at sunset. Call Sandra and see if she's OK."

Mark looked around for the phone.

"It's over there," said Kallabush.

Chapter Twenty-Three

Instead of going directly back into town, Mark took the loop road out to Cape Flattery, parked at the trailhead, and hiked out to the promontory. Standing at the tip of Cape Flattery, well over a hundred feet above the ocean, he gazed at the lighthouse on Tatoosh Island. Golden streaks of sunlight broke through the clouds, and although the sea was grandly illuminated, he knew how deceptive such a picture could be. He hoped Kallabush could learn something useful. For it wasn't only the coastline that was usually curtained in shadows. The native population was reticent and secretive. Even back home, he sometimes felt alienated from his neighbors; here on the reservation, the boundary of familiarity was even harder to cross. Other people were often like foreign countries, their thoughts like foreign languages. He needed real answers. And he needed to know what to do.

Leaving the promontory, he started back toward the trailhead, detouring briefly to look over the north side. A sandy cove was carved out beneath the cliffs, and waves crashed into the mouth of a cave. The water, as the sun struck it, was aquamarine. This tropical color surprised him, for the air was chilly and the sun was fickle as it now disappeared behind the clouds.

A mass of twisted and exposed roots from a couple of giant spruce trees snagged his shoe on the trail, but he caught himself before falling, and soon he was at the trailhead. He started the Rover and headed back along the dirt and gravel road to Neah Bay.

After arriving, he drove through town to the waterfront cafe. He sat at the table he and Sandra had occupied when she'd first told him about her mysterious husband. He ordered steak and fries. A pang of homesickness came over him. About this time, when Erica got back from school in the afternoon, he'd usually be too busy to meet her at the bus stop, so she would come home by herself, let herself in, and call, "Dad, I'm home!" He always left the front door unlocked. He spent half the day designing and drafting, the other half running errands or doing housework. No problem. He came up with enough clients to justify staying home, not enough to support an office—not yet. But where was that everyday world now? It had vanished, and he knew he had to get home. Outside, the bay darkened into deep blue. Soon, it was time to meet Kallabush.

The church was only a few blocks away, and this time he didn't have to sneak into the parking lot with the lights off. He parked next to the Plymouth near the back door. When he stepped out of the Rover he thought he heard a distant beating of drums, but wondered if it could be his imagination. The air was clear and calm. The door on the little porch had a new deadbolt lock, but it was open.

A light was on in the utility room. He went to the cellar door and descended into the basement. The whole fluorescent-lit laboratory was just as he found it before. The curtains were pulled across the shelves along the wall under the stairs.

Kallabush waved a greeting from across the room. "Just got here myself." He pointed to the curtains, walked over, and pulled the longest one aside.

The shelves of human skulls and other remains were revealed. Kallabush put his hands into his jacket pockets and stepped closer, the look on his face sober and resigned. To Mark, the cold and silence of the basement seemed to force the feeling that these bones, indeed, had been sacrilegiously warehoused, for ultimately "the church" had sanctioned the conquering, slaughtering, and exploitation of native populations. But Mark wasn't in the mood to glaze over or sentimentalize a native way of life he'd learned was often brutal, uncompromising, and barbaric. Only a couple of hundred years ago, he thought, these murders might have been the result of tribal conflicts, when slaves were taken during warfare, kept in servitude, and occasionally killed for sport. He had learned from Matsamura of barbarities reaching back into the gloom of history, such as the hideous uses of fresh human corpses for whale-hunting rituals. The tribal past spoke of many things other than white oppression.

Kallabush gazed at the haphazard appearance of the dead. "I guard them, but I will not touch them." He peered down the row. "I'm not superstitious, but I'm not insensitive. They mean cold-blooded murder." He turned away and walked around the lab, looking over the long, sturdy tables and their jars, vats, trays, and scientific paraphernalia. "Quite a set-up, isn't it?" he said. "We built these tables." He leaned against the one hosting long, shallow vats that contained ancestral cedar implements. "Did you know that Makah families own songs and dances? You aren't allowed to record certain ones that are performed on the reservation."

"So I've heard. But that's not what we're here to talk about, is it?"

"No, I guess not."

"Gregory was checking into the idea of a secret society. Did you talk to Bob Silvers?"

"Yes. And Gregory was on the right track. Secret knowledge is passed down among the true believers."

"And you have chosen not to believe any of it."

An edge came back into Kallabush's voice. "I have chosen not to believe my father who is in his grave. I have chosen not to believe my mother who sleeps in a rest home. I have chosen not to believe the past which is gone."

"My past is gone too. And I want to know why."

Kallabush smiled. "Should I tell you that your wife's spirit still wanders the reservation?"

"There's no need for that."

"She was seen again later. A supernatural resurrection."

"Yes, I know. *I* saw her."

Kallabush's smile evaporated.

"There are things I've seen that you haven't, things I know that you don't. But we both know there are manifestations of dead people on the reservation."

The cynicism wasn't entirely missing from Kallabush's voice, but he seemed resigned. "OK, maybe I don't believe that just yet, but I believe one thing: when this village was massacred in the 1920s, the secret society rounded up the murderers and took them out to the sea stacks called Father and Son."

"Where we were wrecked offshore?"

"Yeah, that's the place. Out there, an ancient rite was performed, and the murderers were ritually dismembered."

Dismay was all Mark could feel at hearing this. "Joseph Torrel and his men, you mean."

"Yes. And probably Lucy Torrel."

"But Lucy Torrel hanged herself."

"She was Joseph's wife, and she may have been seriously supportive of the slayings. That is why she committed suicide. They probably took her body out there with the rest. Neither her body, nor Joseph's, nor the other men's, were ever buried. And through the ritual dismemberment, their souls were torn loose out of time."

"It's insane."

"Those souls still haunt the sea. They are remnants of the past, emotions, blasphemies without form. When the bones were disturbed, the past was disturbed, and those who were cut to pieces and cast into the sea possessed others—your companions—who died violently, but with the remnants still using them."

"I can't believe . . ." said Mark.

Kallabush stood poised by the table, grinning slightly at the incomprehension in Mark's face.

"Did you talk to anyone but Bob Silvers?"

"Yes. But I told you, I don't believe this stuff."

Mark was darkly quiet and breathed the cold, damp basement air into his lungs. Earlier, he would have supposed what Kallabush said was deluded, just as he'd supposed Silvers's e-mail was.

"Those who the remnants first possess have had encounters in or near the ocean, then they become *wanderers* who can move in the rain or fog to possess others still, and that's how the souls co-mingle with the living."

"I don't understand why a ritual would exist to create these things."

"This is a matter of debate. Some think the original details of the ritual were unknown in the 1920s. Others say that no one expected the villagers' bodies to be unburied. And if the bones aren't reburied, they say

Sisiutl will come from the sea, as it did a long time ago, and all the souls and those they possess will be swept away into the serpent's heart."

"What does this mean?"

"I don't know—I don't think anyone knows—but the believers are gathering from off the reservation for a ceremony. Did you hear the drums . . . ?"

"Yes, I think so, when I got here."

"They're drumming in the clinic parking lot. They know about Dr. Radwick. They say the bones must be reburied immediately or more people will die. The tribal council won't give in to their superstition, and to fend them off, there's a meeting tomorrow that will discuss the discovery among the members of the tribe, and it's expected they'll announce the date of reburial at the same time."

"What happened to my wife?"

Kallabush became quite sober. "I don't know."

"When I saw her, she spoke mysteriously about children."

"Maybe the children who were massacred."

"What do they say about her?"

"They say she committed suicide."

"But why?"

"Can you guess? Because she went out in the mist and was *possessed* by one who committed suicide."

Mark gazed at him.

"That's right."

"Lucy Torrel."

"The past is repeated," said Kallabush. "The past haunts the present."

"There are too many things I don't understand."

"Half the problem around here is that people think they *do* understand. Haven't you been . . . ?"

Their conversation was interrupted by a noise. They looked up toward the ceiling joists at a point in the middle of the room about fifteen feet away. A distinct bump had sounded, then a lesser but similar sound, as of someone taking an irregular step on the floor above. For some seconds they watched the ceiling. The bare wood had been primed or painted white to allow maximum reflection of the fluorescent lights, and Mark concentrated on the spaces between the joists.

They watched for half a minute, but heard nothing more.

"I'd better go look," said Mark. "You pull the curtains back across the shelving, and if I need you, I'll call."

"Be careful. Maybe it's Hanley."

Mark left Kallabush and climbed the wooden steps. As he came to the top and entered the utility room, he began to experience a fear that had become all too familiar.

Entering the chapel, he looked across the dark pews. The street light outdoors provided some ambient illumination. The shadowy interior appeared empty at first, but as his eyes grew accustomed to the dim light, he noticed a thin silhouette among the pews to the left—a person, a mere shadow, sitting about eight rows away, a forward-facing figure, unrecognizable. Defensively, he stepped toward the side of the pulpit and its riser, thinking he'd be anonymous to the lone figure.

"Who are you?" Mark's voice echoed in the rafters.

The figure remained still, not willing to look toward the sound of the voice. Mark wondered if this person had been spying and had over-heard Kallabush and him.

"What are you doing here?" he asked.

The person didn't respond.

"I'm going to come over there," Mark said. "Don't move." He tried to keep his voice level. "I'm here on business. This is a secure building. You'll have to leave."

Moving as non-threateningly as possible, he walked slowly down the aisle until he got adjacent to the figure, then moved in along the row to the left. It was stupid, he thought, even risky to approach someone like this, but he was tired of cat-and-mouse, and on automatic. The light was quite dim, but he felt almost sick at the confirmation of his thoughts. His heart beat faster as the profile of Garman Hanley became apparent to him. He strained for something to say—but Hanley remained motionless, and it took only a second to see that his posture wasn't normal but rigid, that his neck was straight, and that his eyes did not move or blink.

Mark felt abhorrence, giving way to cynicism. Poor Hanley had reached an impasse in which he'd returned to his own church to sit and face his own pulpit. Mark stayed focused and let a long moment go by, waiting for a response. None came. Coming within a few feet, he could have reached out his hand and touched him. He felt nauseous again. Finally, after he couldn't get any response, he came closer, but didn't know what to do, so he reached out carefully to touch Hanley's shoulder. The slight pressure had an unwanted effect—and Mark suddenly had to grab the man's clothing with both hands to keep him upright. The body swayed toward him, and Hanley's head came down and would have smacked on the hardwood pew had not Mark caught him. *Was he dead?* Along with the weight of his head, Hanley's matted hair and beard pressed on Mark's palm. All he could do was ease him down and lay him on the bench.

Mark felt for a pulse. Hanley's heart was beating. Maybe he'd had a massive stroke of some kind. The situation required an immediate response, since this man had been moving around up here just moments ago. Mark's emergency skills were vague at best. He and Kallabush would have to get help, but first he decided to turn Hanley over on his back. He felt a sense of panic. He took Hanley by the shirt and rolled him onto his back.

Then there was an odd shadow seen out of the corner of Mark's eye. He assumed it was Kallabush, so he listened to Hanley's heart once more and wanted to be sure the man was breathing. Nevertheless, they had to get help right away. He looked up toward Kallabush and started to speak.

But the shadow that made itself known in the center aisle now moved in the dim light from the window. Its skull was crushed and broken. Its head was pale—drained of blood—but recognizable. . . . The clothing that had been worn during the heavy seas was tattered, but the bitter, sarcastic expression remained on the contorted, deathly face.

Staring in horror, Mark attempted to release Hanley, but the muscles in his hands involuntarily tightened. Paralyzed, nauseous, he gazed at the apparition of John Horn. Even with every nerve in his body screaming for action of some kind, Mark was unable to jerk his limbs into motion.

Horn stood at the entrance to the pew. It was a point in a nightmare where the horror becomes so intolerable that one must wake up screaming. But Mark did not wake up, and the horror did not stop. If it was going to take possession of him, it would have to continue forward. Mark, the victim, had become pathetically immobile. But now came the more inexplicable thing. Horn seemed to shorten. As Mark watched in disbelief, he realized this wasn't what was happening, but rather, the ghastly figure was sinking into the floor. Uncannily, the legs began to disappear into the heavy grain of the floorboards. Water dripped off of Horn's clothing, and in the midst of it, he stared ominously at Mark until half of him was gone. The horrifying osmosis continued until only the crushed head, like a white, mashed ball, was left on the wooden floor of the aisle, lingering to stare upward at its former navigator, until the head also sank out of sight in the shadow of the pews.

Fear had purged his lungs, and Mark gasped for air. Beneath the paralysis, sickness, and desperate breathing, he was aware, even as Horn had sunk into the floor, of a person yelling or screaming. Shock had forced away this awareness of a muffled sound, but now he heard it again, and it was coming from below—distantly underneath, except there was no ground, no earth, and so the sound was of someone screaming down under the floor.

Now able to let go of Hanley, his thoughts on Kallabush, he groped shakily for support, then stumbled out of the row. He skirted the place where Horn had disappeared, then ran back toward the obscurity of the pulpit and the room that led into the basement. Once through the basement door, he risked a fall by leaping down the narrow stairs two at a time until he stumbled onto the concrete at the bottom, into the brightness and silence of the lab.

Kallabush was cowering against the far wall. Mark scrutinized the whole room. Then he focused his gaze.

The color was gone from Kallabush's face. He gave an unexpected chuckle, as if he were trying to speak. He raised his arm and pointed toward the ceiling. Mark approached him, and Kallabush's head gave a little jerk, his arm came down to his side again, and he said, ". . . Scared shitless, man. Can't talk. Ah . . . I thought it was you coming through the ceiling!" He laughed as if it were a nervous habit, but his face had a desolate pallor.

". . . Came down . . . through the . . . the ceiling. I thought it was you coming down through the ceiling. Two legs dangling from the ceiling, coming further down, until . . . it . . . came through the ceiling all the way and . . . it came down." His eyes glazed over and he put out his hand in a gesture to keep Mark at a distance. "Heart beating like a scared deer. Wait . . . catch my breath." He leaned back against the concrete foundation, looked at Mark as if to verify whom he was talking to, then stared at the floor where Mark was standing and his eyes grew a bit wider and he straightened up a little as if expecting something else to happen.

"What are you looking at?" asked Mark quickly.

"Just thinking. Just thinking."

"What?"

"He went down . . . there . . ."

"Into the concrete floor?"

"Maybe he's still there. Just under there."

Mark shuddered, but refrained from moving off the spot.

"But there's no water here, or fog, so he can't come back," said Kallabush. "They can't stay out of the water." He shivered slightly, then hugged himself tightly as if an arctic blast was blowing through the room. "Are we safe? My father would know. My father would know, but he has not forgiven me."

Mark's heart also needed calming, and he braced himself against the long table.

Kallabush was terrified. He continued to stare at the floor. "Down there in the ground, the place that's moist and damp. Under the ground in the water table. They seek out the moisture in the ground when there's no moisture above. They remain alive in the water table, then rise up into the fog."

"Take it easy, Jim."

"To find another host. I didn't believe it, but it's true." Kallabush looked up, his eyes darting from place to place. "We must find out from the others what must be done. We need help."

Mark didn't know what to say as he watched his companion's agitated face in the bright fluorescent light.

Chapter Twenty-Four

Hanley is dead."

"My God, how? When?"

"He came back to the church about three hours ago. He must have had a massive stroke. He died just after help arrived."

"Where are you?"

"I'm at the tribal police station. Kallabush and I have been answering questions. Matsamura is at the church, checking on things. He offered me a place to sleep at the motel tonight, but I don't want to leave you alone. I'm starting back in about ten minutes. They took Hanley's body away. It took them forever. I can't tell you everything right now. Do you understand?"

"Did something strange happen that you can't talk about?"

"That's right. You got it. I'm not alone here."

"Mark, it's late. The fog. I keep thinking of Gregory on that logging road."

"Nothing like that will happen to me. I'm not going to stop on the road for *anyone*."

"Isn't there a meeting tomorrow?"

"For members of the tribe."

"Considering your involvement, they might let you in."

"I don't think so."

"Mark, I'm safe indoors. There isn't any fog right now and no forecast of rain. It's more dangerous for you to drive back. Look, I'm sure not going outside for *any* reason. I'd rather you stay up there. I keep thinking about Gregory. I keep thinking . . ."

"I can't leave you alone."

"Fog can drift in anywhere along the south road."

"When I called from Kallabush's, I didn't give you the whole story about Radwick. He's . . . in bad shape."

"You can give me the details later. But we know it's because he went outside. All the more reason you shouldn't try to drive back. I'm inside, and I'm not going outside. If you drive back, what if you run into one of *them* on the road? What if you run into . . . her . . ."

"Maggie."

"That's right. What are you going to do, run her down? That's a narrow road. We don't know what happened to Gregory, but Maggie was with him."

"Damn it, Sandra . . ."

"Look, I'm fine. I've got a fire going. I'm going to call a friend in Seattle and talk to her for a few minutes. Barney is here. I'll keep him in the house with me. We'll be fine. I'd *seriously* be more comfortable if you went to the motel. You can call me and give me your number when you get there. You can tell me more about what happened at the church."

"All right, then. You promise not to go outside. For any reason."

"I was the one who tried to keep *you* inside the other night, remember?"

"OK, I'll call you when I get to the motel. Don't stay on the phone too long with your friend. OK?"

"Sure."

"You must not go outside."

"Of course. You be careful, too."

"I'll call you shortly."

"OK."

Chapter Twenty-Five

In the archaeologists' motel room the next morning, exhaustion caused Mark to oversleep. He hadn't even heard Matsamura leave. He opened the curtains and looked out onto the waterfront fishing fleet while munching down some cold cereal with milk he'd found in the small refrigerator. After that, he showered and dressed quickly. Then he went out into the salty air, got into the Rover, and drove in the direction of the high school. He was going to be late for the meeting.

The school was quite close, as was everything else in Neah Bay. A reader-board near the playfield said, with a politically incorrect irony he admired, "Home of the Red Devils." He parked the car next to a cyclone fence while noticing the large number of other cars.

Two Native American men stood at the door to the gymnasium.

"Tribe only," said one of them.

Mark was in no mood to argue, and anyway, he wanted to stop and see Radwick again before going back to Sandra's.

"Hey, you the guy who saved that little boy?" asked the other man.

"Yeah," said Mark.

"I recognize you. I'll let you in."

"Thanks."

He walked through the door into the back of the gym. A crowd of about two hundred people filled the rows of folding chairs that faced a broad, raised stage. On the wall above center stage was an American flag and to its right a Washington State flag. To the left was a flag that said "Makah Indian Nation," and this had several other names, apparently with older spellings, that were the original villages that had once occupied the land of the Makah: Diaht, Wa'atch, Osett, Tsoo Yess, and Ba'adah. Through the loudspeakers came a familiar voice, and as he took in the scene from the back of the room he saw Ken Matsamura at the podium. Matsamura was finishing a lecture on the results of the archaeological excavation.

Ken had obviously gone public with the story of the bones. Perhaps now, the media would pick it up, and the bones would be promptly reburied.

". . . I want to thank all of you who took on the risk and the responsibility to give us this sacred trust. Our findings and our research were kept secret out of respect for that trust, and the result is that the truth is no longer hidden."

Mark saw Richard and Judy sitting near the back row, with an empty seat next to them. He went over and sat down in the metal folding chair.

"Big deal meeting," whispered Judy.

Richard leaned over and smiled.

Matsamura finished speaking, and quite a number of people applauded as he stepped away from the podium. But the atmosphere was subdued, and Mark wondered if anything had been said about the bizarre events of the last several weeks.

As if in answer, Judy said, "Those guys aren't going to say anything important. Talk, talk, talk." She shook her head. "What happens, happens. They don't know anything. You know more than they do." She nodded at Mark meaningfully. "You go up there and let them know what's going on around here."

"Thanks, Judy. When did the meeting start?"

"About ten o'clock. Ken Matsamura was the second guy to talk."

"Talk, talk, talk," said Richard, laughing at Judy.

"They *can't* say what's on everyone's mind," said Judy.

Another man took the podium, and he immediately began to introduce someone whose name Mark did not recognize. The new speaker got a lot of applause. He was a Native American, about fifty years old, wearing a plain blue shirt with a bolo tie of the kind that was common on the reservation. As he spoke into the microphone, his voice intoned through the loudspeakers with considerable force.

"We have chosen to learn," he said. "And we have preserved the dignity of the dead by keeping out the exploitative eyes of those surrounding us. This has meant secrets. Compromises. Concessions. But we have learned, and the story will be told. In a little while, the dead will resume their rest—but there are those who will not rest."

A murmur progressed through the crowd, and it threatened to continue at some length, but the speaker's voice overrode it by continuing without pause.

"Our history is partly that of strangers, faded photographs and memories that provide much of the detail but little of the lives themselves. Those who died, and those who killed, still shape our world. The history given by Ken Matsamura this morning reaches into our lives by stealth, and so does the river of our past. We are a continuity, a sea of time and tradition. There is the scientific record, but as a writer I know there is another record of lives in the memory of those old enough to have experienced this continuity. Some are recorded or written down. Frozen history, but frozen thoughts and frozen words that have the power of recall. This is the transfer of one memory to another. The critical history and the uncritical memory join together. We are burdened with legacies. Aided by them. Or hindered by them. Someone said: 'History is a reconstruction, always incomplete.' I would say, my memory of this morning's descriptions is a memory of 'what is no longer.' It is also a reconstruction. What I want to say is that history insists on evidence and structure, while memory creates a moment, an image. We must put together and preserve our memories, and we will surely do this in the way an artist does, moving from fragment to concept and finally to truth, for truth emerges within ourselves from the facts outside ourselves.

"Finally there is 'myth,' the symbol of memory and the framework of continuity. Myth is also with us. This is our heritage, our protection, and our guide. It is the heart of our culture, and we must not be afraid of it, for the force of myth has been with us since the beginning of our people, and we have not, and will not, lose touch with it, but work within it. Many others have forgotten, so it is we who must remember. Thank you."

Huge applause greeted the end of this speech, and when the noise died down, the moderator made an announcement. "We ask you to join us next month at the ceremony of reburial. Again, thank you all for coming. We have refreshments here, and welcome you to stay and talk to our guests."

Sporadic applause, and then the crowd rose and began to disperse—though Mark noticed that quite a few remained seated, talking among themselves in groups. A number went to the stage where they could talk to the speakers.

He was disappointed. This was not a meeting of minds, but a public gathering to officially recognize the massacre. No debate or objections were entertained, no question-and-answer. It was clear from the whispers in the audience that some had more on their minds. And reburial was next month.

Mark felt claustrophobic. He decided to go out into the sunlight, where he squinted across the playfield toward the parking area. Cars drove off in all directions, and something about the sunlight or the way the cars drove away caused him to recall, in a strange way, the encounter with Maggie. He couldn't shut it out. It was foggy on the logging road, he was on the ground, his vision was impaired, and Maggie was coming toward him.

Remembering made him sick, but he had to move, had to finish his business in town.

Questioning his emotions, he walked toward the Rover, got in, and by the time he reached the clinic, he was mentally unraveling. He felt adrift. Where was the anchor he needed? His direct experiences contradicted the rational assumptions on which he'd built his life. *Everything* seemed to have a certain validity now, even dreams, and the town streets seemed like shifting sands. Last night's horror in the church, *undreamed*, inserted itself into reality. Accepting it at face value was no solution. The question was what to do, what made sense for Sandra and him. He wanted her safe, and that's what mattered most.

Inside the clinic, under a sign that said "All Patients Check in Here," a medium-sized man who looked like a Native American greeted him from behind the counter. "Hi, what can I do for you? I'm Mitchell, the Physician Assistant."

"My name's Mark Sayres. Dr. Veress said I could come back and see Dr. Radwick."

"Are you a relative?"

"No, but there were special circumstances."

Apparently trying to conceal a look of consternation, Mitchell hesitated. "He's not seeing anyone right now."

"I was with him just before the incident occurred."

Mitchell attended to some papers, apparently expecting Mark to drop the request. But Mark became irritated when the man ignored him.

"I'd like to see him," Mark repeated, stepping toward the hall. "If I may."

Mitchell came outside from behind the counter. "I'm sorry, I don't have permission to allow visitors."

"I saw him yesterday. I'm sure it will be fine. Is Dr. Veress here? He knows the circumstances."

"Dr. Veress isn't here."

"I wonder if he might have mentioned me to you. Mark Sayres. He told me that Radwick might be transferred." A cry came from down the hall, someone shouting an indiscernible word, and it sounded like Radwick. Mark started to walk down the hall. Mitchell came after him.

"I'm sorry. What do you think you're doing?"

"I'm going to see Radwick." Mark kept walking. Mitchell grabbed him by the arm but he jerked away. Then the man got in front of him and put both hands on Mark's chest. "Stop right here. Just stop before this gets out of control."

"There must be a way of persuading you that I have to see him. Has Ken Matsamura been in to see him? You must know Ken, don't you?"

"I don't know him. He might have been here this morning. I'm a volunteer from off the reservation who was called in to sub for the regular assistant. Look, if you'll wait here, I'll go down to Dr. Radwick's room. Just be reasonable and stay here a minute."

He walked down the hall, looked back to make sure Mark hadn't moved, and went inside the room.

In a minute, he emerged and gestured for Mark to follow. Mitchell watched as Mark went into the room.

Paul Radwick lay just as he had yesterday, but with a disturbing difference. One of his wrists was strapped to the railing at the side of the bed.

A woman sat near the window. Mark didn't recognize her and she didn't offer any greeting. Radwick was whispering to himself.

Ignoring the woman, Mark stepped toward the bed.

"Paul."

There was no recognition, only the continued whispering.

"Paul—"

"Done, done, done."

The whispered words could barely be understood.

"Done, done, done."

The woman in the chair remained silent. Was she a nurse or a visitor?

"In the . . . in the . . ." And then Radwick let out a cry. It was just an incoherent, sharp moan, and there was very little emotion in it, as if generated out of habit.

The woman near the window made a little gasp from inside her throat. Radwick lay in silence now and turned his head to the side.

Mark addressed the woman. "I'm Mark Sayres, an acquaintance of Paul's."

The woman spoke from the shadow. Her voice was shaky. She might have been crying, or was about to cry. "I'm Nancy Radwick, Paul's wife."

Mark tried to force a smile, but couldn't. "I was here just yesterday," he said.

"I recognize your name. You were the last one to see Paul before this happened."

"Yes."

"A doctor came in this morning from the U.W. I arrived while he was examining Paul."

"What did he say?"

"Of course he wanted to take Paul back to Seattle." She reached over to a small table for a Kleenex. He saw that she was a short late-middle-aged brunette with bangs cut straight across her forehead. "But someone told Paul to stay here for two more days. I don't know who or why. Paul comes out of this—whatever it is—and he's perfectly normal. Do you know him well?"

"No. We were just getting to know each other."

"He doesn't seem to have had a stroke."

Mark took a deep breath. "I know."

"I'm not going to tell him what to do. But the U.W. doctor can't do any more unless Paul wants to leave. Paul knows what he wants and Dr. Veress complies."

"Did the doctor say anything else?"

"He said a lot of things. Possible brain tumor. Maybe encephalitis. He has to get Paul somewhere else."

"But I know what to do." It was Paul. With one wrist tied, he struggled to sit up against the pillows. He was suddenly himself, completely lucid. It was shocking how suddenly well he looked.

"This person, or combination of persons inside me wants to leave here, but I won't let them leave. I've become aware of them, and I know something about them. You understand, don't you, Mark? Tell Nancy you understand and things will be much better."

His wife had apparently seen this before. "Paul, I've heard what you've said, but why do you want to stay here?"

"Because it's going to end. Those who know are gathering. Maybe tonight Sisiutl will rise and take what belongs to it. Then it will be over, and I will be free."

Nancy Radwick stood up. "Paul, we can't do anything if you won't help. Dr. Turner wants you at the U.W. Medical Center."

"It's all right, Nancy."

Mrs. Radwick looked at Mark in defeat.

"Paul," said Mark, "what do you expect will happen?"

"I don't know. Maybe Bob Silvers knows."

"Paul, it may be dangerous to stay on the reservation."

He smiled. "And for me, more dangerous to leave. I think something is going to happen tonight. There's rumor of a big ceremony. Members from other tribes have come into town or are staying on the outskirts. I don't know who these people are, but it's not merely a Makah ceremony."

Mark rubbed his hand through his hair and glanced at Mrs. Radwick.

"It's all right, Nancy," repeated Paul. "We have to wait this out."

"Where's Dr. Veress, Paul? Why did he strap your arm to the bed?" asked Mark.

"I told him to. There is a person inside me . . . your friend Olson, I guess . . . but the remnant possessed him in the sea and is also here. The remnant, the hidden core, is someone who helped Joseph Torrel massacre those men, women, and children. That's what the elders say."

"Paul tried to walk out of here last night," said Mrs. Radwick.

"Not quite," said Radwick, "*he* tried to walk out of here, or *they*, and I don't know what'll happen if they do get out. Dead human beings act out their own past."

Mrs. Radwick looked at Mark again.

He said, "Paul, you have to get off the reservation."

"They go with you."

Mark took a deep breath. He felt hot.

"The trick," said Radwick, "is to know who the original ones are, and then you know what they'll try to do, because they create the ghost wanderers and use them to repeat their own misfortunes. I've diagrammed out both the who and the what. Luckily, Olson is a calm man, difficult to use, and unlike the devout, alcoholic Reverend Hanley, I don't confuse human personalities or voices in my head with angels. They say Joseph Torrel *himself* is the remnant who possessed your captain—who in turn used Hanley that day in the street."

"How can anyone know that?"

"Knowledge is an elusive thing up here, isn't it?"

"Hanley is dead."

"I know. The news is all over town."

"Horn had left Hanley's body. I saw it."

"Anyone who dies while possessed will return, until Sisiutl rises."

Mark stared at him and then thought of Gregory's return.

"Let's talk about you, Mark." He sounded like a sympathetic teacher now. "First step: Know your enemy. You failed there, didn't you? When your wife disappeared, it took us all by surprise; yet, in a way, we had the answers in hand. We had dug up the answers. And the white men who killed the villagers were ritually murdered for revenge, and now they've returned in incorporeal form to inhabit others. What they say is that your poor wife was possessed by a remnant who committed suicide."

"Paul, when would Maggie have known she'd been possessed?"

"No one can say. Remnants can remain hidden, secret, silent, until they grow strong enough to act or make themselves known."

Radwick was silent for a moment, his eyes like hard marbles. "Who do you think was most responsible for the massacre?"

"Joseph Torrel."

"He is back. And all the others who committed murder. But there was a woman. Remember?"

"Yes, I know. Joseph Torrel's wife, Lucy, hanged herself."

"When she found out what her husband had done. Maybe, like Lady Macbeth, she encouraged him. But we know that she was the only woman involved, and your wife is the only woman who disappeared."

Mark gazed at him sadly, for it was essentially what Kallabush had told him.

"They must have cut her down and taken her away with the others. Perhaps she was still alive when they cut her down. After the ritual, her spirit became one of the remnants in the sea. She came near shore and inhabited your wife, your wife was driven to repeat her suicide, and whomever your wife tries to inhabit will do likewise. You said you knew *something* was wrong with Maggie when you decided to leave San Diego, and you were too late getting here."

Mark felt defensive. "Yes. She wouldn't tell me what was wrong. And she came out of Gregory's truck on the logging road."

"Where he committed suicide."

"I'm afraid so."

"That would fit," said Radwick. Then his expression changed to concern. "There must have been fog or mist. What happened to Maggie afterwards?"

"I don't know."

The memory of the logging road flooded back into Mark's mind. He was on the ground, his vision impaired, and Maggie was coming toward him the *second* time—from the direction of Sandra's truck—and it *was* Maggie coming toward him, though it was Sandra whose face had looked down at him after he'd turned away that second time, and it was her voice that had yelled his name.

"Oh, God, Paul."

Radwick stared at him, his brow narrowing with concern.

The idea that arose in Mark's brain took hold with terrifying force—because it wasn't Maggie who'd stared down at him on the logging road, but it *was* she who had come toward him, and as he'd lain in the road trying to recover his senses, it was Sandra who had yelled at him and looked down at him. But where *had* Maggie gone?

"My God, Paul, I'd fallen, and after I looked up from the ground, Maggie came toward me from Sandra's direction. Then Sandra was leaning over me."

"They can stay hidden," said Paul. "They can be silent in a person until it's too late. We can also guess what happened to Gregory on that road. You understand what I mean?" His eyes became wild. "Don't be too late again."

"I shouldn't have left her. Paul, I've got to go."

"Go quickly," said Paul. His advice was a chilling proclamation.

Mark said goodbye to Nancy Radwick, stepped into the hall, and ran quickly to the lobby.

Two patients gave him a strange look. He passed them and reached to open the front door.

But he didn't quite get outside without overhearing a fragment of an exchange between Mitchell and another woman:

". . . think Dr. Veress went out to the old Torrel house."

That was the fragment. Had he heard correctly? He went to the counter to ask.

Mitchell, standing there, turned to look at the woman behind the counter. She told Mark, "It's confidential. I'm sorry."

Mitchell turned and walked back down the hall to one of the examining rooms. To the woman Mark said, "You already said where Veress had gone—out loud. I just want to know if I heard right."

"I . . ."

"I'm staying with Sandra Torrel. Did you say that Dr. Veress was called out to the Torrel house?"

"Well, Mrs. Torrel phoned here with a problem of some kind, and afterwards Dr. Veress said he was going over to the police station to borrow the keys to the south gate."

"Can I use your phone?"

He dialed Sandra, waited through a half-dozen rings, but ended up with her voicemail. She always answered if she could. He tried twice again but couldn't reach her.

Sandra had sought Dr. Veress's help once before, after her husband had grabbed her by the throat. She must be in trouble. He ran outside, got into the Rover, and started the engine. Radwick had just said people sometimes didn't know they were possessed until it was too late. Slamming his foot on the accelerator, he sped out of the parking lot, squealed into the street, and sped out of town. He forced himself to acknowledge that people call doctors for many ordinary reasons, but why a house call? Why couldn't Sandra get into the truck and come into the clinic? She, too, had a set of keys to the logging gate. Yet a blackout or nausea or something would mean she couldn't drive. He shouldn't have left her. If Maggie had possessed her on that logging road, it was bad enough. What was worse was that *Lucy* might have found her way home.

Chapter Twenty-Six

Time stretched along the road like an invisible barrier. His thoughts blended into a rush of fear and speculation, and he had been nearly unaware of driving. By the time he reached the Torrel house, the muscles in his hands were almost frozen on the wheel, and he had to flex them. He came to Sandra's turn-off, the gate (open) and the muddy road through the swamp; he drove through the dark trees along the twisting private drive until the house emerged on the left. In the distance over the ocean, the sky was blanketed with a diffuse, milky haze.

A white Mini-Cooper with a black roof was parked in front of the house. He pulled up behind it. Barney came down from the front porch, wagging his tail. Dr. Veress emerged from the Mini. He wore a thick burgundy sweater, pleated tan slacks, and no coat. He looked perturbed.

"I got here ten minutes ago. She called me at the clinic. She's not inside, and I checked out back. There's a truck in the garage, and her dog's been here since I arrived. I've been waiting to see if she'd show up."

"Did you try the beach?"

"No. But the front door was unlocked, so I went inside and called for her. I searched all the rooms. I don't get it."

"If the truck's here, she has to be around someplace. We'd better go down to the beach."

"Perhaps she wasn't expecting me so soon." He sounded annoyed, then reached into his car for a coat. "It's not often I make house calls, but I came right out here."

"Did she say she couldn't drive?"

Veress put on his coat as they walked to the cliff stairs. "She mentioned dizziness and a mild fainting spell."

Mark was worried, for if she'd experienced these things before, she hadn't told him. "We have to find her immediately. Paul thinks it's important."

They started down the wooden stairs, but Barney wouldn't follow.

"Come on, Barney!" said Mark.

But the dog just sat and barked at them from the top of the stairs. Or was he barking at the sea? He showed no interest in following them.

"OK, boy, you stay here," said Mark. "Wait for Sandra."

"What does Paul have to do with it?" asked Veress as they descended the stairs.

"Let me ask you something. Why are you keeping Paul at the clinic?"

"Because he requested to stay."

"And that's all?"

"I had a man come out from the U.W. Medical Center."

"Yes, I know." Mark looked back at him as they made their way down.

"I'll admit neither I nor Dr. Turner has seen anything like it. Paul has no history of mental problems. One day he is fine, the next day he's got a serious personality disorder. And he demands to stay on the reservation. You can't force someone to go to the hospital, and I'd rather have him at the clinic than wandering around."

"It's an interesting case for a Native American with an M.D."

"What do you mean?"

"Well, you don't practice medicine in downtown Seattle, right? You are hearing rumors and getting information just like Paul is. You had some strange characters out in your parking lot yesterday beating on drums. They must have said a few things."

They came down the last few steps and out onto the sand. The wind was strong on the beach.

Mark said, "Can you accept the *possibility* that Radwick is possessed?"

Veress looked out at the breakers. "Possibilities," he muttered, "*can* be imagined. Also, pressure has been put on me to keep Paul on the reservation for reasons I'm not privy to. I'm not yielding to that pressure. That's not why he's at the clinic."

"But you haven't released him."

"No, I haven't. Something unusual is wrong with him, and he won't go elsewhere. Why is he concerned about Sandra?"

"It's complicated. Paul thinks Sandra has been possessed by a person—or persons—who have committed suicide. I know it sounds crazy."

"Can't argue with the last part," said Veress.

"Yeah," said Mark. "Perfectly said. Just like me when I arrived here."

"Look," said Veress, "I'm used to hearing all sorts of things like this. She just said she was dizzy and felt a little faint."

"Radwick was disoriented when Kallabush found him."

"But Radwick has a serious personality disorder," said Veress. "Has Sandra been changing personalities?"

"No, she hasn't. But they say the spirits can remain silent. And considering what else I've witnessed lately, I have no reason to doubt anything anyone says around here."

"Yeah, I can see that," Veress said sarcastically.

They stepped onto a rocky part of the beach and looked along the shoreline into the distance. The tide was relatively high. Mark pointed toward the south. "I'm going that way. Maybe you'd better head north. I'll meet you back here in a half-hour. The beach may be impassable not too far in either direction."

"OK," said Veress. "A half-hour. That's fifteen minutes out and fifteen back."

"Yes."

They parted company.

Soon, Mark found himself out of the doctor's sight, walking alone, his worry increasing. The air was misty, but this was apparent only at a distance. He doubted Sandra would have come down here in a heavy mist, and certainly not in the fog unless she'd been led here. And this thought caused further panic, for he didn't know what he'd do if she was gone. It was too painful.

Against the cliff were piles of huge boulders, some as big as houses. If Sandra were lying among them in some big nook or cranny, having fallen from the cliff above, it could take hours to find her. Fear rose in his throat, a sensation of impending tragedy, perhaps, and he struggled to push back his worst thoughts. He just had to find her. This time he couldn't be too late or he'd have only himself to blame.

Coming to a large, jutting rock, he timed the incoming waves to step around it. On the other side was a complex of large, barnacle-encrusted boulders stained brown to the high tide line. Narrow passages between these giant edifices presented choices, while below the cliff, the mist was heavy, the dark clefts among the boulders mysterious looking.

His emotions rising, he stood indecisively, wondering which path to take, wondering what he'd do if he found her dead. Or worse.

Then, as if in answer to an unconscious cue from his frightened soul, a figure appeared from around the biggest boulder nearest the sea, from a shadow.

It was Sandra. She was wearing a red parka and the dark blue turtleneck sweater. Watching her, he felt his heart race, suspicion cloud his mind.

"Mark!"

From between the rocks and through the mist, as if in a dream, she walked toward him. The dark, flowing hair. The loose jacket and jeans. She was walking toward him from out of a misty shadow. Yet her face was recognizable and distinct. He felt a certain joy struggling to flow through him, but he couldn't get himself to move because of his experience with Maggie on the logging road. Then things seemed to blur around her, as if his trepidation was justified; but she was in focus, the center of vision in focus, and everything else hazy as he stood and looked at her coming toward him. He didn't move a single muscle or bat an eye, concentrating on where she was in the center of his vision near the rocks under the cliff, and he was not backing away because the water was right behind him.

She came to within a few feet of him—her attractive eyes, smooth complexion, and physical form. The rocky surroundings came into focus again.

"Mark, what's wrong?"

Although she seemed almost unreal, he was aware of her vividness. His body felt heavy, and it was as though his mind were being pulled in two. This immeasurable weight seemed transferred to her, for her expression collapsed with anxious curiosity. The worry in her eyes penetrated deeply into his own. He began to breathe consciously and rhythmically. Sandra remained steady, she perceived his fear, and like a spectre, slowly and carefully reached a delicate hand toward him, her fingers touching his cheek, and he felt a surge of emotion, his lungs taking in a silent breath of oxygen. Her eyes were pure, her face white, her touch silky. The fingers passed over his cheek; and mirroring his own, her eyes brimmed with tears.

"Mark," she said softly. "It *is* me."

He recovered, raised his hand to hers, and when he found it, their fingers enmeshed and the dreamlike uncertainty faded away like a leaf on the breeze.

Whoever was inside her, however she was changed, she was alive, and she was here with him, for real. He got control, but secondary thoughts lay ahead, for here was Sandra, alive—but maybe in such a way as to defy reason, if Radwick was correct.

"Are you all right?" she asked.

"Yes," he said. "I was looking for you."

"I know what you were thinking."

"I'll bet."

"I'm sorry I was away from the house. I had to get some fresh air. I just felt like walking. It looked safe."

"I was in Roland Veress's office minutes after you called and I overheard them say he'd come out here. He was waiting when I got to the house."

Sandra looked surprised. He wondered if she might have suspected that Maggie had possessed her on the logging road.

"I didn't think Veress would get here so soon," she said. "Where is he?"

"He went north on the beach. I came this way."

"Damn. Let's hurry back, then."

They began to walk.

"It's too late for Maggie, but not for you," said Mark. "I'm going to stay with you if you won't leave, but you've got to think about what's happened."

Sandra looked at him with a questioning expression.

"What are you talking about, Mark?"

"Why did you call Veress?"

"Oh . . . I just got dizzy. I've been feeling strange. In fact, I spilled my coffee on the carpet this morning. I felt faint. I must be coming down with something, and I didn't want to drive into town."

"Sandra, we have to talk about a possibility more serious than that."

"What do you mean?"

"I'm talking about Maggie and the logging road."

"Maggie?"

"The wanderers can possess people without their knowledge."

"Mark, what are you saying?"

"Think about Radwick. I told you the story when I got to the motel last night. Paul told me you may have been possessed by Maggie on the logging road and not realized it."

She stopped and gaped at him. "Mark, that's ridiculous!"

"No it isn't."

"Oh, God . . ."

He reached out, but she didn't take his hand. "You've got to come back with me right now." His mind was in turmoil.

"For Christssake, Mark . . ."

"You've got to accept the possibility that my wife is inside you, and driving *her* is an emotional remnant of Lucy Torrel."

"What? Oh, no. I can't accept this. There's no reason to think this. It's crazy."

He lowered his hand to his side when she pulled back from him. "Sandra, you've got to accept the possibility. We were much too close to her. She came from the direction of the Rover just when you did. I heard the Rover's door slam. I thought you were walking toward me. When I looked, I saw Maggie again. My vision blurred, and then you were shaking me. We were in the fog. There's no point denying that, and now you've called the doctor about having some sort of dizziness. And Maggie probably committed suicide."

"She can't be inside me. I haven't had any indications. I didn't come down here to kill myself. Nothing of the kind."

"Sandra, we have to get away from the reservation before it's too late."

"I know why you think so, but it isn't true or I'd know. She just went away that day. I'd know if she didn't, just as Paul Radwick knows his own situation."

"They think Lucy Torrel is the remnant who possessed Maggie and drove her to suicide. This may have gotten into you. Think for a minute. We didn't see Maggie go into the woods and disappear. Take my hand and we'll go pack your things and get the hell out of here forever."

"But, Mark, what happens then?"

They'd gotten back to the cliff stairs. Veress was waiting.

"I didn't know you'd be here so soon," said Sandra. "I'm sorry."

Mark put his arm around her shoulder.

"I'm glad you're OK," Veress said.

They started to climb the stairs.

"We were both concerned about you," Mark said.

"I'm all right now," said Sandra. "Maybe the walk on the beach did it."

When they got to the top of the stairs, Veress said, "Let's go indoors and take a look at you." He walked to his car and got his bag.

Inside the house, the doctor did a brief examination. Nothing wrong was discovered, though Sandra admitted feeling dizzy a couple of times in the past week.

"We'll want to do a more thorough exam if you have another spell."

"Like Radwick," said Mark.

Sandra refused to react to this.

"Yes," said Veress, "ideally you'd want a more thorough examination."

"What are you thinking?" she asked.

"Nothing," said Veress, picking up his traditional black bag. "I've got to go. I've got patients this afternoon."

"No, wait a minute," said Sandra. "You're not telling me what *you* think happened to Radwick."

Veress walked toward the front door.

Neither could Mark allow him to get away unscathed. "The doctor realizes there's no chance that Paul suddenly developed a split personality."

Veress turned before he got to the door, holding his bag at his side.

"This is not a good conversation," he said.

"This is not a good situation," said Mark.

Sandra became irritated. "I heard about Radwick last night from Mark. So, what's going on between you two?"

Mark said nothing.

"I have to go back to town," said Veress. He opened the door.

"All right," said Sandra unhappily. "I can't force you . . ."

"I'm sure Mark will offer his further medical opinion," said the doctor. "I'm equally sure you'll be just fine if you pay no attention to him."

Veress went out to his car, got in, and drove away.

"Sandra, when Gregory showed up here, you intuitively understood the danger when you stopped me from going outside."

"And you are certain Paul is a victim."

"Yes. When my companion Olson was lost, he was possessed and became one of the wanderers. He might have tried to inhabit me on the beach that day but couldn't maintain his presence because of the clearing mist. The fog was heavy when Paul went outside the cabin. Sandra, remember I told you what Kallabush said. Lucy became a spirit lingering in the sea until the bones were uncovered. Then she was drawn ashore, possessed my wife, and Maggie suspected something was wrong. She couldn't leave the reservation. Maybe someone told her not to leave."

"How can you accept all this?"

"The shoe is on the other foot. Don't forget when you tried to stop me from going outside. I've seen Paul. You haven't."

"I know what happened to Gregory—but you were so skeptical and sure of yourself when we met at the restaurant. . . . Mark, I've had one or two dizzy spells. I'm not blacking out or speaking in different personalities. I've been under a lot of stress, and that's all."

"They can stay hidden."

"Jesus, Mark, you're . . . I don't know . . . you're . . ."

He walked to the other side of the room. She couldn't finish her sentence.

"Paul is trying to stay on the reservation because Sisiutl will rise from the sea and take back the spirits, whatever that may mean."

"What happens to Paul?"

"I don't know. That's what worries me. That's why we should leave now. Maybe the cure is worse than the disease."

"All I've had is a dizzy spell or two. Maybe I'm coming down with the flu."

"Your husband stuck a knife in his throat."

Sandra was quiet and they stood in silence for a moment.

"What are you saying?" asked Sandra.

"I'm saying Gregory was possessed. Paul assumed that Lucy would have possessed another woman. In other words, Maggie. But Maggie came out of Gregory's truck, and Gregory killed himself."

"I'm not accepting this," she said.

"I'm just guessing about your husband. We'll never know for sure."

"Then you're also guessing about me. I want to see Paul for myself."

Sandra went to get her coat.

"What are you doing?"

"I'm going to see Paul."

"Right now?"

"Yes. Now."

She put on her red parka, went to check on Barney, then let him into the enclosed back porch where he would be safe from other animals. After she returned to the living room, she and Mark went out the front door.

The wind was blowing, and westward toward the cliff the sun was gone. An hour ago it could be seen through a dense, drifting haze. Dark purple clouds now formed a wall of sky that looked like a science-fiction water color. The sky formed an immense concavity that made the sea look like the inside of a hollow earth. Mark wondered if his state of mind was creating an illusion—or was the sky as strange as it seemed?

"The sky looks odd," said Sandra.

They remained on the porch for a moment. "There's supposed to be a storm coming," Sandra said. "I checked the Internet this afternoon."

"Then we'd better get going."

Chapter Twenty-Seven

On the way into Neah Bay, Sandra was quiet. A huge, billowing plume of black smoke drifted against the sky to the northeast. "Looks like it's coming from across town," she said.

The terrain made it difficult to tell the exact source of the smoke, and Sandra wanted to get to the clinic before it closed. The clinic was only a couple of blocks from where the road came into town.

"I'll see Paul myself," said Sandra, "if you want to check out that smoke."

Mark soon wheeled the Rover into the clinic parking lot. "I'll be back in a half-hour," he said.

He watched her go inside, then drove toward the black cloud rising above the town. When he came upon some people in the street watching the smoke, he rolled down the window. "Where's it coming from?"

"The church is on fire."

"Which church?"

"First Missionary Church."

Mark stepped on the accelerator and drove past the onlookers. The smoke was now spreading over the low hills downwind.

Coming along a familiar street at the far edge of town, he arrived at the scene. Ahead was Hanley's church going up in flames. On its isolated spot of ground, the building was being allowed to burn. A small fire truck stood by, doing nothing. A number of people milled around, kept back by only two or three volunteers—as if the town were half-deserted. He got out of the Rover and walked closer, feeling the wind and heat. The wooden building was being consumed with maximum

fury, and the gigantic smoke cloud was pushed toward the east. He reminded himself that a storm was coming. The narrow steeple tilted in a
swirl of rolling smoke, then burst into yellow flames. Bystanders
watched as it collapsed downward into the roof. The church was so engulfed that the roof quickly turned into a black, flame-spouting crater.
Mark stood at least a hundred feet away, but a familiar figure wearing a
leather jacket and blue jeans approached him. Richard Walker, his black
hair windblown, had a somber expression. "Don't it beat all. Judy has
left town with the kids. My friend Leonard is dead. Shot to death. You
met him at my party. "

"Shot?"

Richard fixed him with an accusing gaze. "You know about this insanity, I think."

Mark didn't know how to answer.

Walker looked back at the conflagration. "The fire engine was
sabotaged. We're just hoping to contain the blaze. There's a lot of space
around it and the forest isn't dry this time of year."

Mark shook his head as he watched someone nearby watering
down his roof with a garden hose.

"You know what, cowboy?" said Richard. "I thought the tribe
would be immune. Seemed like it was white people disappearing, getting killed. But my friend Leonard, he was killed by a blood-brother,
and that Native has a spirit inside him. That's what they told me. And
sometimes the spirit speaks. I'm not sure, you know, but I tell you,
man, they got three more dead—one white, one Makah, and one visiting Quileute—since last night."

The heat from the church, even upwind, registered on Mark's face.
Walker stared at him, not the church, causing Mark to feel under suspicion, or at least uncomfortable. God knows what Walker thought.

"You know something about the *wanderers*, I think," said Walker.

"Richard, who did this to the church?"

Walker was clearly unhappy with Mark, but he answered anyway.
"Jim Kallabush."

Although this news should have been surprising, it wasn't. But why
did he do it?

"He's in deep shit all right. He and a couple guys got a truck, took the bones out of the basement and started loading them up. Tom over there asked what the hell they thought they were doing. Kallabush gave him this mad look, said it was the bones that brought the spirits ashore, and that the spirits would awaken the serpent in the sea. Do you know what that is?"

"I've heard about it," said Mark.

"My grandfather used to say it was only a fairy tale. But Kallabush believes it! Kallabush, the guy who wouldn't listen to *me* about digging up the graves of the dead!"

Mark looked at him, half amused.

"The elders whisper among themselves," said Richard. "They tell secrets, but they know little. The secret society thinks *they* know what's going on—and that makes me nervous—and the tribal council angry. It's not a matter of revenge any longer. With all these deaths, every TV station in Seattle is going to fly in here, and the tribe has nothing to tell them, nothing they can say without looking like idiots—because maybe it's the bones after all. Legends about unburied Indian bones."

"Did Kallabush say anything else?"

"Some strangers showed up, and they had this big argument. I came right over here just as the word got out. Kallabush said he had the authority to take the bones. The other guys said Sisiutl will take away the spirits, and the bones can stay where they are. They almost came to blows."

"Who were these guys?"

"Secret society—some off the reservation. But one of the people helping Kallabush is old. He says his great-grandfather told him when Sisiutl came hundreds of years ago, many tears were shed."

"What does it mean?"

"Funny, I asked him the same damn thing. He was as serious as a priest at a funeral, and he said, 'There are those whose memories reach back to others, whose memories reach back in a line to the distant past, and some are now crying in fear in the night.' He said, 'They dream of horror coming from the sea.'"

One of the side walls of the church caved in with a crashing sound, and the flames shot higher.

"What happened to Kallabush?"

"They loaded up the bones and drove off," said Richard. "But not before lighting the church on fire with gasoline. Makahs have attended this church since the early 1900s. There's a lot of mad people here. A lot of mad and confused people."

"I have to go, Richard, and get Sandra."

"OK."

"Why did he burn down the church?"

"Only one reason. An old Indian custom. You have to burn down a house to get rid of spirits." As Richard said this, he kept his eyes on the flames.

"Kallabush had good reason," said Mark.

"Yeah? Well, let me tell you something." Richard turned to him. "Whatever his reason, it's going to stay secret. Some powerful families don't want this reputation, and they are going to do whatever is necessary. You better believe it. And we'll have a first-class cover up. Makahgate."

"The town looks deserted, Richard."

The Makah took a deep breath. "Most are indoors. And word has passed about the ceremony on the cliffs south of the Cape. Not a Makah ceremony. I decided to stay here and help see that the fire doesn't spread. Maybe you better go see what's up."

"Have you seen Matsamura?"

Walker looked puzzled, then frowned. "I thought you'd been standing here a while."

"Well, yes, I . . ."

Walker pointed. "See that car next to the church, all black and burned? That's Ken Matsamura's S.U.V. Been parked there since long after his speech this morning. He wasn't in it, and he hasn't shown up." He turned to Mark with the most melancholy expression. "Where do you suppose he was when the fire started?"

They stared at the church.

"It can't be," said Mark. "Jim would have checked inside."

Walker nodded. "I hope you're right, cowboy."

Chapter Twenty-Eight

The burning church flickered in his rear-view mirror as he drove away. When he stopped in front of the clinic, he saw that the parking lot was empty. He found the front door locked. No one answered when he banged on it, so he cupped his hand over his eyes and peered into the window. He couldn't see anyone. But the long wheelchair ramp led to another entrance near the end of the building. That door was open, and he went to Paul Radwick's room. He saw no one in the hall, and the emptiness made him nervous. He swung the door of the room open.

Roland Veress was sprawled on the floor, his head bleeding. Mark bent down to him and tried to raise him up. The doctor was semiconscious. Mark got him to the bed. Paul was gone.

"Roland, are you all right?"

The doctor moaned and put his hand up. The light illuminated the doctor's face. It looked as if he'd been hit on the side of the head. No one else was in the room. Mark grabbed a couple of pillows and helped Veress lay back, tilting his head. At the sink he got a towel and some warm water, then gently wiped away some of the blood from the doctor's face.

"Roland, what happened?"

The doctor spoke slowly. "They took Radwick. I tried to stop them. His wife was nearly hysterical, but she went with them. These guys were not Makahs, and they weren't fooling around. They had knives."

"Where did they go?"

"They took Radwick to the ceremony. It's what he'd been waiting for. But I couldn't just let them come in here and take him like that. They broke their way in here after we'd closed. The receptionist was gone and the nurse ran away. I tried to stop them, but Paul wanted to go with them."

"Where's Sandra?"

"They took her, too."

"Why would they take *her?*"

"You know the answer. They think she has a spirit in her. *And Radwick insisted.*"

"Oh, God."

"This is dangerous," said Veress. "These beliefs are dangerous things."

"I've got to get out of here and find her."

"Go on, I'll be fine. One of them hit me. Knocked me down, that's all. You get going. You better follow them."

"Where?"

"Go out the Cape road. That's where they went. The ocean cliffs. But first call the police from the front desk. The number is pasted next to the phone."

Mark rushed out the door, down the hall, and to the reception counter. He found the phone and dialed the police station.

"I'm sorry," said the person. "There are no available officers to speak to. Is this an emergency?"

"A woman has been kidnapped and taken out the Cape road. I don't know what kind of vehicle they were driving."

"I understand. I'll dispatch someone as soon as possible."

Mark hung up. Why had the woman *understood?* She didn't ask for further details. He ran outside, got into the Rover and tried to quell his panic. He was shaking with frustration. He'd allowed himself to become separated from Sandra again.

He started the engine and sped away. The desolate Cape Loop Road began just south outside of town. It traced an inland path for a length of fifteen miles around a huge piece of territory that on a map looked like the head of a giant snake. But the road was hiking distance to the cliffs from almost any given point. As he drove on the paved road about two blocks from the beginning of the loop, he saw something far ahead—a brief view of a red car. Although it was just a brief image, he would have bet it was Richard Walker's Honda. Had Walker left the fire to see what was going on? The only way to know was to catch up. The paved road ended, but with the 4 × 4 he felt no need to slow down, thumping the suspension over the rough parts without mercy. He doubted that a smaller car could keep that up. Five minutes later he still saw no sign of it, but he was sure he was closing in. Whoever was driving that car was moving rapidly, for Mark slowed only a little around the curves. Then, as he came onto a long straight section, he saw the Honda ahead. It was indeed Walker's. He could see the car slaloming around sections of potholes, speeding up.

Looking ahead, working the steering wheel, Mark passed a sweep of alders, turned the wheel hard, and resisted the temptation to hit the brakes as the car slid around a turn on the hard-packed earth. He slowed down. Walker probably knew this road only too well. The red car was out of sight around a long curve, and the road was now a twisting frustration of bumps and holes. Still, Mark maintained a constant forty-five miles-per-hour.

Long before the hiking trail at the tip of the Cape, and still on the Pacific Ocean side with forest between the road and the sea, he rounded a long right-hand bend and then slammed on the brakes. For what must have been a quarter-mile, cars and trucks were parked along the roadside. It was a surprising sight.

He drove uncomfortably down the line of vehicles, and only when he got to the end did he find space to park—next to Walker's old red Honda.

Stepping out, he put his palm flat onto the Honda's hood. The engine was hot. He looked back up along the road, searching for a trailhead into the forest. It was there, unmarked, overgrown with saplings; and if a lot of people hadn't just trampled through it, it might not have been noticeable.

He walked into the alder thicket and kept moving until he was in the midst of the dark spruce, moist earth, and grotesque underlying vegetation of the forest. The damp trail, camouflaged at the roadside, had been recently cleared. There were many footprints. The cold wind gusted in the trees. He zipped his jacket over his sweater, and a depressing thought came to him—that he was stuck in something he couldn't alter, an unwinding of events that would run to an unknown but inevitable conclusion. As he moved forward, his mind turned to Sandra. He would get her off the reservation and take her with him. Just do that one thing. Retrieve that opportunity.

A minute later, he stopped and stared into the gray-filtered light of the woods. From behind a tree, a figure appeared. A silhouette. The ephemeral quality of a human being. Blood pounded in Mark's ears. He was aware of fearful instability in his legs, but when it seemed as if the seconds would stretch into forever, the figure moved again, closer to the trail—and the silence was broken.

"I waited."

It was Walker. Mark didn't answer.

Richard shook his head. "Can't tell, can you?" he said. "Can't tell if it's me or *them*."

"Maybe both," said Mark.

"Ha! Maybe I'm not so sure about you either."

"Makes us even."

"Come on, let's walk down the trail together so we can be sure."

Walker's face turned toward the late afternoon light in the west.

"You left your fire duty back in town," said Mark.

"In memory of my ancestors," Walker said. "Because in the old days, as I said, when a place was haunted by spirits, they'd burn it down—even their own house—then build another somewhere else. The idea kind of died out after a while."

"No wonder."

"The church was also Christian. And as my grandfather used to say, that's where the white man got his driver's license before he ran us over. 'Be fruitful and multiply. Fill the earth and subdue it.' White men came to the wilderness. But to us, there was no such thing as wilderness. Only creation and relation."

Zealousness had crept into Walker's voice, and Mark thought of Matsamura's burned car, so he changed the subject.

"So while you're busy getting back to your roots, our friend Ken Matsamura is still missing?"

Walker stopped. He turned with a look of irritation, dissolving into understanding. "He couldn't have been in the lab. Kallabush wouldn't have done such a thing. He might have been snoozing on one of the pews, out of sight, but not likely."

"His car was right outside the church."

"They *must* have seen it."

"If they bothered to think."

"I'm not going back," said Walker. "I have to see what happens here."

"You're a member of the secret society, I'd guess."

"Well, not really."

"It'd be like you."

"I can't understand them. But I have to know what they're doing."

"I'm getting Sandra away from here if it's the last thing I do."

"I had a dream," said Walker. "Oh, I didn't like that dream because it was about the slaughtered villagers—and when I woke up, the wind was howling outside the house, and Judy was frightened. This is bad."

"I understand, but we have to find Sandra. That's what we have to do now. They came and took her."

Walker flinched but kept going. "Who came for her?"

"I don't know."

"Representatives of several tribes are here now," he said anxiously. "They'll try to keep everyone who's suspected of being possessed near the sea. They say Sisiutl will come, and anyone near the sea will be purged."

"How will that happen?"

"Depends on who you talk to. I don't think they know. But that's why they try to get all the suspects to the cliff. There, the wanderers can be removed. I don't know how. But I'm worried about the radical members."

Walker was hiking even faster. Mark caught up and took him by the arm. "Richard, Sandra may need us."

"Yes."

Mark took him by the sleeve. "Will you help me?"

"I won't help you take her away yet."

Mark wanted to force him to take sides, but he saw such a look of consternation on Richard's face that he decided against it.

Walker, now ahead of him, said, "You can't always tell if they're inside you. Some get buried in there real deep. Some whisper so quietly that you can't hear them. That is what they say."

Between the trees ahead of them, the sky had a strange purple color.

Chapter Twenty-Nine

Before long, the sound of distant drumming and chanting intermingled with the ocean wind. Mark and Richard soon emerged out of a tangled growth of salal and alder onto the awesome ledges of the southern Cape Flattery cliffs. In front was the gray, rolling Pacific. To the north and south, promontories of rock were separated by rugged gaps, while waves slammed thunderously into boulders and fissures a hundred feet below. The sky was changing from an odd purple into a threatening cavern of black clouds. The yellow flames of campfires burned brightly on the ledges and promontories. Every clear area as far as they could see was occupied by small fires. The pressing vegetation of the forest was thick, sometimes growing out to the very edge of the cliffs, but leaving natural, well-defined spaces of flat, open rock. Nearby, an old spruce tree with knots like huge fists piled on top of one another grew from a crack in the rock. In contrast to these natural surroundings, the huddled people and their fires seemed delicate and tenuous.

"I'll go north," said Richard. "If you can't find her right away, go south around the big fissures. I think the people are spread out along the cliffs for quite a distance."

Mark started south, but he'd gone only a few paces when two figures approached him. Mark didn't acknowledge them at first. One was an old man, the other an old woman. They wore baseball caps and quilted polyester jackets.

"We are from British Columbia," said the man. "Will you come and join our group?" He gestured to a circle of people sitting around a fire on a large shelf of rock, singing and beating on large hand-held drums.

"Thanks," said Mark. "I have to find someone. Sandra Torrel."

The old man, dark and wrinkled, stared into Mark's face. "Someone there knows you," he said, pointing to a different fire. "They said you have come a long way."

Mark looked to where the man gestured, but he couldn't see anyone he knew.

"Yes, I've come a long way," Mark said.

"You are welcome here," said the man. "We are glad you have come." He seemed to search for something in Mark's eyes, then he and the woman turned and walked back toward the fire while a dog began barking.

Was this the end of the world? The sky was dark with the pending storm. How long before sunset? Enough people were here that he couldn't imagine anyone harming Sandra. He walked to the campfire where he was supposed to have known someone. A dozen people were singing or chanting in a hard and steady rhythm. Using drumsticks, they beat on hand-held drums that were either round or octagonal. The singers chanted in sharply rising and falling syllables, and the sound lifted powerfully into the air. Their wrinkled faces were old, their hands dark and leathery, their expressions lit by an ancient glow. The circle did not pause, though some nodded soberly when he approached. They might have been elders of the tribe, yet they were dressed in simple rain parkas, hunting jackets, jeans, and caps that had the insignia of sports teams or industrial companies. One woman wore a straw hat; another, younger woman, swayed rhythmically to the beat, more so than the men whose expressions were sober and steady. Mark put his hands in his pockets for warmth. The drumming and singing dominated and dulled the mind. It was purposeful and territorial, the rhythm and language transfixing. Did these good people know what they were doing? They looked wise, but he suspected they were no wiser than anyone else. Maybe the elders' advantage lay in a traditional acceptance of unknown things, even if they didn't understand the nature of those things. They sang in symbols. They spoke the double-talk of myth. Mark wanted to cut through it all, but the drumming sliced up the intellectual world he had been forced to abandon here on the reservation.

Beyond the knotted tree, another fire burned. He left the circle and made his way along the rocky ledge toward the south. The air was pungent with ocean salt and wood-smoke. He felt lost, separate even from the things he could hear, see, and smell. Were the Indians lost, too? Their campfires were small, their faces turning toward him as he passed. He came to a fissure in the cliff. The only way around was to go into the woods, so he walked into the twilight of alder as the salmonberry stuck to his clothing. It took five minutes of struggle to make it through the undergrowth to the other side, and there were several more campfires along the next promontory. He looked carefully at each, hoping to find Sandra. He noticed one group of people huddling near their fire but not partaking in the songs. One of them, covered with a heavy olive-green tarp, was lying on the ground. Mark went toward them across an area of thin soil that looked as if it had been cleared. When he got nearer, he saw who was lying on his back under the tarp.

Paul Radwick was speaking calmly to a woman next to him. When the woman glanced up and saw Mark, she rose and came to him. It was Paul's wife, Nancy.

A desperate helplessness broke out in her voice. "He still won't listen to me, he'll catch his death out here, and none of them will listen. I've called the tribal council. They've publicly renounced this gathering, but this is not just a Makah gathering and they won't do anything to stop it. These people, they're from all over—some from British Columbia. I can't get Paul away." Her voice cracked. "They took him out of the clinic. They assaulted the doctor, and they say there's a storm coming."

Mark took her by the arm. "Take it easy. What have they told you?"

"That he can't leave until Sisiutl comes to take the spirits." A frantic expression crossed her face. "Do you know they've blocked the main road out of town?"

"Where did you hear this?"

"The Makahs have got a bunch of equipment out there trying to clear a landslide. There was an explosion. These people out here, this society, have got a war going on and I'm afraid they're going to hurt Paul. Paul is sick. He needs help. Where are the police?"

Mark took her by the hand. "Stay with Paul. Keep him warm and he'll be all right. Have you seen the woman who came to visit Paul a little while ago? Sandra—with black hair, wearing a red jacket, not an Indian?"

"They brought her with us, but I don't know where she is now."

"OK, I've got to go, then."

"Paul hasn't been delusional for a while," she said hastily. "They told me the spirits quiet down when the serpent is coming—what serpent?" Tears came to her eyes. She was helpless—and a growing sense of danger emerged in Mark's mind as well. What if he couldn't get Sandra out of here either? What plan did these people have?

He told Mrs. Radwick he'd return. Then he went toward the next campfire. Because of the opaque sky, it was starting to get darker, and without being able to see the position of the sun, he didn't know how long he had before it would be too dark to search.

By the time he reached the last fire on that section of cliff, he noticed several people who had stopped singing. They were looking across the gap that separated this promontory from the next.

A figure was standing on the edge of a jutting precipice. A figure wearing a red coat.

Sandra.

The distance across the gap was far enough that it took a moment to perceive just how close to the edge she was standing. And it was too close. Much too close.

"Sandra!" he yelled, but the sound of the waves far below canceled any hope of his voice reaching her. He moved quickly along the natural parapet he was on and saw three other people across the gap, staring at her and talking to one another. He stumbled as he sprinted toward the woods at the rear of the notch. After struggling through the undergrowth, he passed in front of a small cave formed by the rocks. He couldn't recall when he'd fallen in love. He'd been attracted to her from the first, as he'd been attracted to other women, but had he fallen in love with her after Maggie had appeared on the logging road? This spontaneous thought worried him in an unusually disturbing way. Was it Maggie he'd seen behind Sandra's eyes?

He climbed up a grade, forced to hold onto the limbs of trees. The ground was not as flat and easy to cross. He was short of breath, but he would get there. He stumbled out of the salal and spiny spruce onto an area of rock. He searched again, but she must have been on a ledge just out of view. The angle was confusing, but he headed toward the place where she must be. The three people were near a tree that grew behind the tall, rocky promontory, but she was still out of sight, apparently just below and in front of them. Tormented now, he ran forward over the rough ground. He couldn't allow himself to think she'd fallen. One of the group saw him and seemed to understand what he was doing, maybe who he was, because he said something to the others. If she'd fallen, they'd have known, wouldn't they, because they wouldn't just be standing there. But why were they standing there in the first place? Why weren't they trying to get Sandra away from the ledge?

A man who motioned to him seemed pale and frightened.

"We've been keeping an eye on her, afraid to approach. Are you Mark Sayres?"

"Yes." Mark ignored them and made his way carefully along the side of the ledge, where he discovered a steplike formation overhanging the inlet a hundred feet below. Undulating waves smashed in and out of a cavern in the rocks.

Sandra's profile was toward him. He wanted to rush and grab her, but like the men, he didn't dare. She was too close to the edge, and looking purposeful.

"Sandra."

She turned only slightly, but spoke both logically and emotionally, loud enough to be heard over the crashing waves below and the wind as it whipped around the precipice.

"It was a slow disintegration of love," she said. "Lucy committed suicide in that room. She knew what her husband was doing—that he was helping to send the children away. Later she knew he'd massacred the ones who wouldn't go. And she allowed it, inside herself, because she was dutiful. She might have left, but she didn't. She might have taken Joseph's son, Gregory's father, away with her, but she didn't. She encouraged Joseph in his ambitions."

Mark edged closer along the rock until he was nearly within reach. "You know this?"

"In that house . . ." Her thought was incomplete, but she continued: "After her spirit had rested for decades, Lucy possessed Maggie and drove her to suicide in the sea."

"The storm is coming," said Mark. "Let's go. It's not too late."

Sandra glanced at the sky. "Maggie succumbed to the depression that was both in Lucy's spirit and her own. Lucy and I have something in common, too. I could have done more for Gregory."

"It's over now."

"Nothing comes to an end," she said.

"Sandra, just back up a little, will you?"

"Sure."

But she didn't move.

A dangerous expression crossed her face—the kind that emerges when someone feels privy to greater truths. He was terrified she was about to jump.

The bank of clouds arched overhead like a breaking wave in gray and black. A small fiberglass fishing boat came into view around the jutting of rock. These distractions filtered into Mark's consciousness because he couldn't make a decision. If he grabbed for her, she might fall. If he waited, she might jump.

"Sandra, look at me."

She did. And although her face seemed almost unreal, he was aware of the vividness of her existence. He cared very much about that existence. His legs shook imperceptibly, and she seemed to sense his fear. Her jaw tightened with anxiety. The worry in her eyes penetrated into his own. She breathed consciously and rhythmically, but remained steady and seemed to gather her thoughts about her.

"Lucy is only a remnant," she said. "And Maggie is still here."

He recovered his strength and reached his hand out to her.

"Let me have your hand," he said.

She seemed to be waging some inner battle, then slowly, carefully, reached a slender white hand toward him, and in the moment of contact, with her fingers touching his, he felt a surge of emotion, tears rising in his eyes, lungs paralyzed. Her eyes were steady, her face white, her touch silky once again. Their fingers enmeshed as they had only hours before, and he firmly pulled her toward him while her eyes mirrored his.

"Mark," she said, almost as if surprised. And the *dreamlike* quality of her existence wavered and disappeared, as it had on the beach. Whatever her condition, she was alive and moving away from the ledge. The sickness in him ebbed. He gained control and hung onto her. But there were other thoughts; for Sandra, like Paul, was alive in such a way as to defy reason. It had not ended.

She was tearful and shaken. No one was standing along the shelf of rock any more. He could hear the more distant drumming again, but it had been there all along.

"The spirits are still here," Sandra said. "I have nowhere to go."

Wind swept the cliff, but a haze had developed offshore, reaching down from the darker clouds, and as they moved back along the rock he thought it was distant rain. They went back into the foliage at the end of the notch. He held onto her arm, guided her past the cave, and looked toward the flickering campfires. Did he see people lying flat on the ground? Or was it just blankets? They pushed their way back through the forest, and the man who'd motioned to him previously met them on the other side.

"I'm Bob Silvers," he said. "I have joined my native brothers, but I don't care any more who stays. If you go, we won't stop you. We think we know so much, but we know so little. Perhaps some will leave." His hand was shaking as he gestured. "Yet I feel Sisiutl is coming, as our great-grandfathers foretold."

Mark looked out to sea, but there was nothing except a rain squall moving in. Sandra put her arm around his waist. Silvers watched them, then he walked back toward his campfire to join the others.

Mark wanted to get Radwick out of the storm, so he and Sandra went back north near the woods, coming out again on the wide middle promontory. A few people were standing at the cliff's edge, gazing out to sea. Whatever they were frightened of, the only things seen were the natural elements that had molded and weathered this coast for thousands of years. Mark looked over the edge at the small fishing boat that had stopped to troll near sunset amid the rolling waves. It was such a routine sight, and it contrasted so distinctly with the self-important gathering on the cliffs, that he felt an odd sense of conclusion. There was nothing here. Myth. That was all. Explanations would be silenced by the storm, everyone would leave, the spirits of the dead would—must—fade away, and only a mystery would remain. He could cope with that, he thought, as he watched the fishing boat below.

The wind had almost died, but the front moved in until sheets of rain engulfed the boat. The pilot, hidden in a convertible cabin with plastic side-curtains, started the engine and made a circle as if to leave the area. Mark searched for the location of the fire where Nancy Radwick would be standing or kneeling. He wondered if they could take Paul away now. Then he felt Sandra tug at his sleeve. She was looking down at the rolling waves. Mark looked again, too. The small boat was still going in a circle. It kept going in a circle in the middle of the rain squall until it finally turned toward shore. Then it gathered speed, accelerating quickly.

Mark let go of Sandra and went to the edge of the cliff. The boat emerged from the squall at *full speed*, heading toward the base of the cliff. It didn't turn. It came straight in. Mark watched incredulously, while in an absurdly terrifying way, for no reason he could discern, the boat launched off a final wave and smashed head-on, shattering against a huge boulder . . . and in an instant there was nothing but debris.

The drumming and singing stopped.

Shaken, he turned toward Sandra. She was behind him, but she had seen. She had her hand over her mouth, backing away. He looked at the ocean again, then down toward the scene of the accident. The boat had circled and come straight out of the rain squall into the rocks. Straight out of the . . .

Rain.

Mark stared in disbelief. Then terror. The incoming rain was almost at the edge of the cliff. If what arose in his mind had any validity, it was too late. He knew—not instinctively, but by experience—that the rain was dangerous, just as the fog was dangerous. Although he saw nothing *in* the rain, he moved back as the rock at his feet began to spot with drops of water. The rain had begun, and the drops seemed to strike like steel darts. To the north and south, the small fires danced in the waning light. He had to get Sandra out of the rain. He grabbed her arm and pulled her. Then they both ran from the cliff toward the forest. He remembered the cave. They stumbled through the foliage, then along the rocky ledge he had used before. Big rocks formed the small cave at the end of the notch between the promontories. He escorted her in.

"You must stay here," he told her as they bent down inside the shelter. "Remember when Gregory returned, you forced me to stay inside and not go out into the fog? Now, you must do the same. This is a dry place. Whatever you do, whatever happens, don't leave here. Fight the urge to leave."

She nodded.

"I have to help Paul and his wife," he said. "Sit down and don't move."

Then he heard a scream, but couldn't tell where it came from. He stepped out and started back to find Radwick. The drops were falling. Coming out of the salal with his rain hood up, he walked onto the wide middle promontory. The sound of the rain became a rush, then a roar.

Something pulled at him. He felt dizzy. Then sick with fear. The cliff fires wavered in the rain and seemed out of focus. He thought the rain might put them out. Turning, he looked to make sure Sandra hadn't foolishly followed him.

He went to the edge of the cliff. Some force seemed to draw him, and the danger of water overwhelmed his rationality once again. Whatever he saw or felt, he knew he had to control his terror. That was the myth, he reminded himself. If something came out of the sea in the rain, according to the myth his survival would depend on staying in control, so he put his hand up to protect his eyes and began walking north toward where he'd seen Radwick.

He believed he was in view of Radwick's fire when, a short distance away, a man suddenly ran toward the edge of the cliff. He was holding his head between his hands, covering his ears. His face was contorted. The man moaned, then screamed as two others ran after him. It was too late. Still holding his head, the man ran directly off the cliff to his death. The others stopped. Women were crying and screaming. The men were agitated and terrified. They ran back to the fire near the edge of the forest.

Nauseated and increasingly dizzy, Mark was afraid that he might be forced off the cliff as well. It felt like the same nausea he'd experienced before, and he was too close to the edge, though he couldn't see any danger. What was happening? He tried to back away, but became too dizzy to stand. He purposely fell on the ground and grabbed onto a rock. He still couldn't see anything *in* the rain. The rain poured down, running in icy rivulets in the creases of rocky ground, soaking his clothes. He had to get to his feet. But his disorientation and dizziness increased, and the sky became darker moment by moment as the full force of the storm moved in. The sound of the rain was like the breakers—an intense rush of white-noise, masking whatever sounds might be near him. The wind whipped up, the fires flickered violently lower, and the clouds seemed to hover near the tops of the trees. The mental, whirling sensation was incapacitating, and Mark couldn't get up. He could only hope Sandra kept back far enough in the small cave to be safe and dry. Frightened, he cursed under his breath and knew that something horrible had caused that man to rush to his death. But as he tried to reason, nausea overcame him; his skin felt hot, then cold. Then, unmistakably, there was an unsettling perception at the border of his consciousness. He was immobilized by the pulling, dizzying sensation, but there was something else that impacted on his senses now—a sound that he thought must emanate from inside his head, yet which may have been in the rain itself. He wanted to bring his arm over and wipe the rain from his face, to clear his head, but he didn't dare let go of the rock. Had that man been possessed? Is that the way the spirits are removed? By suicide? The vague perception of something invading his consciousness increased. He wanted to get up and run, but couldn't. Though his hood was up, he tried to cover his head with his arm. The dreadful, increasing noise seemed to coalesce into . . . *voices*. It's in my head, he thought.

He heard another scream, behind him to the left, and he saw another man walk toward the edge of the cliff at the southern end of the promontory. The man's face was contorted, as if he was in pain, and he waved his hands as if to fend off a horde of insects. Two other men came after him. One was Bob Silvers. But the man broke away and went right off the edge, plunging a hundred feet down. This horror played out against the ebbing fires, while the rain fell.

Nothing could be seen in the watery curtain, but from the sea came a noise so terrifying that Mark's grip on the rock became a grip on life itself. Lying on his side now, he could see over the cliff's edge toward the ocean. Was it hallucination? Was the ocean moving strangely? He watched, straining his vision through the barrier of gray precipitation, and as if in a dream, a huge whirlpool seemed to form a mile off shore. Oh, it *must* be an illusion! he thought. Oh, God, it must. It was the spinning in his head, and not reality. But the rain fell harder and the wind rose again to surround him with impossible sound—the sound of a thousand screaming voices. And these weren't in his mind. They were like a throng of incomprehensible demons—an agony of sound multiplied by thousands. He knew the power that could destroy rationality and suck souls into its vortex. They were getting closer. *And they were dead.*

Now the fires flickered and died, and the people on the cliff fled or lay flat on the ground covering their ears or holding onto anything they could find—rocks or growing plants. The dissonant sound of tortured souls came in like a monstrous wave, louder—and he knew it was true—that Sisiutl was a kind of serpent, but not with two heads. Not two—*thousands.* And they were pulling others into its immortal heart.

The swirling haze of rain erased the sea, and those thousands of souls began to pull consciousness off of the rock, out of every body that strained to hold on. Mark opened his mouth and screamed and screamed again—to block out the tumult. No spirit inside him tried to get out, because he was not possessed. But *they* were sweeping closer, and as the wind decreased and the rain fell like arrows, the awful tumult changed, and now he could hear whispers.

A thousand whispers of individuals were speaking and crying, and he felt for the only sanity he had, the hardness of the stone.

At last he had to let go, cover his ears, and depend on the weight of his body to hold him onto the rock. But as he closed his eyes, he thought he heard the *familiar* voice of a dead man. Olson, he thought, had been torn loose from Radwick. And passing by, separating itself from the other voices, it whispered in a monotone. Then he felt another spirit moving in his mind. Not Olson now. Another.

Then the stone underneath him turned to sand, the sand was wet, and there was a fire again in the darkness . . . and he was no longer on the cliff. The whispering voice was replaced by his own footsteps, and his hands were free to move, his legs worked under him, and he was up and moving along a moonlit beach, following dark figures in the moonlight. The people were many yards ahead of him and moving away. They were unaware of him, which, somehow, was his intent, for he'd had a change of heart. The moon shone silver on the crescent waves that slid up the beach at night. Stealthily, he crouched along the inland side, near the trees, breathing quickly, carrying a heavy rifle. He didn't know what to do. It was wrong.

Shots cracked in the night. The people around the campfire screamed and fell. Some tried to get up, but were shot down. They were dying, all of them, the women and children too, and some cried piteously for help, but he couldn't help them. He ran into the carnage, even as the shots were fired—and ducking down, while the killers were brutally executing those who remained alive, he managed to grab a child who was struggling under the weight of its dead mother. He ran with the child into the bushes, and there he hid the child. And when he emerged, he screamed in anger, screamed at them, thinking they wouldn't shoot one of their own—a white man.

But a bullet struck his chest, painfully smashing his sternum into pieces, and another bullet exploded his eye and entered his brain, and he fell dead onto the ground.

Rivers of blood mixed with the water and ran down the beach into the sea.

Rivers. And the dead drifted into the night sky, and the moon was pure and cool and ever-present, and death faded into the stillness.

He who had saved the child was the last to die—to linger and die—and he could feel that pulling, and he wanted to float with the others up into the moonlight. But the others had gone, and he found himself in horror, because there were colors in the darkness.

The dream was wrenched away. The unknown spirit who'd possessed Olson was gone, and so too was Olson.

Mark's heart pounded killingly, and the thousand insane voices became whispers at the edge of perception, and when he wasn't sure if the sound was real or in his own mind, he dared to open his eyes.

He had been possessed just now and had seen the massacre.

The rain fell, and the clouds rushed across the sky as the storm's fury continued inland to the east. The dizziness faded, but the sky had not lost its cloak of gray twilight. The fires were out, and everyone was still but for a few solitary individuals. He heard a woman sobbing loudly in the direction of Radwick's fire. It was quite near. How much time had passed he didn't know. He got up, dripping wet, and walked through the rain that was becoming a drizzle, searching the area around him. A burnt-out fire now lay to his right, and next to it, a woman was kneeling beside the prone figure of a man. Other people stood around them—including Walker.

Soaked to the bone, chilled as much by recognition as by cold, Mark realized who was kneeling and put his hand on the woman's shoulder.

"He's dead," said Nancy Radwick.

Mark stared down at Paul's body. The face was sunken, with a pale, almost lithic texture, the hair white, the mouth open in horror.

"The voices carried him away with their spirits," said Walker, "so he must have died of shock. I am sorry. He was very well liked."

Nancy sobbed uncontrollably, while Mark bent down to her.

"The serpent *returned*," said an old man with great emphasis.

"Paul is dead," Nancy said.

"I . . . I'm sorry," said the man.

"Can you help us get his body back to town?" asked Walker.

"Yes," said the old man. "There are others coming now."

Mark stood up and guided Richard aside. "I left Sandra back there."

"It's nearly dark. You better go get her. Is she all right?"

"I think so. I left her in a dry place."

Walker looked over at Paul's body, keeping his voice low. "There's a rumor going around that Kallabush has reburied the bones and is under arrest. Are we all crazy or what?"

Nancy Radwick stopped sobbing. Mark put his arm around her and helped her up. Then he motioned to Richard.

"Help her to town, Richard. I'm going back for Sandra."

Chapter Thirty

The storm departed and the slate-gray twilight returned to the coast-line. The ledges were abandoned, the wind had calmed, the rain had turned to drizzle, the drizzle to mist. Incoming waves were white-tipped, and the rugged scenery was depressingly empty of visible life. The fading light would not last long, thought Mark. His hair was slick and wet, his face cold, his jacket and jeans soaked, but he thought he could tolerate the cold by sheer adrenaline. He was almost where he had left Sandra, and couldn't allow himself to think the worst. If she had left the cave, only two choices remained. He could cover as much territory as possible while there was still light, or he could attempt to restart one of the fires and hope Sandra would find her way to it. Either choice was desperate, because there would be no explanation for her being gone other than the worst. Below the cliff, the sea was dark. If she'd fallen, there would be no chance to know until morning. But he had to block from his mind the idea that she'd repeated the suicide of the person who inhabited her. Nevertheless, he had gone through the massacre with an unknown person who'd tried to save a child, and he'd heard Olson's voice just before being swept back into time. The spirits had been taken away. Of that he was certain.

He reached the cave, but she was gone.

Putting his hand on a rock to support himself, he breathed long and hard. He was tragically aware of the possibility she'd been pulled over the cliff. She had the suicides within her. Perhaps she, of all, was least likely to survive. His only hope had been that she had remained dry and safe, but the air was damp and she was gone.

Fearful, cold, and physically weak, he chose to use the remaining twilight and restart one of the fires, to provide light and warmth. If Sandra was alive, a fire might guide her to him. Although he still had a flashlight in his pocket, there was too much territory to search, no moon, and the landscape would be completely dark within half an hour.

Finding a smoldering fire with an abandoned orange-plastic tarp next to it, he knelt down as close as he could, shaking from the cold; then he blew on the dying coals, rearranged the logs, and coaxed a flame into life. It had been a big, hot fire and the rain hadn't dowsed it beyond redemption, but it took time to get it going enough for warmth. As the forest and the cliff's edge retreated into dim outlines, he tended the fire and sat in front of the glowing flames with the tarp over his shoulders to trap the heat, his back to the sea. The circle of light would make only a tiny glowing island amid the suffocating darkness, but it was all he could do. He wanted to cry or yell, but at the end it had become a struggle even to think, for his mind and body were almost numb. In the flickering glow, time slowed. The sound of the waves ought to have retained some of their power to frighten, but he was all out of fear. What was left, when he looked past the flames, was the blackness of night. The spirits were gone. The waves and the flames made natural sounds. The fog grew dense, but the fog was empty of souls. He found the small flashlight in his pocket and made a short foray into the darkness. He added wood to the fire. Then he sat down with the tarp over him, and as he warmed up again, he couldn't keep his eyes open. Exhausted, he gave up the vigil for a few minutes, turned his back to the fire and looked toward the infinitely black and empty sea.

"Mark."

Startled, he turned, wondering if the voice was real.

But Sandra was standing across the fire from him.

"Mark, I'm sorry."

The flames danced on her face, and her dark hair hung in graceful, silky waves—as if she'd stayed dry. "It's me."

He was overjoyed to see her, got up, and wanted to take her in his arms. But she knelt down at the fire.

"Let me just warm myself for a minute," she said quietly. "I've abused your trust."

"No, you're safe," he said, sitting down near her, reaching out for her hand. "I love you, don't you know that? What happened? Where did you go?"

They sat close to each other. She took his hand and looked at him with widening eyes, as if she felt love, too, but couldn't speak.

"The terror is over," Mark said. "We can leave the reservation now. Come on, it's dark." He started to get up.

"No," she said. "Hold my hand here for a while longer. I like the fire. I've been so cold, and the fire's warm."

"What happened to you?"

"I was in the cave. But I knew that something was in the rain and it was pulling me out. It wanted me to come out. I was dry, but so close to the cliff. I saw a man run over the edge. When the rain turned to drizzle, I came out and ran into the woods, but fell." She turned her leg and showed the slash in her jeans. Then she showed a cut on her hand.

"Did you hear the *voices?*" he asked.

"God, yes, faintly, but I got up and kept running. I thought I'd be forced to join them, but I'd stayed out of the rain until the last, and I found a dry place where I hid under a huge log. Oh God, Mark." She looked away. "I knew you'd come to look for me, but I stayed away until the drizzle turned to this mist."

"It's all right."

Then she looked back at the fire and was quiet. He took his arm from around her and stirred the coals with a stick he'd set aside. "Others ran away too," he said. "The hot-shots up here who knew something was going to happen."

She sighed, then looked at him. "I'm still afraid."

"You've been through hell," he said. "That's why you ran. You had to escape."

She said nothing.

"Let's go back to the house now," he said. "We'll talk there."

"It was *her* house. She's gone, I think, gone with the voices when I left the cave, even though it was only drizzling then, but they were after me too, and I could hear them whispering as they faded away. I've been so lonely. So lost. I've been in the gray places, the wet, damp places, but I could hear them in the distance for days, getting closer all the time. No living person could hear them, but I could, and I was lost and alone. I couldn't even control where I went, because Lucy used me for her own loneliness and guilt, and I couldn't find you until the logging road, but she and I were crying for all the children and I couldn't talk to you then, although you recognized me. And I'm so sorry for the phone call."

Mark stared in horror, unable to breathe.

"Lucy had possessed me, but I didn't know, though I seemed to feel her inside me, and when I found out, it was too late. I wanted to be free of her when I called you that day on the phone, but she took me and walked me into the sea one night. I'm so sorry. You tried to get here, but you couldn't know what was happening. Now I live in some-one named Sandra. I own a mill in Forks. There are questions concern-ing my husband's death. I stayed well hidden, didn't I? This is where I, and she, should be. The house is where Lucy died—but I'm leaving now, I think, and Lucy is gone, isn't she. It's one thing I know, because the remnants get pulled into the whirlpool and are swept away forever, because their time has come, and they're gone—all the old ones. Wan-derers like me temporarily escape by staying away from the sea, because they're still strong. They try to hide and escape. That's why those peo-ple came and got us, because they thought I would escape unless I came down to the sea."

She shivered and shook her head. "And so at last I'm free of Lucy. Isn't that right? But I can feel myself fading. Mark, will I go home? I miss Erica. Can I go home now? I miss her so much. . . . Mark, I can't see you any more . . . and I have to tell you something. I have to tell you that I love you. Whatever has happened, I love you."

Mark couldn't move. Tears came down his cheeks, and at last, after a moment, he said: "Maggie . . . I love you, too."

She stared into the fire, unblinking, and was quiet.

Mark froze in the stillness. He waited for an eternity while she stared into the fire. Perhaps Sandra, in a trance, might die right in front of him, as Paul had done when the spirit left him. But he could do nothing. So he waited with tragic awareness, his thoughts tightening into a bundle of lonely, indecipherable emotions. He had come to this coastline for a reason. The reason had never changed.

She blinked and looked up at him, confused.

"I'm ... sorry," she said. "I was thinking about something . . . thank *God* you're here. I think Maggie was in my mind. But she must be gone now. This mist is damp."

"Sandra."

"What? I can't remember sitting down here. I saw your fire, though. Thank God you waited. It was too dark once I decided to come out of the woods, and I'd never have made it without the fire."

"Sandra."

"What . . . ?"

"Nothing. I'm so glad you found me. So glad." He nodded and wiped the tears from his eyes.

"I ran away when the rain stopped," said Sandra, "into the forest, and I was afraid to come out. I stayed until the storm was completely over. God, it's dark. How long have you been waiting here? If you're angry I don't blame you. Mark, I'm a coward. You were so near the edge and I couldn't bring myself to help you. I saw that man go over the edge. I don't know why, I just had to stay away and out of the rain."

"Sandra, it's all right," he said blankly, trying hard to get control of himself. "We'll go back to the house and pack. I would like to get off the reservation. It's important."

She didn't move. Rather, she stared at him.

"What's wrong?" he asked.

"I don't know. I seemed to have blanked out for a while."

He felt a horrible tug of emotion, but chose not to reveal anything. She'd never know he had spoken to Maggie. She'd stayed dry and ventured out only after the storm had abated. It wouldn't matter if she didn't know everything.

"I want to go away with you," she said, "but . . ."

Mark pulled the tarp tight around himself.

"I can't," she said. "I can't leave the reservation, Mark. This isn't the way it's going to be—not with me as a substitute for her."

"It's not like that."

"Maybe the nightmare is over," she said, "but leaving won't work."

"Sandra ... you can't be a substitute for anyone. Maybe I thought so subconsciously, but it's not true. Falling in love was the last thing anyone could have done under these circumstances," he said with a hint of desperation in his voice, "but I couldn't help it, and neither could you, not because of our spouses, but because of us."

"Then send for your daughter and stay with me. We have the mill and I should be here. This is where I have to be. The dead are gone, regardless of where I am. This is where I belong, at least for a while. People like me, white people who come here, have nowhere else to go. That's why they come. Gregory and I came here for a purpose, but we also escaped here as a couple. Once you come to the end of the world, there's nowhere else to go. You have to stand your ground when the serpent comes, don't you, because there's nothing else you can do. Death is the only other place you can get to from here."

"You're thinking too much, asking too much."

Sandra looked at him strangely, and her face contained that same distillation of clarity and beauty he'd noticed when he first saw her. Secrets were not part of her character. Her decision to stay rested in her troubled eyes. And Maggie was really gone.

The wind rose again. It was getting colder. The ocean sounded bleak and threatening. It was the cold Mark sensed the most.

He couldn't stay. Couldn't bring his daughter up here. But he mentally clung to Sandra. He needed her, loved her. But perhaps he had to let go.

He said: "You have been captured by the serpent anyway."

She looked disturbed, then smiled, but only a little. "Maybe," she said.

"Let's find the trail," he said. "I've got a flashlight."

Chapter Thirty-One

From inside the small cabin of the fishing trawler, Mark watched the lonely man outside zip his jacket up against the cold and thrust both hands firmly, perhaps bitterly, into his pockets.

Ken Matsamura stood at the stern of the trawler, starkly silhouetted against the bluish-green water as the docks and old buildings of Neah Bay receded into the distance. Having him aboard provided the only solace for such an early morning departure. Although his car had been parked at the church yesterday, he'd walked to the town meeting, then driven with two tribal council members to inspect the landslide on the road along the straits. By the time he'd returned, the church was a pile of cinders.

Mark now pictured Sandra, alone in her house on the cliff. Amid all the chaos and cruelty, she couldn't break free of the dream Gregory had unknowingly created out of his ancestor's tyranny. Now *her* dream was living at the edge of the world and awakening each morning to the sight of the endless ocean. That's how she thought of it. She might sell the mill, or she might not, she said. She just needed some time. For Mark, the town and its encompassing culture retreated into the distance as if in another kind of dream—the familiar one of loss—while the swelling wake of the fishing boat made separation more complete moment by moment.

"I don't know how you talked me into this, cowboy," said Richard Walker as he navigated the boat around a pillar buoy at the entrance to the bay. "If my brother doesn't get his boat back by next Tuesday, and in one piece, I'm horsemeat."

"I didn't talk you into anything," said Mark. "I'm paying you."

As they rounded the terminus of the breakwater, Walker looked over his shoulder at Matsamura through the little window behind him. Then he turned to Mark. "Look at him on deck out there. He isn't a happy man. It's hard for him to believe what's happened. Radwick's death was a shock."

"Yeah."

"And you guys might have waited to leave town until the road was cleared—three days at most."

"I suppose."

"Gray's Harbor is a ways from here."

"We'll make it. Besides, I told Kallabush I'd stop and see his mother in Hoquiam."

"What are you going to tell her?"

"I'm going to tell her the moon isn't red any more."

Walker shook his head. "That's cool."

"Then I'm going to tell her that her son is in jail for burning down a church—but that he should consider himself lucky."

"Everyone should consider himself lucky," said Walker.

"Even you, my friend. Kallabush and friends stole the bones and reburied them just as the storm moved in. We'll never know if that was as important as some believe. But you, Richard, ought to appreciate the possibility."

Walker gave him a slightly testy look. "You want to catch a bus south?"

The boat started to pitch and sway as they motored out into the straits. Matsamura came into the cabin to get warm.

In a while, they rounded the Cape, skillfully navigating landward of Tatoosh Island, admiring the old lighthouse. Walker was quite familiar with the waters. As the coastline angled to the east below the Cape, they headed south-southwest in order to put distance between themselves and the rocky cliffs before the coast angled outward at Cape Alava. Although the three of them were in close quarters, they didn't have a lot to say to each other.

Mark would take a bus to Portland, then fly to San Diego, bringing Maggie's suitcase. He wondered what he would do when he got home. How would he break the final news of Maggie's death to his daughter?

How would he continue his work? How would life be without Maggie? Though the land of the Makah was retreating into the gray spaces, nothing that had happened to him was really over. The present was an open-ended conduit. Memories, like love, never entirely fade, possibilities always remain.

When they neared the latitude where the *Lenore* had collided with the sea stack, he went out on deck, put his foot up on a large rusty cleat and tried to see where the Torrel house might be. He wondered if Sandra was watching for him to pass. He thought she'd be standing on the cliff or at the upstairs window. But they were already miles out to sea, and nothing on land was visible across that distance. So he came back inside to stay warm and listen to the low, steady pounding of the engine as it carried him farther and farther south.

Printed in the United States
79304LV00005B/19

9 780977 173471